Behold The College Girls

Mary Ngwebong Ngu

Langaa Research & Publishing CIG
Mankon, Bamenda

Publisher:
Langaa RPCIG
Langaa Research & Publishing Common Initiative Group
P.O. Box 902 Mankon
Bamenda
North West Region
Cameroon
Langaagrp@gmail.com
www.langaa-rpcig.net

Distributed in and outside N. America by African Books Collective
orders@africanbookscollective.com
www.africanbookscollective.com

ISBN-10: 9956-552-14-3

ISBN-13: 978-9956-552-14-6

About this Book

Behold The College Girls is the story of how students in an exclusive girls' mission boarding school interact with one another, on the one hand, and with their principal and staff, on the other. It portrays the power play between senior and junior level students, particularly the obstinate Form 2 students. Other struggles show students taking on the challenge of inadequate meals as well as the prohibition to entertain romantic relations with boys of other colleges within the city. It equally highlights key events like spending a day with boys, and the Vocational Week aimed at recruiting reverent sisters. The story brings to the fore the shared views of four key actors on main occurrences, with one of them featuring in every event, and thanks to whom the setting changes from the college campus to the outside world, particularly the village. In the closing chapter, readers cannot help but sympathize with the key protagonist due to the quandary she is facing— to pursue higher education or not, and if so, where? Thus, *Behold The College Girls* ends with a suspense. Answers can only be supplied through a sequel.

About the Author

Mary Ngwebong Ngu was born in Santa, a village in Southern Cameroon. After graduating from high school, she pursued her education at Yaoundé University, where she studied Modern Letters. She obtained her BA and Maîtrise in English, and years later an MA in Information & Communication Sciences. By then she was already working as a reporter, desk editor, program presenter and news anchor at Radio Cameroon which later became Cameroon Radio Television, CRTV. Mary enjoys writing. Apart from numerous articles published in local newspapers and foreign magazines, Mary has written two poetry collections, *Earth, Breath & Touch: Inspirational Poems for the Beloved*, and *Escape from Prison*. She is also the author of *My Foolishness Prevails: How I became the Star of My Own Epic Drama*, her memoir.

Dedication

To my parents, Sylvester Che Ngu, and Justina Bih Ngu
And to my sister, Mafor Bridget

Acknowledgements

I extend my initial gratitude to the young woman who chose to forego her personal self-improvement as well as youthful pleasures to sacrifice a chunk of her salary to sponsor me through college, my elder sister, Mafor Bridget. I equally extend my thanks to all my senior siblings for the extra support they gave me, namely, Aza Bertha, Che Vincent and Fon Munga while I was a student. My younger siblings, Ngum Delphine, Azunda Odilia, Fruawah Grace, and Chi Augustine provided constant support and deep affection only possible in an exemplary family.

How can I thank my father, Ngu Sylvester Che, who braved all criticism from fellow villagers, to educate his children, especially the girls? Alongside his firm resolve, my mother, Bih Justina, gladly wore faded clothes to ensure that her girls would have school fees.

I will not be able to name all the neighbours and extended family members who gave me timely help, from hosting me, giving me bundles of needed food and precious coins to buy a pen or to hiring a taxi at critical moments. Among them are my uncle Mr. Max Fru Munga, my cousins, Mrs. Helen Siche Asongwe Chumba, and Mrs. Monica Mangwi Asongwe Tantoh. Manyi Tenda Rose Tange, Ma Paulina Ngwekeum Tange, mothers from the big compound next door, wives of my father's elder brother. Florence Fruawah Tange, and Rose Ngihkwihi Tange, my father's nieces. Ma Susana Lum Ndimah, and Ma Rufina Bihnyui Ndimah Nsuh, my mother's cousins. Ma Martha Nganteuh, and Mami Kein Ngong, Ma Sohngwe Ngong, our neighbours. Mami Mary Mangay Nwana, my father's niece, who was forever grateful to him for having babysat her.

Immense gratitude to my nephew, Ayeemelee Durrell Waji, who spurred me on after he read the first scripts. The joy and excitement he expressed, chapter after chapter, put a high value tag on the initiative. His suggestions helped to give a more artistic stroke to my brush, especially in areas that needed the enmeshing of intricate details.

My sister, Ngum Delphine stepped in to proof-read some of the chapters that I rewrote. I am thankful for her constant support and words of encouragement.

Finally, and most importantly, I express deep gratitude to my dear friend, Philippe Vivier, for joyfully creating the conducive environment where I was able to plan and begin writing, right to the end. May the rest of the Viviers as well as dozens of friends in Fleurus, Belgium, accept my thanks for the indirect support they gave me throughout that period!

Table of Contents

Preface

In writing *Behold the College Girls*, I set out to recapture some of the most exciting moments in boarding school during my time, for the reading pleasure of both young people and others who never had this experience as well as seniors who would enjoy reminiscing over it. For me, it was an attempt to write the type of book that I would have enjoyed reading as a student. I had searched through practically all bookshelves in our college library in vain.

Early in the process I began sharing my writing with my nephew in the USA, who is working in the domain of health, particularly psychology and counseling. He was hooked from the very first chapter. "I can't wait to find out what happens next," he would say. There were days when I slept late or woke up in the wee hours of the morning to complete a chapter quickly for him. "Oh, wow! What a revelation!" he went on. As the work progressed, he began saying, "if only the boys in my former college had known this, their behavior towards girls would have been different." As someone who had attended a boys' boarding school, he was learning something new about women.

His eagerness convinced me that I was creating something that many others would cherish. So, I kept on. *Behold the College Girls* was no longer just for entertainment, as I had originally thought, but more so, informative and educative. "Thank you, aunty. I can't thank you enough for sharing this wonderful story with me," he often said. "We befriended those girls, spent time with them, and thought that we knew them, now I know we didn't."

Soon, I got to the chapters about my vacations in the village which portrayed how I was juggling between studying my class notes and doing intensive farming. "I never knew this about my grandparents," my nephew went on, "though I spent some vacations with them." At that point I realized how instructive it was for a young man who had grown up mainly in the city! "I am very disappointed, even indignant," he once said, with a sigh. "My grandparents should have become millionaires given their consistent efforts to overcome daily challenges."

I kept on following my inspiration and writing daily. Then, I got to the final chapters. "My goodness, this one feels like I was right there myself," he said. "You know what? — you can publish it just the way it is, aunty" he suggested.

Finally, I finished writing and began reading over while editing. After reading through, I let it go for a while. A few weeks later, I picked up my manuscript and read it again. Oh, how fascinating, fresh, and refreshing! It was like I was discovering new stuff each time. How stimulating that I was being absorbed by my own work!

In the end, the writing process, a recollection of the five-year romance of privileged students at a renowned boarding school, raised pertinent questions that hardly crossed the minds of students as well as parents back then, much less received any attention from policy makers and planners. That is why *Behold the College Girls* ends in suspense, hopefully a life-changing experience for the reader. In other words, it is an equation that the writer is kindly inviting the reader to help solve.

While you are brainstorming, rest assured that you will relish the rest of the account in the sequel to this story, entitled, *In Search of My Molecule*.

Chapter 1

Examination Results

It was 9.00 a.m. at Virgin Mother's College, for short, VMC. Teachers began distributing report booklets according to classes; they were reading names out loud. Each recipient quickly flipped through to the final page. The results of the end-of-year examination were like light rays emitted from an overhead electric pole, flashing through the assembly of students.

While the boldly scripted "Passed" and "Promoted" on the last line immediately lit up the lives of some, "Failed" dazzled others. Facial expressions revealed the status of each student. Even introverts found it hard to hide their feelings. Others could not contain themselves; they were shouting for joy and dancing.

"Hmmn, what will I do if I fail?" whispered a Form 2 student to her friend.

"Let's just calm down until we receive our reports," responded her friend.

Some of the anxiously waiting students cupped their mouths with their palms while others were trembling.

The more report booklets received, the more spontaneous and random reactions. They were going off like alarm bells. Students roared as if they were inhaling laughing gas. Others shrieked out, as if being injected by a nurse.

Between the two extremes, a tiny third category remained silent. They looked unshakable like baobab trees. Shock gripped and arrested them in a somewhat meditative mood. Meanwhile, deep tears quietly rolled down a few cheeks. Even some of the Form 5s were sighing and frowning as their results were a vital prognosis. However, they were luckier since theirs was the Mock GCE; their failure was not a final blow.

At last, instructors finished their job, but they could not move away immediately. The multiplicity of theatre scenes before them was compelling. Two-hundred-and-something students were simultaneously acting in individual dramas on the same stage.

Impromptu joyous tunes were blasting out in a cacophony of one-liners. Laughing, giggling, sighing, clapping, the quickening of steps. Elsewhere tears were gushing out. Successful friends and sisters were holding hands and singing mirthfully. Next to them were others covering their wet faces in their hands. Even more pathetic were the three students who crashed to the floor.

Despite crisscrossing sounds, some utterances stood out. "Mamamiéééé!" repeatedly exclaimed students with nice surprises. They were the loudest. Their promotion to the next class animated their limbs. Indeed, they took over the spectacle. The boldest began parading the stage, showing off; they had become the newsmakers of the year. Hand in hand, they danced, jumped, and hugged each other. Some began sweating, though it was a cold morning in Mankon, Bamenda. Others were skipping high up enough to touch the ceiling while exclaiming, "Yeah!" "Yeah!" "Yeah!"

Meanwhile, a group of disappointed students took to the backstage. They were shivering and looking guilty as if their failure had disconnected their energy supply circuits. Mimicking mourners in the village, they were wailing and dragging their buttocks on the floor. It was like an attempt to earth an electric equipment to prevent future shocks. One of them lifted her hands, expressing regrets, "O, what shall I do?" "What would my parents say?" Obviously, their pain was draining energy. Thus, they gradually toned down their moaning like dying batteries.

Meanwhile, Sister Maura, the principal, stood by, helpless. She had already made several unsuccessful attempts to hush down students.

"Hello, girls, hello, hello," shouted the principal.

She was eager to complete her holiday wishes, but who was listening? So, she gave up, waved goodbye, and walked away, smiling ruefully.

As for tutors, they were both congratulating and consoling students. They had never witnessed such an outpouring of feelings after the publication of exam results.

"This is beyond anything we expected," said Mr. Babila, the Arts teacher.

Incidentally, it was the first time that the school administered multiple-choice testing. More than 60% of the questions in science subjects were multiple-choice questions. A total of 8% of the students had failed. It was the highest number of students to repeat a class since the past half-decade. Also, up to 35% had scored only the average mark.

"This exam was misleading," complained dozens of students, loudly and bitterly.

"Why did they give us multiple-choice tests?" asked a Form 3 student.

"It looked like a simple game, but tricky," a Form 2 student remarked.

After completing each test paper, a lot of students were unable to say whether they would pass or fail. Thus, they had maintained a wait-and-see attitude. Now that they were facing the outcome with generalized low performances, they wanted a return to the traditional essay, with open-ended and open-response questions. To them, it was a more practical test of knowledge.

"Only those who grasp the key details can pass in the multiple-choice test," explained a Form 5 student.

"Are you saying that I did not study well?" retorted a Form 3 student who had failed in Biology, one of her best subjects.

"To me, it was like playing a game while blindfolded," said another Form 2 student who had passed.

True or false, those who failed argued that they had adequately prepared for the exams. They used the surprise passes as well as unexpected failures registered across the

3

board, to buttress their case. The Form 2s and Form 3s who failed blamed their misfortune on what they called the ambiguity in the choices. Others, mostly the Form 1s, complained that teachers had not sufficiently drilled them on the techniques of taking multiple-choice tests.

Thus, the obvious question was, what had gone wrong? Who was to blame? Teaching methods? Study tactics? The formulation of multiple-choice questions?

Despite energetic protests, winners were set apart from losers as far as the North Pole is from the South Pole. While the former was poised to move on triumphantly, only two outcomes awaited the latter: repeat the class or drop out of school.

The obligation to leave college without a certificate had tragic consequences on the family of the student. Some recalled what happened to a former student, Memboh. The year before, her mother, Mami Tidzie, had lamented over her daughter's failure as if she were mourning. Her weeping had left a more ominous cloud over her yard than the blinding smoke escaping through the grass rooftop of her firewood kitchen. Later, she had lost control of herself at the open Food Market while responding to her friends' inquiries about her daughter. She had burst out into hot tears.

"Instead of a bucket, Memboh has taken a basket to the stream to fetch water," Mami Tidzie cried. "What shall I do?"

Memboh's failure in Form 2 had equally broken the hearts of her elder sister and uncle, who had been contributing towards her school fees. Their two-year investment towards her education had evaporated. Mami Tidzie was inconsolable, repeatedly saying that her failure had deprived the family of "the water of knowledge." How would her children grow, much less bear fruit? She compared her children to stunted plants.

The sad mother could not bear her burdens alone. She visited her neighbours in search of consolation and ideas. At each stop, she cried, refusing to eat whatever they offered her.

Meanwhile, her husband, a polygamist with three wives, was infuriated. He could no longer spend precious cash earned from his carpentry business on school fees, especially on his daughters. "Didn't I tell you to groom her for marriage?" the irate man had asked his third wife.

It was common for miserable mothers like Mami Tidzie to give away their teen-age daughters to wealthy families in large cities like Douala and Yaounde. Allowing Memboh to go live with strangers was like playing the lottery with her last coin. The young girl joined the list of undocumented babysitter-housekeepers. Her future was as blurred as a nimbus cloud.

The bell began ringing. It was the end of the assembly. The late morning sun began shining bright. Its rays were piercing through the maroon wooden windows and reflecting on the red brick walls.

Classmates began grouping to compare marks. However, all ears were eager to hear the complete results of the notorious Form 2s. Failing in that class was like committing a crime. "Who has failed?" was the recurring question. According to tradition, anyone who repeated that class received the label of "rotten potato." The in-coming Form 2s would jeer at such a girl, especially if she had bullied them while they were "foxes." Besides, senior students would intimidate her at every turn. They would mock her, saying she had suddenly become a wild dog with fallen-off fangs.

On a more sympathetic note, there were four Form 2 students who were everyone's concern. If any of them failed, they would have to pack their bags and return home, never to come back, like Memboh. They were a foursome in a category of their own. Their haughty classmates secretly referred to them as *Moukouta* (an untreated fibre bag for carrying freshly harvested food) girls.

Despite the disparaging label, the rest of the class envied the four girls for their record performances. Indeed, they never dropped below the red line in any subject despite attendant personal difficulties. So far, each of them has obtained the best score in at least one course. No personal setbacks ever discouraged them. From time to time, one of them would come close to the edge of a crisis; yet she would bounce back. Another would be feeling sick; still, she would attend classes. The four girls ended up gravitating towards each other as if they were quadruplets. Indeed, they often did their homework together. Eventually, the rest of the class fondly referred to the determined foursome as the "Four Rocks."

The report-booklet-comparing session finally ended. Students began dispersing towards their dormitories or to the refectory.

Meanwhile, some of those who had failed were still sobbing.

"What will I tell my parents, ooh," wept a Form 1 student.

"This is not a *cry-die* (a dirge during mourning), it's not the end of the world, Suzie. You still have another chance," consoled her Big (assigned caretaker).

Other senior students, friends, and Bigs were equally holding the "weeping willows" by hand and comforting them.

Meanwhile, the news was already spreading around that three of the Four Rocks had passed. Indeed, their success had caused part of the fireworks created by excited students.

On their way to the refectory, the three girls suddenly stopped midway and looked back, worried. One of them was missing.

"Where is Maahtou?" asked Eposi.

"Hey, I've not seen her since we received our results," said Nubodem.

"You are right. She was on the line at the beginning, but then where did she go afterward?" asked Ngwe.

Indeed, by the time instructors finished handing out report booklets, she was no longer in the hall.

So, on the spot, the three Four Rocks changed their direction and rushed to Ave Maria, Maahtou's and Eposi's dormitory. They did not see her. They rushed towards the locker room while calling out her name, but she was not there.

None of her dorm mates had seen her. Though the three friends were each starving, they decided to first find her. Each of them went to the other three dormitories.

Chapter 2

No Second Chances

Maahtou suffered from a dizzy spell while students were gathered at the assembly waiting for their report booklets. For fear of falling, she had pressed herself against the wall. She could not ask for help since each student was suffering from anxiety.

As soon as she received her report booklet, she quietly waded her way through the unsuspecting crowd of students. The moment she was out of sight, she plodded towards the opposite direction of the assembly hall. She walked slowly until she reached the Laboratory block. There, she sat on the green lawn and closed her eyes. Not only was she feeling weak, but she was afraid to open her booklet. She took a deep breath and picked it up. Then, she threw it back on her lap. What if…? She imagined what she would do if she had not made it. Oh no, the thought was too scary. She would faint. She could not summon up the courage. She inhaled and exhaled several times while pressing both palms against her chest.

For the second time, she closed her eyes. Then, she opened them furtively and peeped at the light blue booklet on her lap. Her hands were shaking. So, she paused for a while and imagined what would become of her life if she failed. Repeating the class would be a better outcome. Worst still, her guardian could not afford to pay double fees.

For the moment, she was afraid to pursue the worst-case scenario. Another thought quickly came to mind. Hadn't she done her absolute best to study? Hadn't she and the other Four Rocks revised every subject? At the end of her self-introspection, she felt no tinge of guilt. However, what if she had not paid careful attention to each question in the various subjects? Yet, of what use were those questions when the stark reality was merely the flipping of a page away? It was too late to make amends. So, she decided to rather keep hope alive.

In the event where her optimum effort does not grant her promotion to the next class, she would plead with her family to support her in an alternate pathway to life. At that instance, she imagined her mother hugging her and consoling her while repeating that it would be okay.

Within a second, a feeling of calm came over her whole body. So, she picked up her report booklet and opened it. What she saw quickened her entire being. "Yeah, yeah," she cried out for joy. Then she raised her hands, and energy began flowing into her veins. Happiness was hugging her with a warmth that spontaneously got her to her feet. She skidded forward and backward.

Where were her friends, the Four Rocks? Had they passed? How could she speedily convey the good news to her parents? She began walking towards the dormitory. Her mind was darting between her friends and her family. She quickened her steps. At the same time, she was longing to be with her parents and younger siblings in Santa as well as her elder sister, Bongshee in Victoria. She was dying to shout out a thank you to her elder sister. She was grateful to her for having given her the chance to attend one of the renowned colleges in West Cameroon.

Maahtou stopped in front of the stairs and opened her report booklet again. She turned over to the last page. Yes, indeed, she had passed. Her eyes ran down the page, subject after subject. She had top grades in Chemistry and Literature.

Right there, she began imagining her family's response to her performance. Immediately, her mother would stand up, wherever she was, tighten her wrapper around her waist and sing one of her on-the-spot compositions, with hands lifted to the sky. Her father would smile while energetically polishing his shoes in continuous strokes to a perfect shine. As an expression of his joy, Baba (her father) would kill the fattest cock, which Mama would prepare to celebrate her success. Or better still, if Baba had enough money, he would buy the head of a cow.

As for Bongshee, her sponsor, she would laugh and let her face relax and lull into a dream of better days ahead, ushering in rest and merry making. Besides, she would rush and tell her *ndjangui* (savings and loan) members that the money she borrowed the previous year was already yielding profits.

Indeed, during the endless hours of preparing for exams, Maahtou had been feeling a recurrent throbbing in her body. Bongshee's anxious face kept appearing before her. Her guardian's caution against dashing away their family's hopes kept ringing in her ears like a mobile instructor. It was like the humming of a bee, ready to sting if she lazed away. Above all, she desired a bee that would rather pour out its sweet honey to crown her success.

Just before stepping into the dormitory, Maahtou opened her report booklet again. Yes, yes, she was not dreaming! Her total score in Form 2 was an outright improvement from the borderline pass in Forms 1. She recalled how the previous year Bongshee had sighed while shaking her head in disapproval. Having passed, she was going to begin the senior section in college. She could not help imagining herself graduating successfully.

Maahtou could not contain herself any longer. She began thinking of the rest of her classmates. She was dying to see the Four Rocks. Instead of entering the dormitory, she gripped her report booklet and started running towards the refectory. Nubodem, one of the Four Rocks, was first to notice when she stepped in through the door. Exceptionally, they were all sitting at the same table. The prefects had been lenient in allowing girls to relax by sitting wherever they wanted. Maahtou stared at them, one after the other, hoping to read their results on their faces. They were all smiling.

"What is your direction, Maahtou?" they all asked in chorus in coded language.

"Ascending," Maahtou said while holding her right thumb up.

"And you," asked Maahtou. Each of them equally held their thumbs up. "Almost reaching the top of the Buea Mountain," said Eposi with a broad smile. Maahtou shook her body in celebration before pulling out the empty chair reserved for her. As if remotely controlled, the Four Rocks stretched out their hands and clasped them together at the centre of the table. Maahtou was eager to hear the details of each of their performances.

"Show me, I want to see for myself," Maahtou requested while passing her report booklet to them.

They each opened theirs one after the other, Eposi, Ngwe, and Nubodem and piled them up in front of Maahtou.

"Yeah," "yeah," "yeah," "yeah," they exclaimed with bubbling joy. Each of them had performed better than the first year. With an overall score of 75% in the core subjects, Maahtou had moved upwards by 10% compared to the last end-of-year exams.

"Shiii," Nubodem cautioned. They began speaking in low tones, out of respect for the Form 3 girl who was sobbing at the table next to theirs. They gave each other high fives and proceeded to twist their thumbs over the middle finger, producing a cracking sound effect.

Having exchanged their report booklets, they began telling Maahtou all that they knew about the rest of their classmates. For those of them admitted into Form 3, their overall scores ranged between 55% and 85%. The headline news was the rise in passes in Mathematics and Physics. That meant that six more students were going to automatically join the club of the Logical Oversabis (Pidgin for "knowing too much"), the proud group of students who, since Form 1, had maintained at least an average pass in Mathematics and or in Physics. Members of the club often took pleasure in parading around the campus with a Physics or Mathematics textbook in hand. The last of the Four Rocks to become a member of the Logical Oversabis was Ngwe after she passed in Physics in the third term of Form 1.

The Four Rocks were among the last to leave the refectory. The girls were so happy that they helped the kitchen staff in picking up some of the bowls and plates scattered on tables here and there.

When the Four Rocks got outside, they found it hard to separate from each other. So, they stood out by the hibiscus shrub near the terrace wall and shared their vacation plans. Maahtou was the only one who was going to two places—first to Santa and later to Victoria. The others found out that she was the only one among them that was being sponsored by her elder sister.

"What a wonderful sister you have!" exclaimed Eposi.

The three girls became even more curious when they learned that Maahtou's elder sister-guardian, Bongshee, was not even up to ten years older than her. How did Bongshee become Maahtou's sponsor? Maahtou's friends were curious.

"Do you remember that I arrived here at the campus only three days after college resumed?" asked Maahtou. "My fees were the cause of that delay."

"Yes, of course, I still remember" answered Nuboderm and Ngwe. "You had on a beautiful dress," added Ngwe. Nubodem nodded.

"I still remember when you and your mother first entered the dormitory," said Eposi.

"I was so happy when you offered to show me the locker room," said Maahtou to Eposi.

Spontaneously each began pointing to some unforgettable event of their first day at college. While walking to their various dormitories, Maahtou's mind began straying into the unforgettable scenes of the day she first set foot on campus. That was two years ago.

Though Maahtou's mother kept entreating her to concentrate on her schoolwork, her eyes were capturing everything on the road. It was also her very first trip to

Bamenda. Deep down in her soul she was struggling with two pressing matters—Firstly, would she be able to catch up with the two days she had lost? Secondly, would she find friendly girls? It was the first time in her life to leave her family to live with total strangers in an unfamiliar place.

Chapter 3

Behold the Campus

The yellow taxicab from the crowded city centre made its way into a paved road, leading up onto a hill. The driver slowed down to allow pedestrians to cross the street. Some were carrying loads on their heads. Others were dragging food bags with strained hands. There was a truck filled beyond capacity with bunches of leeks and *njama njama* (huckleberry leaves).

After a hundred meters or so, the driver slowed down again and turned right. Some young boys were playing football at a primary school field. They were running excitedly and raising dust in the air. The narrow, unpaved road was scanty, but for a few people descending on foot. Soon, the car got lost into a forest of giant eucalyptus trees. The air was fresh and permeated with a distinct minty, pine smell, oozing out from the densely packed leaves of the trees. Hundreds of long branches gently danced to the wind. They swung in from both sides, joining together and forming a closely-knit canopy in the middle of the road. For a while, contact with the sky was cut off. It seemed like driving through a trail of nature's healing potion.

Suddenly, a grey Land Rover, followed by a black Mercedes car, bypassed the taxicab. Instinctively, the taxicab driver increased his speed. The remainder of the road got steeper as it swerved its way out of the forest.

Without warning, tall, pale green and yellowish grass bushes appeared on both sides of the road. Then, right ahead was a series of terraces. A long, reddish brick building was sitting on a wide and long patio to the left of the entranceway.

"That's your college," Mama said to Maahtou. From the back seat of the car where mother and daughter were sitting, Maahtou raised her head and began peering in front from left to right without saying a word.

She had been quiet all along. Her eyes had been too busy capturing every object in sight. It was her first-ever glimpse of the college. Within seconds, the whole view spread before her in the form of several buildings, amidst terraces here and there.

Slowly, the taxicab pulled up, and made a right turn to the top edge of a terrace by the right. Two girls, wearing slippers, one in a loose gown, the traditional *kabba*, and the other in a green knee-length dress, were chatting in front of one of the buildings. Mother and daughter guessed that the series of parallel long red brick buildings, to their right, must be the dormitories.

It was the very first time that Maahtou stepped foot onto the grounds of a boarding school. She was glancing left and right. The natural, maroon-coloured concrete on the walls of the terraces contrasted with yellow, red, and blue flowers by the sidewalks. Virgin Mother's College was captivating. She felt like jumping and exclaiming in praise of the striking sight before her.

While Mama was getting her balance from the driver, Maahtou was steadily taking a glance of the first general view with the camera of her eyes. They moved from the environment to the students. They were in pairs and groups, strolling in various directions. Before she realized, the taxicab was driving off.

Mama carried her snack bag while Maahtou lifted her suitcase. Her rolled-up straw mattress was lying on the ground. In which direction should they go? They wondered without saying a word as their eyes moved from building to building.

Within minutes, the two ladies, probably in their late teens or early twenties approached them from the long building situated to the left side of the road. They were each carrying a ledger in hand. They stopped in front of them and said, "welcome." Then, they asked for Maahtou's name. Immediately, one of them proceeded to flip through the pages of her ledger. Within a few minutes of staring at the page, she wrote in it with her pen, lifted her head, and smiled at Maahtou and Mama. Within minutes registration was over. The other lady opened her ledger and flipped through the pages. She stopped at a page, wrote something, and patted Maahtou on her back. Then, she offered to take Maahtou to her preassigned dormitory.

Mama was following closely and hoping they would let her in too. Promptly, Mama's request was granted. The young lady took Maahtou's suitcase. Mama held her bag while Maahtou picked up her mattress and placed it on her head. As they were walking, Maahtou began wondering what part of the official welcome ceremony she had missed. It was already the third day since schools reopened.

Though Bongshee had written to the principal to that effect, Maahtou was feeling a little disoriented. What could be going on right now? She hoped that she had not missed a crucial part of the welcome of fresh students.

They finally reached the first building, which was to their right. There was a flight of six steps, or so, leading up to the door. The dormitory was a single-floor hall, stretching straight from one end to the other. A dozen students were sitting on their beds. A tall student, looking more mature, quickly stood up from the first bed at the entrance and gave Maahtou and Mama a handshake.

Next, she asked for Maahtou's name. Then, she turned around and picked up a sheet of paper from her bed and stared into it. "Follow me," she said. They moved close to the end of the hall, towards the left-wing, adjacent to another dormitory, which was visible through the window.

She stopped and pointed at a bed. Then, she helped Maahtou to place her mattress on the bed. Maahtou quickly opened her suitcase and took out her two white bed sheets, a pillow, and covers. The senior student stood by, waiting. She picked up the edge of the bedsheet and helped Maahtou to make up her bed. Mama's eyes glowed with joy as she smiled broadly. She kept saying, "thank you, "thank you," thank you, *ma pickin*," (my child) non-stop.

"Yes, Mama," the mature girl answered. When they finished making the bed, Mama embraced her.

"*You take care, na ya small sister, ok?*" pleaded Mama. (Please, take good care of her, she is your younger sister). *Wetiy be ya name, ma pickin?*" asked Mama. (What is your name, my child?).

"Grace," the student said. "*You be na ma pickin sef sef,*" Mama said with broad smiles while embracing her. (You are my very own child).

While Grace walked away for a while, Mama sat on Maahtou's bed and gave her final instructions. Then, she stood up, embraced Maahtou, and bid her goodbye. Of course, Maahtou walked out with Mama and saw her off.

As soon as she returned, Miss Grace, who by now, Maahtou realized was the dormitory captain, announced the rest of the program for the evening. Maahtou nodded. Then, she returned to her bed and began unpacking her bags. She had to put away her stuff quickly to get ready for supper.

While she was still arranging her valise, one of the girls who was sitting five beds away at the opposite roll, came over to welcome Maahtou. She was called Eposi.

"Come and see the locker room," said Eposi.

Maahtou trotted behind her, curious to see the place. Grace had mentioned it and pointed to it, but she had barely nodded. It was a new word to her.

Eposi pushed the door open and ushered Maahtou in. There were more than a dozen wooden shelves carrying dozens of suitcases, buckets, and bags, here and there. Eposi showed her the shelves reserved for new students.

She thanked Eposi and returned to her bed. She continued to sort her toiletries from her clothes. When she finished, Eposi and one another girl, Bih, came over and helped her carry her suitcase and bag into the locker room. Eposi and Bih were also new students like Maahtou. She immediately asked them what they had done during the first two days. "Don't worry," said Eposi. "Classes have not yet begun," said Bih.

18

When Maahtou finished arranging her stuff in the locker room, the dormitory captain requested Eposi and Bih to show Maahtou the bathrooms and toilets. There was still time left before supper. So, the two guides walked Maahtou from block to block, pointing to the other dormitories. The girls reassured Maahtou that she was not the last one to arrive. The only thing she had missed was the Orientation wherein rules and regulations were given and explained.

The bell started ringing. It was time for supper.

When they got to the refectory, there were over a hundred students already. Maahtou's guides took her to a table at the entrance where a senior student was looking through several sheets of paper. She asked for Maahtou's name and quickly flipped through her documents. Then, she pointed to Maahtou's table. There were two other Form 1s at her table.

The meal that evening was plantain and *njama njama* stew. Maahtou ate the vegetables but did not touch the plantains. For someone coming from Victoria, those ones looked somewhat shrivelled. Besides, she was not feeling hungry. She was more eager to discover the rest of the school and get to know the other students.

Maahtou did not have to wait to find out who was who. Girls, especially the Form 4s and 5s, were chattering away about the big news for the evening– the welcome party for fresh students. No wonder there was so much excitement in the refectory. That equally explained why there were only a few students at some tables.

Chapter 4

First Campus Party

Immediately after supper, students rushed to their various dormitories to get ready. Maahtou almost missed the route to her dorm, but for a Form 3 student who pointed Ave Maria to her.

The locker room was busy. Each student was digging into her trunk for their best dress. Others were rushing in and out, asking for a belt or scarf to match their dress. Maahtou asked why such exhilaration. One Form 3 student explained that Social was the rare chance for each student to be dressy. It was an exclusive chance to show off individual tastes, personalities. Girls seized the opportunity to flaunt their new and best outfits.

At first, Maahtou was not sure what attire to put on. However, she began thinking of her most treasured outfit. She had recovered it from Mama's trunk as soon as she got to Santa. For years she had not won it. It used to be her ceremonial dance costume in the village. Since it was a special night, she imagined that nothing could be more appropriate. It was the multi-coloured, raffia wrap-around skirt worn for Makongui dance. The last time she wore that costume was the week before traveling to Victoria during a big *cry-die* (death ceremony) in the village. The girls' dance had performed alongside women's and men's dances. The fourteen girls ranged from ages eight and twelve. As soon as the announcer called up their dance group, they were ushered in amidst thunders of applause. Their uniform was quite an attraction; everyone congratulated them.

While dancing to the drumbeats and singing in response to their leader, their little feet raised a lot of dust. At the climax, they began digging their toes into the ground, thrice on each side, in rhythm to the music. Spectators applauded as they displayed their multi-coloured cha-chas (pompoms) into the air from left to right. Their parents and others came around the circle and rewarded them with precious coins.

Though three years older, Maahtou still cherished the raffia skirt. She and her mates had each weaved their costumes. The task had taken weeks to accomplish. Firstly, they had peeled off the thin fibre from piles and piles of the palm frond. Then, the weaving process began. It required making a long rope for a band to the desired width. It was on it that they wove in the rest of the fibre along the full waistband.

Finally, they went by the stream in search of the colouring plant. Each person harvested the leaves bearing their desired colours. After pouring boiled water onto a handful of leaves, the colours came out. Then, they steeped sections of the skirt into the solution. In just a matter of minutes, the dry beige fibres took on bright, beautiful colours - green, blue, yellow, red, purple.

While in Victoria, Maahtou did not miss her skirt because she did not belong to any children's traditional dance group. However, that skirt was her treasure. During her return journey to the village, she began reminiscing over the past glory of their dance group.

Social must be the occasion to show it off, she thought to herself. If not, when else? She proudly pulled out her fibre skirt from the trunk and smiled. She beheld the green-blue-yellow colours still shimmering as if it had been newly weaved. She was delighted after she tried it on. She was grateful to Mama for having advised her during the crafting process to make it longer than her size at that time.

Next, she pulled out the yellow blouse that Bongshee had bought for her the previous year. She first put on her white cotton underskirt, and then the matching top, after which, she wrapped the Makongui skirt over the underwear. She was feeling triumphant. Though the Form 1s were informed that there were not going to be any cultural dances, Maahtou thought that her costume would serve as a tribute to the Santa Girls' Mokongui Dance.

To her utter dismay, loud shouts and screams greeted her when she stepped out from the locker room into the dormitory. Girls laughed and clapped their hands while falling on their beds. Others came and pulled the frays of her skirt while those at the other end made traditional dance steps back and forth. The rest of the students laughed. Of course, they were not cheering for her. Quite the contrary. What had she done wrong? Maahtou wondered. She just stood there, feeling embarrassed.

"Is that what you are going to wear, Maahtou"? A Form 3 girl, who was later confirmed as her Big, asked.

Maahtou was so stunned by the question that she just stared at her, lost.

"Look at other girls. Do you see their dresses?"

Maahtou looked down at her outfit. "What's wrong with it?" she asked.

"Are you a *villageoise*?" (villager), asked Pamela and Christy, Form 3 girls.

"What do you mean?" Maahtou asked with tears in her eyes.

"That means that this is not the village," Christy explained.

Maahtou was obliged to rush back into the locker room. The only other non-uniform dress which came to mind was what she had upon arrival. It was her most elegant outfit, a multiple-coloured floral dress with a white background. She put it on with her three-inch, heeled, covered black sandals. Quickly, she rushed out of the locker room and followed the trail of girls flogging out from each dormitory.

Within minutes, all students were pushing their way into the assembly hall, where familiar tunes played from the record player. Maahtou sat at a corner by the entrance and kept watching. Every girl was in her best dress. A lot of them wore beautiful, imported ready-made gowns of various styles and colours. Some had glitters on their dresses. Most senior students wore longer gowns, evening gowns commonly called "*soirees*."

The girls who were in charge had arranged the hall to provide ample dancing space. There were also two long chains of tables along the inner wall on which soft drinks and chewables including chin-chin and biscuits, were displayed.

Soon, the principal arrived in the company of staff members. A student was ahead of them to give the signal. Everyone stood up and welcomed them with applause. The authorities smiled and waved at the students. The usher quickly accompanied them to their seats.

The first part of the program was formal. A Form 5 student, Miss Maggie, was the Mistress of Ceremonies, the MC. Immediately after the greetings, she introduced all students with offices of responsibility, beginning with the senior prefect.

After that, it was the turn of the Form 1s. A Form 5 student helped them to form a long line, facing everyone. There were thirty-eight of them. One after the other, they shouted out their names and the names of their hometowns.

When the introductions were over, a thunder of sustained applause followed. The principal and members of staff moved forward and greeted each of them. The school prefects followed suit.

Next on the program was the serving of drinks and snacks. Soon, it was dancing time. It began with the opening of the floor. The principal and staff members had the honor. After that, a second tune came up. Everyone was free to choose their dance partner.

After two more singles, it was time for all the fresh students to dance. It was a disco piece. The music was loud. The MC encouraged each of the girls to show their styles. Everyone knew the famous tune that was playing. It was Mr. Bigstuff. Maahtou particularly liked it. She often danced to it back home in Victoria. She recalled how Bongshee usually got her dancing in the living room, Saturday evenings, especially when her friends were visiting. They would all sit back, singing along, and clapping for her. Each Form 1 girl was dancing and twisting her body from side to side. Meanwhile, the rest of the students clapped for them.

Dancing went on until 8:20 when the MC announced one more tune, and the party was over.

The following morning, during breakfast, the welcome party was the talk of the tables. Students recalled scenes that had caught their attention. Surprisingly, Maahtou received a lot of compliments for her dress, from both senior students and her classmates. They said that they particularly liked her dress because its flounces flipped up and down while she was dancing.

Maahtou could never have imagined that she would feature among those who had stolen the show. Even in her class, three girls stood up at the front, during break time, and imitated Maahtou's three-steps dress. They were moving the edges of their skirts up and down to the tune of the hummed music.

The talk about her dress continued during lunchtime at the refectory. Some senior students pointed at her. She turned around and looked inquiringly, as broad smiles greeted her. Form 3 students at her table explained to her that they were talking about her dress.

Maahtou thanked them and smiled back timidly. Then, she began thinking about the secret linked to her cute dress. She wondered what their attitude would be if they found out.

Indeed, it was one of Bongshee's hand-me-down dresses. In a painstaking process, Maahtou had managed to transform it from a size 16 to 6. Overall, it took Maahtou one week. The task consisted of calculations, measuring, cutting, and stitching the pieces together. It provoked a lot of sweating. She would make a mistake, stop and blame herself, and then correct it. With the excess material, she cut out the three extra layers, which caused the hearts of so many students to flutter. None of them knew the headaches, frustrations, and gymnastics she had gone through to change it into hers. From the armholes, the width to the length, the dress went through drastic modification. During the sewing, she mistakenly sewed the wrong side of one of the layers onto the good side of the others. She had to undo it and take it all over. Without excess material, it would not have been possible.

Even Bongshee herself had no clue what physical strain and mental stress Maahtou had gone through to transform her old dress. All the work on the dress was done during Maahtou's free time, when Bongshee was either at work, visiting, or attending a meeting.

The compliments from students were totally a nice surprise. Maahtou beamed. She was so proud of herself.

However, she kept wondering whether fellow students would have congratulated her or treated her with disdain if they knew the truth. Would they have still admired the dress, had they found out in advance that she was the one who had made it?

In any case, she tucked away the details in her heart.

Chapter 5

Punishment Without Crime

Ave Maria dormitory feast day was barely weeks away. Each year students came up with new activities to keep the community bubbling with excitement. While some senior students were exchanging ideas on types of amusement as well as the show of talents, Mercy, a Form 5 student came up a huge project. She wanted to direct a play. It took two days to decide on the cast of her chosen play. Apart from two Form 3s and one Form 4 student, she selected her actors and actresses mainly from the newly arrived Form 1s. Maahtou was among the six girls selected for a speaking role.

After their first meeting, Mercy duly handed out respective parts to each of them. She proceeded to conduct a dry run on the spot, leading to the switching of some roles. Then, she gave them four days to memorize their parts.

On Friday, as the last class was about to begin, Mercy appeared stealthily by the window of the Form1 class and waved. She held up a sheet of paper with the name of the play and the rehearsal time written on it. One of the girls by the window got the message and passed it on. All the girls with parts to play were to meet Mercy after lunch.

Friday afternoons were free of prep. So, instead of beginning weekend chores like laundry, they had to do the first rehearsal of the play.

Everyone was excited except Maahtou. She had forgotten to memorize her part. What was she going to do? By then, the Geography teacher was writing on the board. He had not noticed when his class was being distracted from outside. As the others started pulling out their copies from their lockers, Maahtou realized that hers was away in the dormitory. No luck. She could not ask for permission because the ongoing class was the introductory class. Even if she did, there was not enough time to memorize her part.

The only time she had was during lunch. That day, she rushed over her food and arrived at the hall before the others. Shaken and shivering, she tried to run her eyes through the five speeches that made up her part. It was impossible to grasp them all. So, she came back to the first page and started repeating the two first speeches. Luckily, they were not long, but that was only as far as she could go. Mercy arrived while Maahtou was doing a trial run with her acting mate. So far, it was beautiful.

The general rehearsal started with Maahtou taking off smoothly. However, she stumbled and paused at the second speech. Mercy was enraged. Maahtou apologized while promising to do her best to catch up before the next rehearsal. Mercy frowned and raised up her forefinger in anger.

Instead of continuing with the rest, Mercy stopped the rehearsal. She started yelling and insulting Maahtou. "What is wrong with you, stupid girl?" In the meantime, she asked the other girls to continue working on their parts while ordering Maahtou to follow her.

Maahtou had no idea why Mercy was taking her away from the hall. The senior student was moving so fast that the little girl was running after her. When they got into the dormitory, almost all fifty or so dormitory mates were there. Maahtou thought that Mercy was looking for someone to replace her.

No, not so. Mercy ordered Maahtou to stand in front of the entrance. That spot, near the dormitory captain's bed, was the imaginary podium from where the prefects made announcements.

As soon as Mercy stood there, the whole dormitory became silent. All eyes were on her. Instead of making an announcement, Mercy began pointing to Maahtou. Girls began sitting up on their beds. In her opening statement, Mercy declared that Maahtou was disobedient and disrespectful. Then, she went on, elaborating on Maahtou's crime.

Some students began exclaiming and calling it "the audacity of a Form1." Their spontaneous reactions seemed to offer more cud for Mercy to regurgitate. So, she moved two steps away from Maahtou, and stared at her from head to toe, like dazzling light. With one hand at her waist, she moved from end to end, as if she were performing on stage.

"Look at her, stupid thing, dull girl, poor fool," she blasted out while throwing her hands in the air, with increasing rashness and harshness in her merciless smearing of Maahtou.

Meanwhile, forty pairs of eyes began scanning Maahtou to determine her degree of stupidity, dullness, poverty, and foolishness. Yet, she remained stiff like a "pillar of salt." Though her eyes brimmed with tears, indignation was building up inside her. She would not cry. If she did, she would tarnish her natural beauty, blur her sight, blunt her mind, thereby lending credence to Mercy's vituperation.

The only thing for which Maahtou was desperate was for someone in the dormitory to stop Mercy, or at least, plead for mercy on her behalf. No one did. The prick of loneliness began stinging her like a bee. More tears were filling her eyes and swelling up in readiness to gush out.

"I think it's because Maahtou had arrived three days late," explained Bertha, Maahtou's Big. Finally, someone spoke up. Maahtou inhaled and breathed out in relief.

Mercy turned around and stared into Bertha's face as if to say, how dare a Form 3 student challenge a Form 5 student? At that instance, Mercy raised her voice. She insisted that Maahtou had deliberately refused to memorize her part. She had defaulted on purpose.

Of course, Maahtou knew that Mercy was misjudging her. Since no one else came to her rescue, she began mumbling words to refute Mercy's condemnation. Mercy shouted down at her, and carried on, increasing the severity of her insults. It felt like torrential rainfall, with hailstones crashing on Maahtou's head.

"How dare you?" "Look at your ugly face," said Mercy. "Idiot, who do you think you are?"

What had Maahtou's person as a Homo Sapien to do with forgetting to memorize drama texts? Mercy was crossing the line of decency. Maahtou was enraged. She wondered why Mercy was not taking the blame for having chosen a poor, ugly, stupid girl as a character in her play. Had she been wise herself, she would have created the role of a nincompoop for Maahtou to perform.

Still Mercy went on berating Maahtou. The indifference of the other girls infuriated the lonely girl, who was subjected to shock treatment. Why were they silent as if Mercy were merely acting? Maahtou was taking the full blows; she was hurting so badly.

The lonely victim was dying to shout out in pain, yet she could not. Instead, she began shivering. The seeming hours of torture were becoming unbearable. Maahtou wanted so badly to cry, but something deep down inside was fighting back the tears. Mercy did not deserve the honor to see her embattled state. It was better to weep in the locker room with her face plunged into her trunk. Yet, for how long could she hold back the avalanche?

Just when Maahtou reached the breaking point, Mercy dismissed her with the sweep of the back of her right hand as if brushing off a buzzing fly. Tarnished, sad, embarrassed, and alone, Maahtou burst out crying, while moving towards the locker room. Blinded by tears, she bumped into a student. Maahtou began excusing herself while the student instead dug into her heels, blocking the passage. Maahtou removed her hand from her eyes and looked up.

"*Kor kwiie nguier mbar, Neumour,*" (Don't cry anymore, Sweetheart), said Philomena, in a gentle voice. Maahtou now realized that instead of being an obstruction, she was providing a wall of protection. The sympathetic Form 2 student stretched her hand and rubbed Maahtou's back while she sobbed. Maahtou soon calmed down.

Meanwhile, Maahtou's Big, Bertha, and two other senior students confronted Mercy. They expressed their disapproval at her method of discipline. She brushed them off and walked away.

"Wow! I didn't know that Mercy was so arrogant," said Grace, the dormitory captain.

"Maybe she is mistaking Maahtou for their house girl or something," added Bridget.

The bell for supper began ringing. That evening, Maahtou sat at the refectory, heavy like a wet lug of wood, with swollen eyes. She remained silent all evening, even during prep.

Later, she returned to her dormitory, where she quickly put on her nightdress, long before anyone else. For almost half an hour, the obloquy scene came back to her repeatedly. Gentle tears rolled down her cheeks. She stood up and stepped outside, though it was pitch dark. She wanted to dissolve her tears in the tap water near the shower rooms. On her return trip, she sat on the stairs and contemplated her predicament. Then, she overheard her Big and another sympathizing student remarking that Mercy had exaggerated in her tirade.

"Why did she insult her like that?" questioned Bertha.

"She should simply have dismissed her from the play," said Delphine.

"I don't know why some students think that they are better than others just because of their privileges," added Bertha.

"This palaver of fair complexion, where shall we go with it?" asked Delphine.

Maahtou's failure was not idiosyncratic. It was commonplace for Form 1 students to blunder within the first weeks and months of arrival. Some lost their panties while others forgot their towels in the bathroom or laundry line. Similarly, they broke the rules inadvertently.

However, in cases of blatant disrespect, a senior student would summon the culprit and warn her. As for outright rebellion, top students punished specific intolerable acts like rudeness, lying, or purloining. They ordered such students to either weed the flower bed or to scrub the stairs while her classmates play.

Regrettably, Maahtou's case stood in a category of its own. Students wondered whether Mercy knew Maahtou prior to her admission to college, and if she was settling some old scores.

The day was over; it was lights-out time. Feeling lonely in a dark dormitory, Maahtou tried to harness uncontrollable thoughts running through her mind, like free radicals. Although Philomena was no longer standing by her, Maahtou could still hear her soothing words as well as feel the soft touch of her gentle hands. It was relieving as a Mentholatum balm on an aching body. It seemed to be producing instant heat on her freezing body. Yet, she felt a ball of pain stuck in her throat as if her body's defence mechanism were out of order. She did not want to cry anymore, but the tears flowed out freely and wet her pillow. How she wished she were at the laboratory for a Chemistry class! The teacher would have given her laughing gas. She did not want to pass for a pitiful actress with swollen and red eyes.

The following morning, Maahtou's classmates heard the news of her tragedy. Three other classmates who had gone through similar, but less severe ordeals, shared their pain with Maahtou. Upon seeing her swollen, red eyes, her classmates came to her desk and surrounded her.

"Where is the link between a student's family status and failure to memorize a script in time?" they all wondered.

"Or is it because Mercy is fair while Maahtou is dark in complexion?" questioned Rachel, who had an ebony complexion.

"No, I guess it's because Mercy is from a wealthy family while Maahtou is from a poorer one," said Miriam.

"None of that. It's rather because Maahtou's parents are villagers while Mercy's are city dwellers," said Ngwe, whose parents lived in the village.

"Don't worry, Maahtou, one day, she will fall into a worse trap," concluded her classmates.

Two days after, when Maahtou and the other victims had recovered from the numbness imposed by Mercy, they began looking for ways to hit back.

"Does she think that we came here only to act in a play?" questioned Nubodem.

"Even if we came here to perform drama, she doesn't qualify to be a director," added Miriam.

"Who does she think she is? Even teachers are not so strict," commented Odile.

The three other girls, including Maahtou, came to a final wishful conclusion—Mercy deserved to play a permanent role in the stage of life, wherein antagonists would shout the hell out of her. That was not all. They began brainstorming for an appropriate label for Mercy. Suggestions came up, spontaneously. Some of them were "Longmouth," "Villain," "Mami Talktalk," "Vanity," "Chakara," Kushkush."

It turned out to be such fun that the girls started giggling. Maahtou laughed out loud and bent over, leaning on the others. What a healing potion it was! The girls insisted on coming up with a tag whose meaning no one could easily detect. It had to reflect the fact that Mercy was both pitiful and vicious. Soon, Judith, who was attracted by the laughter, suggested that they each imagine that they were doctors and that Mercy had come to consult them.

After brainstorming for a while, they finally coined a label that scientifically reflected the abusive use of her tongue. They concluded that Mercy was suffering from a disease called Tongsilitis, which they abbreviated as Tongsi.

The following Tuesday, Mercy invited the rest of Form 1 students to resume the rehearsal of her play. Meanwhile, she had dismissed Maahtou.

The girls assembled in the hall on time. Rehearsal began. Everything seemed to be going on smoothly as from the opening scene. However, by the time they got to scene 2 in Act 1, one actress suddenly paused, and began saying, "Ah, ah, ah." Then, she bent her head and tried to peep into her script.

"No, Ngwe, you can't look into your script," Tongsi shouted.

Once more, Ngwe tried to recall her lines. She made it through the first speech but lost the second.

Next, Tongsi called out to Nubodem, who started boldly. Tongsi began nodding. However, Nubodem began stuttering before the end of the first speech. Had she indeed forgotten her lines?

"Nubodem, what's going on? Didn't you say your lines well the other day?"

Tongsi gave her another chance, but it did not work.

Next was Eposi, who began by directly reading from her script.

"No, you can't do that," shouted Mercy. She ordered her to drop her script and go on without it. "I'm sorry, Miss Mercy," said Eposi while shaking her head.

As for Gertrude, she managed to do the first and second parts well, but the third was a total blackout. "What is going on?" shouted Mercy.

Next was Miriam's turn. She strolled in from the door, turned around, and began reciting her part exceedingly well. Mercy was thrilled. She held both hands up in jubilation. Suddenly, Miriam paused. She wanted her script desperately, but Mercy began prompting her. Finally, she finished her part well. Mercy was so happy that she jumped up smiling broadly.

When it was Martha's turn, she recited her part perfectly. Everyone applauded her. Nonetheless, Mercy said that her intonation, as well as her facial expression, did not match her speech. So, she ordered Martha to take it over. Instead of holding her head up, as she did before, she moved around the stage with her head down.

"Are you a machine?" Tongsi shrieked.

Tongsi stood up and asked if any of the previous actresses wanted to take a second chance. Immediately, she warned that she was not going to tolerate any lapses. There was total silence; none was willing. Each actress looked away. They were instead thinking of the History assignments that their teacher had given them.

In desperation, Tongsi dumped her scripts and asked the girls to quit immediately.

The girls walked out sighing. However, as soon as Tongsi's back disappeared into her dormitory, they all burst out laughing, "ha ha ha ha."

Apart from Miriam and Martha, who had gone away, the other three signalled to each other. Together, they walked towards the class and stopped by the stairs.

"Miss Talktalk, Kushkush, Tongsi, serves her right," said Ngwe.

The girls gave each other high fives and rushed to class. Mercy had again misused her tongue due to 'tonsillitis.' Her new 'name' had passed the test.

As soon as they entered the class, the dismissed actresses each embraced Maahtou, informing her that she had missed nothing.

There was an open invitation to another activity. Maahtou and the Four Rocks, including Miriam, decided to join Miss Grace's Choir.

Finally, on Saturday evening, during the feast day of Ave Maria dormitory, Maathou and all her friends, who had been considered inept for Mercy's play, sang, and performed exceedingly well in front of the whole school. Spectators, including staff and guests, gave them a standing ovation. Maahtou and Miriam received a special mention for clarity and the sweetness of their voices.

Miss Grace, Maahtou's dormitory captain, had chosen both Miriam and Maahtou for the duet as lead singers in one of the songs entitled, "Sing Hossana."

Chapter 6

Judgment Day

Finally, the annual Judgment Day (JD) arrived. All students were thrilled except for the Form 1's who dreaded it. It was the last Friday following the end of graduation examinations. JD rituals went on simultaneously in all four dormitories. For years, it had become a tradition, notwithstanding undercover. Students observed it dutifully, but without the knowledge of authorities. They compared it to the seclusion of pregnant women during delivery. Indeed, JD was a birthing exercise. It brought about shrieks from the "cutting of the tails of foxes," following which new "babies" were born.

In preparation for the kick-start, all girls, but for the foxes themselves, that is, the Form 1 students, spent the day regurgitating whatever offenses foxes have committed against them from day one. As from the first term, most vengeful students began nosing around for 'crimes' like sniffing dogs and taking notes.

Early in the morning of JD, grievances and resentments, concealed in every heart, began spewing out while girls took their showers. From then on, and throughout the day, all fingers pointed at foxes. Everyone who frowned was supposed to be frowning against them. Repeated wrongs, as well as flagrant wrongs, headlined all conversations. After classes, students began sharing their lists of 'crimes' so as not to forget any malapropisms.

However, while most of the student population got involved in the ritual just for the fun of it, the spiteful ones delved into it religiously. They grabbed 'crimes' here and there, turning them into personal grudges.

Palpable individual crimes included untidiness, ruffled uniforms, lateness, recurrent naughtiness, untidy hair, bedwetting, selfishness, stubbornness, lying, laziness, gossiping about senior students, caught writing letters to or discussing boyfriends, and disrespecting higher-level students. The worst of all crimes were stealing and owning lost-and-found items.

The Form 2s played a distinct role on JD. They were exclusively in charge of the operation of tail-cutting. They were the actors, the executioners. They often prided themselves on being the daily police, restoring law and order. Exceptionally, they were going to act as soldiers on JD.

The question was, why the Form 2s?

First and foremost, tail-cutting was considered a thankless job that was best suited to the Form 2s because of their notoriety. Most senior students labelled Form 2s as "intolerable," "obnoxious," "offensive," "incurable," "undaunting," and "elusive." Those 2nd-year students seemed to possess unsettling powers. Even their mere presence often raised the heartbeats of others. If a group of them stood chatting or better still, 'plotting,' other students assumed that they were concocting some form of ammonia. That was why they bore the brunt for ills committed on campus, long before any investigation began.

Thus, by assigning tail-cutting to the Form 2s, senior students hoped that it would serve as a remedy to their class-specific sickness, if not, at least, create an extra occasion to manage their stubbornness.

Secondly, the Form 2s were semi-foxes. Vestiges of their cut tails were said to have hardened and protruded on the most stubborn among them. Indeed, such residual tails were wreaking havoc on the established order of the institution.

After two years on campus, and despite multiple warnings, a lot of the Form 2s remained stoic like pebbles or rocks, resisting falling hailstones. Like rocks, they equally withstood scorching sunshine, no matter its duration or intensity. Whenever the girls in charge of discipline were tough on them, rebellious Form 2s became like flints that produced fire when hit by steel. That is, the more anyone tried to hush them down, the more they became self-assertive. Unlike foxes who were still clueless, they claimed to know it all. Thus, they were commonly nicknamed Oversabis. Indeed, some of the very timid foxes of the previous year surprisingly became bold semi-foxes. The audacious ones intruded into the conversations of senior students in the dormitory, sharing their points of view.

"Who asked your opinion?" Mercy was fond of holding them in check.

"Who knows if passing into Form 2 means getting drunk without drinking alcohol?" wondered Anna.

"Have you noticed how, even though they cling together like sheep, they still move up and down, especially on Saturdays, like run-away goats," asked Bridget.

Having mastered life on campus, the Form 2s retained the most undesirable characteristics of foxes. They became experts in finding their way around, not only physically, but also socially speaking. Many also referred to them as Partial-Knowledge Crazies (PKCs) since they often challenged the rules with a cunningness that made them look more innocent than guilty. Overnight they became quick at justifying their deeds and misdeeds, some of which were downright stunning. For example, some Form 2s sewed large pockets into their skirts, into which they hid snacks that they discretely ate in class or during siesta.

So far, all studies over the years indicated that passing into Form 2 was as good as graduating from timidity to fearlessness. They were eager to prove their independence from their Bigs. Instructions from their Bigs became a matter of take-it-or-leave-it. After all, they already mastered difficult tasks like ironing their uniforms.

However, whatever blames were levied against the Form 2s, a few had concrete reasons to celebrate their severance from their Bigs, to regain their independence.

A handful of Bigs constituted a thorn in the flesh of their Smalls. They often scolded them in front of the whole dormitory. Others were fond of prying into the trunks of their wealthy Smalls. Then, they coaxed them into sharing either their goodies or body creams with them. On special occasions like feast days, they borrowed unique dress articles from their well-to-do Smalls.

Nevertheless, senior students with low tolerance for stubbornness perceived the internal changes that Form 2s were undergoing as a personal affront to their authority. Thus, they began looking for the least opportunity to punish them. On Saturdays, they assigned the Form 2s to clean the stinky gutters, apart from other tough or dirty jobs.

Instead of becoming more compliant, the Form 2s claimed they were mere survivors of "comical absurdities." Engaged in a fight for their 'survival,' they did not stop at becoming headstrong but started learning and applying defence mechanisms. Those included the outlandish use of newly acquired vocabulary like favouritism, discrimination, adamant, nonplussed, non-negotiable, and manipulate. They mimicked characters in Literature and History while using phrases like "much ado about nothing," and "vaulting ambition," both from Shakespeare. We are learning "to fly without perching" from Chinua Achebe. They equally flaunted their knowledge of recently learned concepts in the Sciences like osmosis, translucent or opaque to show that, on the one hand they are absorbing knowledge for self-defence, or will remain unmoved in the face of bullying, on the other.

Besides, the Form 2s secretly indulged in the mockery of vindictive senior students, labelling notorious oppressors as Hitler. Similarly, they tagged some Fiendish or Lady Macbeth. As for hypercritical senior students, they dismissed them as girls suffering from MLMs (Multiplicity of Loquacious Maladjustments).

Nonetheless, no one ignored the resourcefulness of the Form 2s. They performed tasks that were best suited to their experience. Dorm captains and prefects admired their general knowledge of Who's Who as well as their navigational mastery of their immediate environment. So, they often requested Form 2s to carry out specific tasks. Those included arranging the locker room, taking the food of absent or sick girls to their bedsides, transmitting messages from dorm to dorm, plaiting and braiding hair, stitching detached buttons, and fixing hemlines of skirts.

Finally, the countdown to the staging of JD activities began. The excitement began mounting in each dormitory. Tail-cutting proper was scheduled for the last hour before lights out; that is 8.00 p.m. The Timekeeper's bell began ringing while the whole dorm started counting down from 20.

The dormitory captain, who chaired the ritual, was, for the occasion, called Madam Mediator. She stood up and made a short welcome statement.

"Hey girls, here we are all gathered on our long-awaited night of the dignity of identity. According to our laws, we strongly condemn habits that tarnish our common identity. However, as usual, we begin by celebrating qualities to emulate…"

Then, Madam Mediator called up the dexterous Form 2s, who for the night were termed "the soldiers of the Conversion Army," assigned with the role to rid the community of foreign and unwanted attributes. They walked up to the centre of the dormitory. Each of them was armed with a pillow. As they stood waiting, Madam Mediator ushered in a Form 4 student. She was supposed to be an extraordinary personality, the renowned Angel Gabriel coming from heaven.

After that, Madam Mediator invited the exceptional category of well-behaved foxes, known as the Shining Stars or Seraphims, to come forth to receive their compliments.

Angel Gabriel mounted the podium and called out the names of the Seraphims. Students applauded each of the outstanding winners. Angel Gabriel went ahead and explained why senior students had selected them as Seraphims.

"It's thanks to your laudable behaviour that you were nominated. Today, we celebrate you. We encourage others to emulate your enduring qualities that include neatness, politeness, kindness, gentleness, punctuality, and honesty."

Then, suddenly, Angel Gabriel's light-hearted tone becomes more solemn.

"Thanks to your good behaviour, you were not a nuisance to others. However, you cannot deny that you have tails. Indeed, it would be a crime not to cut them."

At the end of Angel Gabriel's speech, Madam Mediator invited all the Form 5s to stand up and hug each Seraphim.

Though organizers initially nominated Maahtou for Seraphim, they eventually dropped her name. Mercy had strongly opposed it. However, after a long argument between those for and those against Mercy's motion, they arrived at a compromise. Maahtou was going to receive the Gentle tail-cutting reserved for Seraphims as opposed to the Harsh one, though she had not been openly acclaimed.

Gentle Tail-Cutting was carried out only by the humorous and kind-hearted Form 2s.

Stage two of the ceremony opened with the ushering onto the stage of another Form 4 called Dragon. Mercy had opted to play that role, but all the senior students had opposed it. Ever since the institution of tail-cutting, only Form 4s have played Dragon. Senior students were relieved that Mercy was a Form 5. Her mistreatment of Maahtou at the beginning of the year still lingered in the minds of many.

With a loud, threatening voice, and a whip in hand, Dragon appeared on stage. She marched like the General of an army. Suddenly, she stopped and stared at the Form 1s sternly from one to the other. Then she proceeded to condemn the misdeeds of foxes. She began shouting them out from the long list of crimes in her hand, compiled during the day.

At the end she handed the paper to Madam Mediator. Then she resumed speaking. "Your terrible crimes have caused pain, disorder, and multiple forms of wastage of time and energy." She paused, sighed, and shook her head. "Since your crimes stink, we are inviting you to let go of them as from today," Dragon went on furiously while hitting the floor with her whip.

The whole dormitory roared as she moved along the queue of culprits, staring each straight in the eye.

"Nevertheless, you will receive the special Converted Models Award (CMA) if you change for the better. We are here to help you do just that," concluded Dragon.

On that note, Dragon ordered the foxes to lie on their beds, face down. Soldiers assigned to each bed stepped forward, on the orders of Dragon. The most notorious foxes paid the highest prize. They had the heftiest soldiers.

Dragon again enumerated the crimes of foxes. Meanwhile, soldiers warmed up. They waved their pillows up and down. The rest of the dormitory booed.

At the end of the reading, the Timekeeper rang the bell. It was the signal to soldiers to start lashing out at the foxes. Pillows were flying in the air, countless times.

Meanwhile, to keep themselves energized until the end of the operation, soldiers started venting out their anger.

"Stop leaving your slippers under your bed," "stop showing off your riches," "stop blowing your nose at the dinner table," "stop smearing the dormitory with your bedwetting," "stop complaining daily about the prefects."

Madam Mediator had earlier advised the soldiers to also offer a word of counsel to those whose weaknesses were easy to redress.

"Stop frowning and begin smiling." "Try to wake up early like others to study." "Fatty, stop munching snacks between meals, you need to lose weight." "Stop talking about boys, and study."

While the venting and cutting were going on, foxes were equally allowed to plead for mercy.

"I beg, please stop," "Okay, I will never do it again."

However, the more the hitting went on unabated, alongside the venting, some culprits suddenly burst out into hot tears. Unlike the Seraphims who had spent time imitating cry-babies, upset and hardened foxes were shedding real tears. Woe betides any student with grass mattresses! Their beds were absorbing the full shock of the lashing. In contrast, foam mattresses were merely bouncing up and down.

Finally, finally, the ringing bell stopped. Five minutes of tails-cutting, which felt like half an hour, marked the final elimination of the ugly tails.

The following morning after tails-cutting, some Form 1s remarked that seniors had discriminated against them. They claimed that they were equally qualified to have been selected as Seraphims.

"Now I know that no one cares about us," said Dora of the Assumption dormitory. She was complaining to other Form 1s who equally received the Harsh Cutting. They were venting out their discontent in front of the refectory after breakfast.

"Miss Maggie did not even remember me though she often assigned me to bring her food to the dorm," complained Florence of the Assumption dormitory.

"If you are complaining, what should Maahtou do?" asked Eposi. "She was nominated among the Seraphim, but they dropped her name because of Tongsi Mercy."

"Really?" all the girls cried out.

"Hatred flows in Tongsi's blood, but she cannot change, neither my identity nor my destiny," responded Maahtou. "I hope our paths never cross anymore."

Meanwhile, other disgruntled Form 1s claimed that senior students had taken advantage of their neophyte status. How come their Bigs placed them within the category of "the disobedient?" They had never disobeyed any of their orders.

"Are you aware that there is a clear difference between someone who obeys with enthusiasm and another who obeys while frowning and grumbling?" asked Miss Gladys.

The complaining Form 1s turned around and looked at each other without saying a word. They bowed down their heads in shame.

"If you think it's easy to govern, wait until your turn comes," said the Manual Labour prefect, Linda.

Though the aim of tail-cutting was character reformation, some disreputable students remained indifferent. Among them were those who seemed to be untidy by nature. They seemed to either lack the patience or were unable to make the difference between neatness and shabbiness. Their clothes always looked like they were coming out of a dog's mouth. Even the counterpanes on their beds always looked ruffled.

Similarly, a few others were overtly disrespectful, claiming that no one had the right to discipline them. Those ones received Camel-Water Scrubbing (CWS). Beyond the tail-cutting by soldiers, prefects in each dormitory jointly meted out punishment to them. They ordered the handful of obstinate girls to kneel in the middle of the dormitory. Then, the "scrubbers" surrounded them, and repeatedly condemned their 'sins,' as if hailstones were falling on them nonstop.

'Scrubbing' often led to a lot of weeping. When it was over, each senior student followed up her assigned case. They became like live-in coaches, watching over, and administering potions to 'deliver' their 'patients' from chronic 'sins.' Some of the supervising students were the relatives or family friends of the culprits. They eventually collaborated with their parents towards helping to prune their intolerable habits.

Despite all the care and attention with which senior students handled unreasonable behaviour, resistance was not uncommon. Jessica, a student of the Imma-Concept dormitory, continued to revolt against discipline. She was fond of parading the campus, frowning, and grumbling. It was not long before she won the title of the naughtiest girl. Some even wondered whether there was a link between her 'incurable' gripe and her incessant colds.

"You girls should leave me alone," says Jessica each time that her close friends tried to correct her.

Having chosen a gloomy world of her own, no one envied Jessica. Though she never ran out of snacks, none of her friends was keen on eating her *chin-chin* (hard biscuits). She always willingly offered her chocolate spread at the breakfast table. Yet, hardly anyone accepted it except when the tin was freshly opened.

Before long, the 'blemishes' of tail-cutting soon evaporated. Anxiety for the upcoming exams results as well as excitement for the third term vacation were tugging at each heart.

Chapter 7

Mother and Daughter

Maahtou woke up on Tuesday in the village. It was her first summer vacation to be spent with her parents and junior siblings after a long while. Unlike in Victoria where all she did was household chores and playing, she was going to go to the farm.

Though farm jobs were tedious, she was curious to see all the changes that her mother had been recounting over the weekend. Mama had also prepared her for harvesting and pruning by giving lighter jobs arounds the house the previous day.

Meanwhile, Mama had been preparing something exceptional that Maahtou could never have guessed. A series of lectures for her. She needed to fill in the information gaps that Maahtou's departure had created between mother and daughter.

The only challenge was that of time and place. If she took Maahtou into her room, surely distractions would interrupt them. The random influx of guests, in addition to the ever-present domestic duties, would beckon for attention. She had been thinking about it; so far, the best option was at the farm. Right there, surrounded by nature, the tranquillity of the environment would be conducive to working while having a tête-à-tête.

Early in the morning, Mama stepped out and examined the sky. She decided that it was not going to rain, at least, not anytime soon. She was relieved. They were going to be able to keep their appointment.

She went into the food pantry and parked some bags in two basins. Then, she opened the kitchen. She had left a big iron pot on the fire to steam overnight. She took three bundles out of it. To that, she added more food. Then she took along a three-litre gallon for drinking water.

By 8.30 a.m., they were on their way. They were conversing on general issues. Meanwhile Maahtou was thinking about Ngwe in Akum village. She imagined that she might be helping her mother on their farm too. Maahtou had talked about the Four Rocks and other friends on the very first day of her arrival. Her parents did not know Ngwe in person, but they knew her grandparents.

On the way, Maahtou was just like a tourist. She was observing the changes that had taken place since she left the village. Mostly there were newly built houses here and there. Mama was doing an excellent job as a tour guide. She would stop, point out, and explain who the proprietor of this or that house was which was already completed or still under construction.

In less than half an hour they got to the farm. Maahtou was excited to see the land again after four years of absence. She recalled how they had toiled alongside their parents from season to season. It looked almost the same apart from several trees that were growing here and there. She equally noticed that new cypress trees had been planted at the border.

Mama chose the furthest end. They placed their basins under a large avocado tree that had not yet borne fruits. Next, Mama took Maahtou to the other avocado tree which was bearing its first fruits. Some of the branches were full and bent over. Maahtou picked up six fallen avocados, which she put into the folded edge of her dark blue shirt, serving as a bag. There was a kola nut tree nearby. Mama picked up four kola nut pods lodged between ridges and threw them into the small raffia basket attached to her waist.

Mother asked her daughter to take the fruits to their basins and return. Maahtou did promptly. Mama was about to show her around. It was an unfailing ritual. Each time one of her children returned home, she would show them what was new, while pointing out the boundary line again. With a stick and a cutlass in hand, she paved the way through the tall spear grass on the parts of the farm that were lying fallow. They stopped at the areas that their neighbours had long contested, though the borders were delineated by the cypress trees that Maahtou's father had been planting over the years. Each time a tree was felled, they promptly planted a new one.

Mama held Maahtou's hand. Instead of returning to the chosen place of work for the day, they moved further away. Then, they began hearing the roaring of the river. The flowing water was becoming louder and drowning their voices. Indeed, they began to speak at the top of their voices.

Finally, they were standing barely fifty meters from the river called Nkie Custom. About two hundred meters to their right was the Ntsouofou waterfall. Maahtou held onto Mama until they got to the banks. They were awestruck at the sight of the high speed of partially mud-stained foaming water rising and falling. Nkie Custom was gushing from upstream and slashing down with an extreme abandon on giant rocks. The massive clashing of the waves over rocks formed a cloud of white foams that filled the surrounding area. Escaping drops of water were massaging their faces. Mother and daughter stood there silently watching, carried away in their thoughts. It was refreshing and soothing to the skin.

Mama began pointing to the river. "You see this river?" Mama said, literally shouting out. "It's the same as human life."

"What do you mean, Mama?"

"The water encounters obstacles, and it has to wind its way over hills, around rocks, and through crevices."

It was difficult for them to hear each other distinctly. Mother signalled her daughter. It was time to return to their work site. When they were out of earshot of the sound of the river, Mama resumed her explanation. "That's not all I wanted to tell you."

After a while, they walked back to the harvesting section. They stopped at Maahtou's portion for the day.

"You know that while you are still chewing on kola nut, it is bitter," said Mama. "Tell me, what happens when you drink water?"

"It becomes sweet," Maahtou answered confidently.

An expression of satisfaction glowed on Mama's face. They were on the same page. Maahtou smiled and nodded in approval. Filled with energy, they went to work, giving their utmost best to tilling the section for vegetables. Silently, they worked for over an hour.

Maahtou stood up, cleaned her hoe of moist earth, and dropped it.

"Should we stop now and take a rest?" asked Mama. Both were feeling thirsty and hungry. Mama made two seats with two large cocoyam leaves on the ridge nearby and sat down. Then she asked Maahtou to go and bring their food basket from under the big avocado tree. Maahtou's mouth was watering at the thought of *keuka* (fresh corn pudding), cooked with fresh shallot and palm oil. Mama had placed two large avocados at the top of the basket. Maahtou was not surprised. Ever since she was a child, no meal was complete without avocado, except when they were out of season. There were also steamed cassava, some fresh boiled groundnuts, and bananas. Mama was known in the whole village for feeding her family exceedingly well. Similarly, each guest who dropped home was sure to be served a meal.

They washed their hands and began loosening the bundles of *keuka*. Mama pulled out another item from the basket. It was a pleasant surprise she had reserved for Maahtou. It was a bowl of stewed beans.

"Ah ah, Mama!" exclaimed Maahtou. "Where is that coming from?"

"I cooked it yesterday on the second fire," explained Mama. Beans stewed in tomatoes and shallots was the favourite of every child in the village.

Maahtou clapped her hands and looked at her mother, saying, "*meeya, meeya, neumou*," (thank you, thank you, my

50

darling). Like all children, Maahtou enjoyed eating beans. Mama took the bowl over to where the fire was fuming and placed it by the heat. She stood up and cut two more banana leaves. She placed them on the ridge between them to serve as an extended table. She sat down, took one of the ripe avocados and sliced it.

Halfway in the meal, Mama went back to the burning heap. She dug out three, large, sweet potatoes with a stick. She pressed them one after the other; they were soft.

"When did you do all of this?" asked Maahtou.

Mama had buried the sweet potatoes into the hot ash while they were working. She picked them up and put them on the cover of the bowl, which she carried to their temporary dining spot.

"My friend in Kumba might be sucking on fresh cocoa seeds right now," said Maahtou. She was referring to Eposi. She recalled how she and her friends in Victoria used to harvest cocoa pots and suck out the juicy, delicious beige pulp enclosing the seeds. Now she was eating the type of food that she had almost forgotten about. She smacked her lips and looked up into the sky to show her appreciation to her mother.

"With whom is your friend living in Kumba?"

"With her parents."

"Is she a good girl?" Maahtou looked at Mama and smiled. She was going to look for time and tell her mother about the kindness of the Four Rocks.

"Do you guys meet boys in college?"

"Not in school, Mama. Only during outings."

"Good. You know that soon you will reach marriage age."

"Me?" asked Maahtou. "Not me; that's too early."

"I know, but I want to introduce you to your grooming spouse," said Mama.

"My grooming spouse?" asked Maahtou with an inquiring frown.

"He is an invisible spouse," said Mama.

"Then how is it possible to introduce such a person?"

"You may not know him, but he is the one paving your way."

"Ah ah!" exclaimed Maahtou.

Since they were still eating, the delicious taste of fresh leeks and ginger got Maahtou nodding. The food was so delicious that she stood up and embraced Mama.

"Enjoy, my daughter. You need to put on some more weight before returning to school." Maahtou smiled.

"I was trying to say that your grooming husband is like a foundation built on rock." At that point, Maahtou realized that Mama was saying something profound. Mama had finally gotten her attention.

"If you walk according to his way, you will never be lost or miserable," Mama went on.

"Can you say that again?" Maahtou asked, bending her head forward towards her mother. "So, who is this grooming husband?"

"Your education," my daughter."

"And you make it seem like a person?"

"Yes," said Mama.

"Why?"

"Because it is about a relationship."

"Really?"

"Yes. If you keep him close like the umbilical cord linking an unborn baby to its mother," she went on explaining.

"I like the way you put it, Mama," said Maahtou with her face lit up. "But why call him a husband?"

"In the past, a lot of women were sponsored in college by their husbands." said Mama. "For those who couldn't go for higher training, they depended on their husbands for all their needs."

Mama went ahead and illustrated her point, citing examples of women who Maahtou had heard about. She laid emphasis on the need to treasure and nurture her grooming spouse.

"Your grooming husband prepares you for the right legal husband."

Hebey, Mama!" Maahtou exclaimed. She fixed on her mother in total admiration.

"Rather than rushing to say yes to a drunkard or a sand-sand boy, let your grooming spouse do his job."

Maahtou stood up and clapped for Mama. Then, she sat down. She wanted Mama to tell her more. "How about you, Mama? How did you meet your husband?"

"It's a long story. But suffice it to say that it was ordained. My mother-in-law chose me for her son while my breast had not even fully formed."

Maahtou began connecting some dots in episodes of their family history spanning decades, snippets of which she had heard in adult conversations. She, like her siblings, regretted that they never had a chance of knowing their paternal grandmother. That is why she was listening with rapt attention.

Suddenly Mama stood up and picked up her hoe. Maahtou wanted more details of the story. Mama was thrilled, but proposed that they till more ridges before taking another break. The two could not converse while working since they were at different ends of the selected piece of land. They remained silent for over an hour, except when Mama needed to demonstrate easy weeding with her hoe.

Suddenly, Mama dropped her hoe, picked up one kola nut, and began opening it. "My dear one, God forbid, but if you ever stumble and fall, keep the pregnancy." Mama paused and breathed deeply. "Never ever try to kill yourself, do you hear me?" she stressed, pulling the edge of her right ear repeatedly with the tips of her thumb and forefinger.

They had barely two ridges to complete the section. Mama asked Maahtou to leave that for her. Those wide ridges, more than double the size of the others, needed expert attention.

Maahtou took the jerrican and walked to the stream. Upon her return, she noticed that more avocados and kola nuts had fallen. She hurriedly brought the water and picked up a bag.

When she came back, she met Mama sitting.

"My daughter, sometimes plans don't work out."

Maahtou listened without saying a word.

If ever you become pregnant before time, please, keep the baby and bring it to me." An uneasy feeling came over Maahtou.

"I hope it doesn't happen, but one never knows," Mama went on.

Maahtou took a deep breath and raised her eyebrows.

Then Mama paused. She became silent for a while as if she were allowing her words of caution to sink into Maahtou. Her stare tarried on the freshly made ridges in front of them that were all rid of weeds.

"A baby is precious, even if it comes from off the sand," Mama resumed.

She stopped again, took a death breath, and shook her head.

"What do you mean by sand, Mama?"

"I mean getting pregnant out of marriage."

Meanwhile, Maahtou began staring at her right foot that was digging idly into the loose dark soil beneath. It was not the first time she was hearing her mother speak on those terms. She often counselled her sisters and other girls in the village. However, it was the first time that Mama was addressing herself directly to her. It seemed to be uncalled for, but Mama's solemn tone obliged her.

Mama bent down and began weeding the grass on the next ridge while Maahtou turned around and looked away into the far-off hills. Ever since she was a child, she always marvelled at the frog-shaped plateau, equally visible from their yard. The undulating evergreen hills were far off, but apparently quite close. It seemed like a massive green carpet that had gradually descended from the sky and neatly landed there. Her eyes panned the beautiful scenery from the ground to its meeting point with the blue sky. The imaginary green carpet was hemming in the hills and descending into the valley. Yet, its edges were rising towards the top, concealing the other side.

Maahtou turned her back and looked closer to where she and Mama had tilled. She scrutinized their immediate surroundings. Her eyes settled on a new avocado tree. Another set of birds was chirping away excitedly. The heat of the sun was giving way to a refreshing breeze that was caressing their faces.

Meanwhile, the stillness of the continuous stretch of hills, miles away momentarily captured her attention. She began longing for a long recess from the labour of the time-consuming earth. Everything above soil level seemed to be tranquil. Only she and Mama were somehow unsettled.

Mama picked up some browning cocoyam leaves, which Maahtou had cut. She threw them on the ridge and sat down. Her movements shook Maahtou out of her reverie, a form of therapy lavishing itself from nature's harmony.

Maahtou began talking of her friends at college, the other Four Rocks. "My friend, Nubodem must be at the Mankon market with her mother."

"Shopping?"

"No," answered Maahtou. "Her mother trades in nuts and spices."

"If you like to sell something, I have a lot of foodstuff in the house."

"I know, mother, but I am not used to it."

"Should we go back to the house now?" asked Mama.

It was only then that Maahtou realized that she was hungry. How taxing is reality! The freshness of the air had been so filling, so pacifying.

"I have some keys to hand over to you?" said Mama.

"Of the room?"

"No, not at all. Keys to unlock the doors of life."

"Mother, mother," said Maahtou, thrilled. "I like it when you and Papa speak in *captsoo* (proverbs). I just want to stay close and listen to you all day."

"Next time, we will pick up from there."

Chapter 8

Grooming Spouse

Thursday morning 6.00 a.m. The air was fresh. The light was piercing through the cracks of the wooden window of the concrete bungalow. Maahtou's father had left at 5.00 a.m. to tap raffia wine from his orchard some two miles away. Her mother was in bed in her room rapt in her usual morning talk with God, with her open Bible lying on her belly.

At 6:30 Mama got up and went out to ease herself in the toilet outside, at the far end of the house. She was grateful for the sun. She would be able to pursue her lecture with Maahtou.

By 7:30, they were on their way. They were moving with brisk steps. They crossed the highway and entered the part of the road without houses. All was farmland. They meandered through, bending down to push away leaves. Corn ears were stretching out and blocking the road on the narrow pathway that led to their farm. For the day's duty, Mama had chosen a new section, much like leaving the classroom for the laboratory. Mother was in front using her cutlass to trace the way. Maahtou was behind her with her basin on her head.

"Why did you bring your hoe when there is no tilling or weeding today?" asked Maahtou.

It was the harvesting season. The yellowing leaves of corn as well as the browning leaves of beans and potatoes were desperately beckoning for gathering hands.

"Does a student go to class without their books or pen?"

Maahtou laughed. Like a diligent student carrying his or her notes along everywhere during the exam period, Mama never stepped out to the farm without her main instrument, the hand-held hoe.

The locally invented handheld hoe was every woman's primary farming tool. It was a circular blade-edged, flat piece of iron. Its wooden handle was tightly fitted at an acute angle into a hole of folded iron at the back of the metal. The wood itself was a tree branch with two sides naturally touching each other at an acute angle. The engineers peel off its bark and then smoothen the upper and outstretched arm to protect the palms. A hoe for adults is about half a meter high when sitting on the flat blade. Its user bends over fully to till the soil. Women in the village use the traditional tool for the tilling of acres of land, all day long.

Barely half an hour since their arrival, Mama stopped and began stretching out her hands up and down, in and out.

"You should have taken some rest today," said Maahtou.

"You are right, my daughter," Mama responded. "But if we don't come to harvest the crops quickly, the rain will spoil them."

"Let's hurry then and do as much as we can before we get too tired."

"That's right, *neumour na* (my mother). I'm so grateful that you accepted to come," said Mama.

They picked up their food bags while Mama delineated the day's harvesting area with her pointing hand. Mama and Abong, Maahtou's younger sister, had done barely a fifth of the work in that stretch of ridges the previous week. It was going to require an extra week of work to complete it before moving to another section of the almost two acres of cropland.

The main harvest was the corn as well as the beans. Mama asked for the short cutlass. Maahtou was picking the visible crops, plucking off corn and loading bean stalks into separate bags. Meanwhile, Mama was digging potatoes and arranging them in small piles over the ridges. In less than an hour, Maahtou signalled to Mama that their basins were already full. They had harvested more crops than they could carry. Mama explained that they were going to secure most of the potatoes in a hideout for pick-up the following day.

Three hours of harvesting was enough work for the day. They were both tired. Maahtou was thirsty, so too was Mama.

Mama cut off some banana leaves and made seats on two ridges. Meanwhile, Maahtou rushed to the nearby stream with their jerrican. On her return trip, she stopped and searched into their lunch basket for the bottle of sweet, fresh palm wine. Baba had specially reserved it for her. Maahtou poured out the milky drink into their plastic cups while Mama pulled out the bundles of *keuka* (fresh corn pudding).

"*Azumeh anyuiteh*!" (What a delicious thing!), Maahtou exclaimed.

"That's authentically your father's wine," Mama commented.

Mama gave the bigger bundle of *keuka* (fresh corn pudding) to Maahtou. The latter smiled and shook her head, because of its size. Mama insisted that she take it. Each unwrapped her package of olive-green oily plantain leaves — the orange colour of *keuka* and the characteristic inviting smell of fresh corn hit their nostrils. From the very first bite, Maahtou stood up, bent over, and kissed her mother. Sweet *keuka* was a seasonal staple in the village.

"This is so, so delicious," she said, smacking her lips. "I can even finish two bundles."

"You can have some of mine," Mama offered.

When they finished eating lunch, Maahtou stood up and picked up another empty harvesting bag, but Mama asked her to sit down and allow time for digestion.

"You know that I am your mother," said Mama.

Mama's solemn tone indicated that she had an important subject matter to discuss. Maahtou stared into Mama's eyes for a clue. Silence ensued. Mama seemed to be searching for her words, something that was unusual.

"My daughter, life today has changed tremendously from what it used to be. People have trampled upon honesty and respect like a pig smashing upon mud in its sty," she said while sighing and shaking her head.

Maahtou listened, preferring to absorb everything like a crack on the dry earth swallowing up water.

"When I look at you, my children, I wonder what future awaits you – deception is everywhere, even the sweet promises of familiar people are no longer worth a penny," she went on.

"But you and Baba are working hard daily to provide for us."

Maahtou was beside the point. She knew better to wait until Mama showed her where, and how to step in. The substance of her talk was safely hidden like Mama always did in packaging items for dispatch to any of her children. If she did not release her unique formula on how to unknot it, it would require a sharp knife and many hands to unwrap it without damaging its contents.

"Yes, it's true, but I'm not talking about the efforts of your father," answered Mama.

Maahtou kept staring at her mother, wondering what was on her mind.

"During our days, a respectable man was one who built his own house. Then, with the help of his parents, he chose a well-bred girl for his bride. Both families came together, and after meeting the demands of the bride's family, they organized the marriage in sync with the customs and traditions of our people. Only then could he and his bride start their own family."

"Of course, I know all of that, mother."

"But nowadays, things have changed," Mama went on. "More and more educated men prefer educated women. Some married men go as far as dumping their wives to run after a woman who brings home money."

"Is it because parents no longer choose their son's bride?" Maahtou asked.

"Not only that, my daughter. It is *alehme* (blood). Whether it is the type of food that they eat these days or what, we don't know what happened." Mama sighed and shook her head. "People now prefer money to good character. In some strange cases, men who choose working women still end up making light of their commitments to their wives."

Evidently quarrels and disagreements in marriage were on the rise. It was a topical issue too. Men and women of the older generation were becoming frustrated. Their adult children were becoming more and more detached from them. They would not sit down long enough for a sustained conversation with them. Unable to justify the creeping irresponsible habits of the younger generation, parents in the villages blamed the negative outcome on *alehme*. Was it the reckless and rising consumption rate of intoxicating drinks, particularly beer, that was tampering with the quality of their blood? Otherwise, what was going on?

"People seem to be more interested in satisfying their immediate desires," regretted Baba in a conversation the previous Saturday with some guests.

"Of course, it's due to bad blood," answered Pa Aloh.

"I keep wondering what precisely is responsible for that," said Baba.

"It has to be what they eat and especially what they drink," suggested Mama.

"That should be it, Mama," said Mami Kein.

"Listen to most young men these days. They speak without regard for their elders. Neither do they show any concern for the children in their midst," said Pa Aloh.

"The number of those who have decided to choose their wives themselves, is increasing too," said Baba. "Yet, they are unable to keep the firm promises they made."

"Count how many cases of divorce and troubled homes we hear about these days," said Mama.

"Men get drunk and beat up their wives," said Mami Kein

"How sad for those who are still growing up!" exclaimed Baba.

While Maahtou recalled that conversation, she could not wait for Mama to get to the punchline. How did all this directly concern her?

Firstly, Mama scratched her head and remained immobile for a while.

"A woman is like farmland," said Mama.

"What do you mean?"

"For a farmland to become productive, one has to first clear the grass, till the soil, make furrows before sowing seeds, right?"

Maahtou nodded. How captivating to compare a woman with cropland! She had never heard such similarities, not even in her Literature class.

Maahtou smiled and fixed her eyes on her mother with raised eyebrows. Mama went ahead and explained that nowadays young men with an independent mindset, deprive the parents of the bride-to-be of 'the preparation of the soil.' They bypass her family and try to persuade a girl to marry them. It is as if they are more content with harvesting wild vegetables and wild berries than giving the best chance to their future.

"Can a marriage last without parents properly grooming their children?" asked Mama.

Maahtou shook her head. Mama was not certain that Maahtou had fully grasped her message, much less its importance. So, she thought of using other symbols to illustrate her point. "*Ndaar Anwarneh* (education) is like the sun," she began.

"How?" asked Maahtou.

"You see clearly with the sun, right?"

"Yes."

"But I am not talking about something that you can see and touch."

Maahtou twisted her face and began wondering what her mother was alluding to.

"It is your kola nut gift."

"Kola nut gifts?" What is that?"

"Given the right exposure, a student will not only discover her unique kola nut gifts but equally sharpen them."

Maahtou scratched her and shifted closer to her mother.

"It's an eye-opening illustration, but we don't have enough time now."

"I can't wait to hear it."

"For the moment, I want you to start cherishing your *Ndaar Anwarneh* (education) more than you have ever before," added Mama. "It is your grooming spouse."

"The same grooming spouse you had talked about?" asked Maahtou with a nod of surprise.

"Yes." Mama went on explaining. Given the right exposure, that peculiar husband will help you as a student to discover your capabilities. By the time of graduation, each diligent student would have been equipped with a professional identity, able to render effective service to the community.

"*Irlie*? (Really?)," asked Maahtou in amazement while clapping her hands and slightly inclining herself.

"*Aire*" (Yes)," agreed Mama confidently with a nod.

Both became thirsty. So, Maahtou went to the spring to fetch water.

"Can you give a name to my grooming spouse?" asked Maahtou as soon as she returned.

Mama looked up and started scratching her head. Maahtou was confident that her mother would come up with one. She was good at making up names on the spot. Indeed, in the village Mama was an expert in christening children. Parents often invited her to name their babies. Once, a baby was named *Mbirnkoum*, literally *"coffin-carrier"* because the mother of the child had died during childbirth. Mama picked up the baby for the first time in her outstretched arms, shook her head in disapproval, and called out the baby, *Nyuiebong* (God is good).

There was another case where a family named their baby *Ngeheh* (suffering) because his father died weeks before he was born. Mama rejected the name and replaced it with *Abonneenteume* (a soother of the heart). Thanks to her timely interventions, the base of registered names in the village gradually enlarged. Besides, all her names had specific meanings compared to most traditional ones that were merely appellations.

"*Ndoumnyui*," she finally whispered in Maahtou's ear.

What did that mean exactly? Maahtou was thinking hard. It was a compound word with *"Ndoum,"* meaning either "husband" or "the way" while *Nyui* stood for Creator. Thus, Ndoumnyui was *"the Creator's way" or "the Creator's husband."*

Maahtou picked up the empty pot and went towards the trees by the raffia bush to search for mushrooms. On her return, she started analysing her grooming spouse's name.

"You cannot split the two main attributes of his name, my daughter," Mama said.

Maahtou could not help laughing out loud; it was as if Mama were reading her thoughts.

"Let's sit for a while and rest before leaving," Mama urged.

They sat there, admiring the work they had done. Maahtou stood up and counted; they had harvested twelve ridges. Each of them was about five meters long and one meter wide. They had accomplished a lot in a single day.

"Though *Ndoumnyui* may seem as elusive as your shadow, know that he will be as steady as Ngoorh (Rock)," said Mama. "If you take time to sharpen the endowments he reveals into your life, he will help you withstand any circumstance," Mama reassured Maahtou while looking at her straight into her eyes.

Then, before Maahtou realized, Mama jumped up and brushed off the gluey mud from her hoe. There and then, she began chanting a song spontaneously while dancing in rhythm. Maahtou sprung up and joined her.

One line after another, Mama's song exposed the attributes of Ndoumnyui. Then, she put rhythm into it. Each time Maahtou called out on the grooming spouse, Mama would respond with a new trait.

"*Ndoumnyui: Atsa ndoum (3) tsim tsim (2)*
(It is better than any other way).

"*Ndoumnyui: were abonne (3) teum teum (2)"*
(It is gentle all through).

"*Ndoumnyui: were ferme (3) titi ngwanke (2)*
(It shines with brightness)."

"*Ndouminyui: were agaah nzie (3) nghwin tsim tsim (2)*

(It makes everyone wise)

"*Ndouminyui: boho kong o* (3) *O ferme, ferme ferme* (2)

(We love you. You are radiant).

Maahtou was overjoyed.

"Next time, you will tell me about kola nut gifts, right?"

"Yes, my beloved."

Chapter 9

Steer Clear of Boys

School reopened on Thursday. It was partially rainy and sunny. The first group of students arrived on the campus by 2.00 p.m. Excitement was at its peak. Among the Four Rocks, Nubodem was the first, followed by Ngwe. Maahtou joined them one hour later. Eposi only got to the campus at 5:30. The girls spent the rest of the evening sharing holiday anecdotes as well as the various types of food each had brought along.

Dormitory captains were very busy on Friday assigning students to various dormitories. As for the rest, they were preparing for class resumption on Monday. The principal instructed the senior prefect to read the rules and regulations to the whole school, and not just to the new students.

It was imperative to respect all rules and regulations in college, written or not. The law that received the severest sanction from authorities was the one to do with entertaining relations with boys. They were strictly forbidden. The only occasions for direct contact with non-residents were during the Sunday mass and the weekday early-morning mass, both at the city Cathedral. Apart from two or three Muslim girls, who were exempt, all students mandatorily went to the church during scheduled services.

Despite the prohibition of contacts with boys, not everyone stayed in line. The principal, sister Maura, became curious when she noticed that some students were receiving personal letters frequently. Which parents could afford writing to their daughters every week? It was the question that called for an investigation.

On Thursday there were a lot of mails. The principal disregarded the kingship names of the senders inscribed on the envelopes. She opened a selected number of them. What? She could not believe her eyes. What did she see? She was shocked upon reading the salutation on the first mail, "My steaming hot Honey." She did not read through it.

Instead, she dropped it and opened the second — "Your piercing eyes set my heart throbbing. I just can't hold my peace until I hear from you," wrote the second lover. "My heart beats for you, morning and night faster than the speed of sound," affirmed the boyfriend of the third student. "I can't wait to cuddle you until you crumble in my hands while I'm kissing you," concluded a fourth boy in his letter.

The principal's hands began trembling as she was folding each letter. Urgently, she summoned teachers to her office. She gave them a list of names of students, among whom were the four recipients. She requested their test scores as well as their conduct in class. She further instructed the teachers to consult class prefects for more details on their behaviour in class.

At the end of one week, teachers handed their reports to the principal. Their remarks varied— "Talkative," "non-participation in open class discussions," "distracting in class," disturbing during prep time," "sad and looking lonely," "copying from others during tests," "poorly done homework," "good scores in tests," "poor scores in tests," "eating in class" among others.

After receiving the first set of reports, the principal summoned dormitory captains. She requested them to observe and report on the behaviour of the girls on her shortlist. It was done according to their respective dormitories. Of course, the Form 5s and the Form 1s were exempt.

In the end, dorm captains compiled several lists of complaints. Some of their remarks were, "talkative," "making noise after lights out," "disrespect of senior students," "untidy," "lazy," "looking sad," and "isolated."

There was an outstanding case concerning two Form 2s of Assumption and Imma-Concept dormitories. The two were fond of "showing off pictures of boyfriends" and "sharing letters from boyfriends and causing distraction on campus." The dorm captains concerted among themselves and decided to withhold those extreme cases. Their disclosure could cause the principal to bypass issuing a severe warning to outright dismissal.

The principal compared the dormitory captains' reports to those of teachers. First, she summoned the two Form 4s who had the most disturbing details by their names, one after the other. Both admitted that they had fiancés and that their parents were aware of it. They argued that rather than being a distraction, those fiancés were giving them all the support they needed. The principal had no more to say but to dismiss them with a wish of good luck.

Next, the principal summoned the notorious Form 3s. They were up to eight in number. Rather than talking with them individually, she received all of them together. Firstly, she congratulated them for the progress they had made so far. Next, she emphasized the importance of reaching the finishing line. Their parents had made enormous sacrifices, and they should not let them down.

Then, she brought out all the withheld mail. She requested each addressee to open their mail right there. It turned out that two of them were from their relatives. As for the rest, she made a schedule whereby each of them had to meet her in her office. Only one letter out of the six was from a fiancé. She warned the five others and ordered them to write to their boyfriends to stop writing to them. Otherwise, the principal was going to invite their parents or guardians to school.

Next was the turn of the Form 2s. All ten of them had received letters from boys, potential or confirmed boyfriends. Their numbers were unexpectedly high. So, the principal sought help through the Church. She solicited counselling from a highly respected women's group leader. Her charge was to address the importance of education vis-à-vis relationships with boyfriends.

The whole school was invited to attend that Friday talk, in the presence of staff members. Students could ask as many questions as they wanted. The following week, the principal issued a newly written rule: henceforth, defaulters were going to be punished, with the risk of being dismissed.

After a month of observation, it was clear that all the efforts that the principal was making were yielding good results. The number of in-coming letters dropped by close to 70% though some of the girls on her tracking list still received letters. She proceeded to open all those whose senders did not sign at the back of envelopes as well as those whose senders were not on her pre-screened list.

The principal was still disappointed. She read love declarations in some of them that made her shriek, proving her suspicions right. As before, she withheld the most indecent ones. Soon, she began informing parents in writing, making sure to include some quotes from received letters. Henceforth, during the Morning Assembly, the principal would issue a severe warning to students against distractions from boyfriends.

Though the principal was sounding an alarm, bold culprits quietly blamed her for trespassing.

Nevertheless, after keeping count for a few more weeks, the number of suspicious mails dropped drastically. The principal celebrated the success of her procedure. Little did she know that students had switched from using the Post Office to the traditional hand-mail delivery methods. Almost double the mail that used to come in through the Post Office was being sent as hand mail. No one knows who initiated the system, but it was clear that it took a lot of brainstorming and collaboration to set it in place.

On Tuesday morning, at 5.00 a.m., the Lebanese bakery owner, Hassan, delivered bags of bread to the kitchen as usual. He got back into his van and took off. However, after bypassing the three first dormitories, he slowed down and stopped at a corner by the terrace wall. Two Form 4 and two Form 5 students, who had been waiting for him, rushed to the van. Nothing seemed unusual. A few girls often bought sweet or soft bread once a week. They preferred it to the simple one served at the refectory.

However, that morning, there were two additional girls waiting for the arrival of Hassan. Both were from the Ave Maria dormitory, the closest building to the entry. They were both Form 5s. It was the first time they had woken up that early to approach Hassan. They were not looking for bread. Indeed, those students wanted something more desirable than food. They stood a few steps away and waited until Hassan had finished selling bread. He, too, was waiting for those two Form 5s. They came up promptly. He picked up a carefully folded plastic bag and discreetly handed it over to them.

The Form 5 girls rushed back to the dormitory. The rest of the girls were still sleeping. They went back to bed. As soon as they had taken their shower, they invited other Form 5s to help them in sorting out the letters. Each dormitory had its share. The Form 5s were the only ones responsible for distributing the mail. They had a rule that was to be strictly applied— the Form 2s and Form 1s were not allowed to receive letters from boys. Period. Meanwhile, all girls from Form 3 upwards received their letters intact while the rest had to undergo a second sorting. They opened all letters that were not sent by relatives.

Of all the Form 2s, two girls notably received the highest number of letters. Form 5s in their respective dormitories examined their cases. They were Youla from the Regina dormitory and Maahtou of Ave Maria. Strangely, the letters of the former were coming not only from a single boyfriend but from two of them. Although that was shocking, no one was surprised. Indeed, Youla was one of the few who featured on all the reports of notorious students. Indeed, she was one of the two students whose notoriety dorm captains had withheld from the principal.

Maahtou's case was also surprising. She was quiet and obedient. She was even the type whom some senior students described as "one in whose mouth butter could not melt."

Though intriguing, the Form 5s restrained themselves from opening her letters. They gave her the benefit of the doubt since she avowed that the sender was her brother.

"What if Maahtou is slow water that runs deep?" One of the Form 5s wondered.

"You are right," confirmed the second Form 5. "There is no art to find the mind's construction in the face." She was quoting a line in <u>Macbeth</u>, one of the drama books that was on the curriculum for GCE exams.

Thenceforth, Form 5s began keeping an eye on Maahtou as well as other students who wore innocence on their faces like a permanent identity aura. Or was it a veil? So, dorm captains added Maahtou's name to the list of girls under observation. The news finally got to a third-year student by the name of Esther, who was in Regina Dormitory. She was the girlfriend of Maahtou's elder brother, Moonbih. Esther promptly went to Maahtou's dorm to defend her.

Incidentally, on that same day, Maahtou had received a letter. A Form 5 student stood by her and ordered her to open it. It was ironic that the student was suspecting Maahtou when Esther's statement in defence had reached some of the Form 5s.

Unlike Youla, who was putting up a good defence despite the evidence, Maahtou did not dare to speak out. It was not easy for junior students with Maahtou's reticence to express their genuine feelings to the senior students, particularly those who held their credibility in doubt. Besides, older students were often keener on bullying than questioning. Maahtou perceived the futility of arguing. She quietly thought to herself how amusing it would be when they would finally find out the truth.

Nevertheless, Maahtou shivered a bit. What if Moonbih had introduced her in absentia to a boy at his college, Rock of Ages (RAC)? Indeed, some girls had received letters from boys that they had never met. The Form 5 students kept staring at Maahtou sceptically. Maahtou knew that if the letter in hand was not from her brother, no one would ever believe her anymore. They would punish her more severely than Youla. She took a deep breath and opened it. Quickly her eyes ran to the signature line. O, how relieved! She relaxed.

Despite the clear proof, two Form 5s shook their heads. "Brother, brother, you know us Africans," the first Form 5 said. "Everyone is related to everyone else, even to their boyfriends."

The others burst out laughing.

"Exactly," the second Form 5 agreed. "Let's dig deeper," one of the Form 5s proposed. "Which brother writes letters up to two times a week to her sister?" she wondered.

Just when the two Form 5s were about seizing Maahtou's letter, Esther arrived and confirmed Maahtou's statement.

"Moonbih is my guy," declared Esther.

"Fine, but what is the relationship between him and Maahtou?" one of the Form 5s asked.

"Siblings," Esther said, nodding her head.

"Are you joking?" the other Form 5 asked, with eyes wide open. They knew to whom Esther was referring. Moonbih was a Form 5 student at RAC. He was one of the best-known dandies who enjoyed dressing *à la mode*. He and his fashion pace-setter school mates were among the first guys who wore the pants popularly called *"Mpang,"* *"Apaga,"* or *"Pas d' éléphant"* (elephant foot trousers).

The girls were stunned because of the differences between the siblings. Unlike Moonbih, Maahtou was quiet, simple, self-effacing, and looking innocent like a newly hatched chick. Maybe that was even why Esther never associated with her like other girls who spent hours chatting with their 'sisters-in-law.'

On her part, Maahtou made no effort to draw close to Esther. It would have been great to receive gifts and a lot of attention from a senior student apart from her Big. Yet, she was not jealous of the other pampered "sisters-in-law." She was not the type with the aptitude to partake in romantic chitchats.

On the flipside, she wanted to be left alone. Time spent alone was her best chance to focus on her raison d'être. She often took advantage of the extra time beyond official schedules to study. It was also during those private moments that she wrote to her brother and equally read through his replies. She had requested her two elder brothers to write to her in French, except when providing answers to her science questions. She equally enjoyed reading extra-curricular material. She was one of the students who borrowed books from the college library on a regular basis. That is why she even had a personal daily schedule. The time from when she woke up until breakfast as well as the time between prep and lights-out time were marked out for a particular subject.

Maahtou and the other Four Rocks often wondered how girls coped with multitasking, opposing objectives like academics and emotional desires. The Four Rocks often watched Youla and company and clapped their hands in dismay.

While senior students frowned on Youla's case, the rest of the students, from Form 3 upwards, saw the underground mailing system as a godsend. It brought more excitement on campus than did the Post Office. Tuesdays, Wednesdays, and Fridays were both delivery and pick-up days by Hassan. Girls with replies discreetly handed over their letters to their respective dormitory Pigeons, a newly created post that neither the principal nor the staff surmised. For the fun of it, girls would call the name aloud even in the presence of authorities, but the latter always thought that they were referring to Pidgin English. During breakfast, at least 5 percent of students were more content with mails from their boyfriends than the bread on their plates.

The system went on smoothly. After the first successful delivery, only one girl at a time was responsible for picking up as well as depositing at the rotating central distributing dorms. There were four rotating volunteers, one from each dormitory. In barely two weeks, Hassan knew who the assignees were. Not even the kitchen staff were aware of the existence of the underground system.

The only shortcoming was that the underground system was limited to the students of Rock of Ages College (RAC). Their college was the one with whom Virgin Mother College girls maintained the highest number of college-to-college affinities. After all, girls who had boyfriends in institutions other than RAC tended to be discreet about it. Virgin Mother College (VMC) girls considered RAC students as their perfect match, what they commonly called the "reigning guys."

Three days a week, Hassan shuttled between the two institutions, RAC and VMC, located at the two extremes of the town. Those three letter-shuttling days incredibly changed the mood on campus. Girls reported confirmation of loving relationships with heightened excitement. Some of them underlined in red ink the most affectionate sentences. All day, they shared with friends and classmates.

Of course, some letters brought terrible news. There were declarations to the effect that supposed or hoped for chemistry by a VMC student was null and void. Thus, while some boys directly wrote to jilted girls, others used silence to make their new stance clear.

There were equally a few cases whereby two girls received letters authored by the same boy. The two letters bore similar degrees of zeal in the boy's love declarations.

Thus, the impact of letters from RAC created both fireworks and torrential rains on campus. Right from the breakfast table into class, the two outcomes were as visible as sunlight or dark clouds. On the sad side, some girls' eyes swelled up while their noses flew non-stop with sudden catarrh. At the extreme, some shocking letters left a girl or two in bed, sick all day. Their friends would come to their bedside and try to comfort them in vain.

Despite the Form 5 prohibition, Youla continued receiving letters from her boyfriends. However, the boys were using an alternative channel. Discreetly, her letters were delivered during or after the daily mass. Apart from Maahtou, Youla often received more letters than senior students. Instead of keeping her notes to herself, she would quickly disclose the contents to her classmates. She was fond of memorizing lines and repeating them to her classmates. "You are the love of my life." "I found love when I met you." "You are sweeter than honey."

"Are you in a platonic friendship or what?" asked Maahtou to Youla who was bluffing in class as usual.

"Whether I am standing on a plateau or I am as tasty as tonic, when are you ever going to taste one?" retorted Youla. The class burst out laughing. Maahtou smiled. Youla had just forgotten that Maahtou grew up in Victoria. She used to drink soda almost at will. As for Youla, though she was a smart student, everyone knew that she had no clue of the meaning of the word.

Youla was always agitated like an erupting volcano. While almost all her classmates were still far from ready to entertain friendships with boys, she openly declared that she had more than one. Some classmates expressed their concern for her. Instead, she took pleasure in trying to prove to them that they were missing out on the real fun of life.

Despite her boldness, Youla threatened that if any of her classmates reported her to senior students, she was going to deal with them accordingly. Most students took her threat seriously though none could verify if they had any backing. Her family lived in Mankon, the locality of the college. It was probable that she had a power base not far from the campus.

In the meantime, the class kept waiting for the Geography teacher. Youla took out a tiny bottle from her desk and sprayed it on her neck. Then she invited students to come and smell the perfume she was wearing. Those sitting by her did, but for Nubodem; she kept reading as if nothing was the matter. Ngwe shook her head and smiled. Bih, Jackie and Rita from rich families, who were used to deodorants, smirked at her.

Meanwhile, Eposi stood up and walked up to Youla. "I know better perfumes than that," said Eposi.

"Have you ever smelled a rose," asked Maahtou, who was sitting two rows away from Youla? Youla didn't answer.

Instead, the following week, she took out a 500 francs banknote from her Math textbook, raised her hand, and flipped it up and down. She proudly stated that it was a gift from one of her boyfriends.

"She thinks that 500 francs is a lot of money," said Bih to Jackie. Both girls were the children of top personalities in the country.

"You think that having money is more important than passing your exams?" Maahtou spoke up. "Aha," the rest of the class concurred.

"Are you trying to tempt us?" asked Odile.

Instead of responding to the questions raised, Youla raised her open display to a climax. While her classmates were still staring at her, amazed at her daring, she did something that took everyone by total surprise. She lifted the arm of her beige uniform blouse and showed off her light green brazier. By then, less than ten girls in class were wearing braziers. She boasted how her boyfriend had bought it for her.

"What is wrong with her?" the class prefect spoke up.

"*Okrieka*," (second hand), Rita scribbled on a piece of paper and passed it to Jackie. Then, she asked her to forward it to Bih. The three girls smiled. Maahtou, who was sitting close to Bih, saw it. She did not say a word. She too had bought a brazier from *Okrieka* during the last outing. She shunned discussing the matter. She recalled how uncomfortable she was after trying it on for the first time. Her breathing had been interrupted. Promptly, she had taken it off. Neither were any of the Four Rocks wearing braziers. They had exchanged notes and decided to give themselves more time.

As if the scene that Youla had created was not enough, she asked if any of her classmates had ever stepped foot into Club Cent. It was a newly opened nightclub that was becoming the talk of the town. Most students just stared at her while some dismissed her with a sigh. The truth is, no other students had been there yet.

"There is a time for everything," said Maahtou.

"Hear that one," retorted Youla.

"You mean to say Maahtou isn't right?" asked Bih with a frown.

"So, some of you are beginning to speak up, even you Bih, when you are still like a baby?" Youla hit back.

"Let's forget about Youla and concentrate on our assignment," said the class prefect. Youla kept speaking.

"*Laisse-nous tranquille, bavard!*" (Leave us alone, talkative). Maahtou tried to hush her down in French.

"Yes, I know that you are good in French," said Youla. "But who eats that?"

"Stop talking, Youla," ordered the class prefect.

"Who is she talking to?" asked Youla angrily.

"You are disturbing, and we are fed up with your nonsense stories"

"Who do you think you are?" Youla thundered back while beating her chest.

Youla's raised voice drew the attention of the discipline master. Soon, her shocking adventures as well as her nuisance in class reached dormitory captains and the head prefect. Her Big tried to call her to order. Senior students often punished her severely for noise making especially. Surprisingly, she would take on each task speedily and energetically. Then, in the end, she would stand up and beat her chest, chanting that she was a survivor. "They will all get tired," Youla mocked repeatedly.

"These Form 2s think that they have reached the moon" was the remark of horrified senior students.

"Wait and see if you will go through and climb up to where we are, then we will know you are tough," others commented. It was the typical chorus repeated each time a Big realized that their Small was showing more interest in extra-curricular matters than in studying.

The conclusion throughout the campus of about two-hundred students remained unrefuted— for the past five years, Youla had received the most discipline. Yet, she continued to be the most stubborn. Harsh tail-cutting, direct insults, and warnings, all seemed to her like throwing water on a duck's back. Instead, it appeared as if finger-pointing warnings and subsequent punishment somewhat hardened her back like a tortoise's. Her notoriety was evident even in her looks. Except for Mondays, her beige blouse uniform was frayed at the edges. It had not taken up to the end of the first term for her often-twisted rhubarb red skirt to distinctly fade.

Despite her defiance of student authority, she had a knack for comic relief. Her loud, imposing voice caught the attention of all in the same way that hot pepper increases both the flavour of food and the appetite for it. On the spur of the moment, she would craft a tale, a lie, or merely a dramatized physical feat to resist punishment from senior students. They would relax and let go. Even teachers, who were quick to punish a stubborn student, laughed away her trespasses. In the end, she was not a typical student by VMC standards but a piece of drama on call.

On Saturday, Youla seized an opportunity to render herself indispensable. Thus, she became an award-winner, albeit, in an odd way. It was during the weekly Saturday manual labour. Students armed with brooms and lances had already finished cleaning the campus. It was visibly perfect. There were no more weeds on the walls, corners, and in-between the terrace stones.

Nonetheless, there was a daunting challenge staring into each face. For lack of implements, prefects could not find a way to get rid of the trapped muddy mess of wet gluey garbage in the gutter. The spot was open to the view of passers-by, just a few steps away from the stairs leading to the principal's office. Neither gloves nor spades were available. To the surprise of all, Youla boldly stared at the Form 5s and asked, "What are you afraid of?"

Each face was twisted from merely looking at the trash and imagining the most dreaded wastes, hidden underneath the concrete slabs.

"Give me the way," Youla spoke out loud while stretching out her arms. Bending over the mountain of a mess, she spread her legs and planted her feet firmly at the edges of the gutter. The girls standing on both sides steered clear. Youla paused for a while and closed her mouth tightly. Everyone was watching her. Without a word, and within a split second, she quickly dipped both hands into the stinking mountain of rotting trash. Then, she began dumping bundles of garbage into the waiting large Moukouta bag and black plastic buckets. It was a mixture of dead leaves, plastic bags, and who knows what else? Almost instantly, everyone started clapping and calling her Champion. Prefects congratulated her and promised her goodies of all sorts.

As for Maahtou, she was among Youla's classmates who applauded the loudest. "At last, she has shown us her mettle," said Maahtou.

"Oh, yes, not just talking about boys, but making good use of her hands," said Pamela, a Form 4 student.

"Yea, yea, yea" shouted Youla's classmates while others smiled and nodded. They were happy that Youla had finally given them reason to admire her.

"Now we have a different story to tell about Youla," added Maahtou. Though she was one of the quiet students, Maahtou would speak up whenever she was moved. Her classmates always admired her diction as well as her balanced sense of judgment.

Chapter 10

Invitation to Elope

Sister Maureen, the Chemistry teacher, was expected any minute. While some students were going over the Periodic Table of Elements, others were being entertained or shocked by Youla. She was reading portions of the latest letter from her boyfriend. She had underlined parts of it in red and was displaying them to those doubting her.

"You are my oxygen. I love you so much that I will give you the moon and stars," she repeated.

Everyone in class was already used to anecdotes about Youla's boyfriends. However, many more students were beginning to join the conversation.

"Youla, are you even old enough to have a boyfriend?" asked Martha.

Others applauded while insisting that she answer the question.

"That is her business," retorted Beatrice, who also had a boyfriend.

"But she has to be careful," Martha insisted while shaking her head and pointing her forefinger at Youla.

"Even if age matters, who says she is too young?" interjected Judith.

A lot of girls giggled because they knew that Beatrice and Judith had boyfriends. Stories had been told of those two girls— how they often met after prep time in the dark, outside to cry over how much they were missing their boyfriends.

"Okay, let me not see anyone come and ask me for money," Youla stated boldly.

"Even if I lack money, I won't go to a boy," Maahtou stated categorically.

A girl stood up from her desk right at the back, came forward, and patted Maahtou on her back. Meanwhile,

Nubodem gave her a high five. Eposi and Ngwe held their thumbs up.

Two girls who had been wearing braziers since Form 1 joined in the conversation.

"What is your bra size?" asked the two girls. Instead of answering, Youla shoved her right hand into the left armhole of her beige blouse. She pushed down the straps of her brazier on both sides, lifted her beige short-sleeved blouse and unclipped the brazier. Then she pulled it out, looked at the size label and lifted it for all to see.

"Mamamiéé!" girls exclaimed in total dismay.

Laughter burst out in torrents. Shock gripped some while others kept giggling. Of course, chitchats about boyfriends were still as elusive to most as stars in the sky. No one could fathom how rapidly Youla had short-circuited the shocks of puberty. Her daring was not a laughing matter. Unease and timidity were on many faces.

Though Maahtou spoke up occasionally, she was one of the bashful ones. As far as she was concerned, comparing bust sizes or bra measurements was like walking through fire. She shivered at the very thought of broaching it in an open class. Her first-time experience with wearing a brazier, a few weeks ago, was still haunting her. The discomfort she experienced was still fresh in her mind. She had suffered a gnawing malaise that caused her to have palpitations, sweating, infrequent heartbeats, and dizziness. Even her ears whizzed with echoes of the quiet shredding away of her protective innocence. That day she was so distracted that she hardly heard what the Physics teacher was explaining.

Even tougher than dealing with braziers, all girls were more anxious about dealing with the onset of menstruation. It could happen anywhere and anytime. Not only do those biological changes cause discomfort to the body, but what embarrassment if the flow begins unexpectedly in public!

"Look at me strapped in a bra which I'm struggling to hide, yet Youla is showing hers to everyone," said Bih in a low tone to Maahtou and Nubodem. "Had my mother not obliged me to wear it, I wouldn't," Bih went on.

"Just the mere thought of the monthly flow scares me," said Priscy.

"The worse is when others first notice that a girl's skirt is stained," added Nubodem.

That anxiety was written over each face like a terrible and unavoidable adolescent illness. Approaching womanhood seemed like a threat to liberty. The terrifying truth was that none could stop their breasts from forming. Though Youla, whose breasts were still to develop fully, was proudly showing off her brazier, a lot of girls would have opted to postpone the arrival of breasts.

"Our neighbour ironed away her daughter's breast," said Judith.

"How is that possible?" asked Bih

"They use hot stones," said Beatrice.

"And what if they never come back?" asked Maahtou.

While the girls were still discussing their biological clocks, the class door flung open. Everyone became silent. It was the Discipline Master, Mr. Molongo. He pushed in his head and began searching with his eyes. Molongo was his nickname, meaning a cane or whip. A group of students who had gained the notoriety of becoming his regular victims had labelled him thus. All eyes instantly turned towards Youla, while three other students tiptoed back to their seats. Had Youla undertaken one of her daring deeds again? Everyone was wondering.

Instead, Mr. Molongo's big eyes rolled and settled two rows away from Youla. Each one held their breath until he finally called out a name. Surprisingly, it was Maahtou. What had she done wrong? Students wondered. Maahtou's heart began beating faster. Indeed, her trembling hands dropped a notebook on the desk. Her yellow pencil started rolling towards the greyish cement floor.

"Follow me," Molongo announced and walked away in his usual bouncy steps, supporting a muscular and hefty body. By the time Maahtou reached the door, Molongo was far gone. There was no one else on the long stretched-out veranda where Maahtou was running after him. He was moving towards the stairs leading to the entrance of the college.

He finally got to the bottom step and stopped. Maahtou's body tilted to the left to catch a glimpse of his face, from an angle. That very second, he turned around and pointed ahead of him.

"There is your aunt," he announced and walked past a waiting lady.

Her Aunt? It was an error, Maahtou thought to herself. She did not know the woman. She tried to focus, but the dazzling precious stones on the woman's outfit flashed into her eyes. She started thinking of her Uncle's wife, who lived in Mbatu. How could she have changed so much within the past year when she last saw her? Except she was returning from America. Or was it one of her two cousins who lived in Mankon, having lost almost half their weight? There was an error, Maahtou concluded. Nothing made sense to her. How she wished Molongo could come back and solve the puzzle!

Instead of speaking up, the strange woman started scratching her head and smiling. According to tradition, a younger person was supposed to be first to greet an adult upon recognizing them. Maahtou did not know her, but she said, "good morning, Ma."

"How are you, Maahtou?" the woman finally spoke up.

Immediately, Maahtou recognized her voice. It was Kandji, a young woman from Santa. She was renowned in the village for being a pacesetter in the latest ladies' wear. However, that day, she seemed to have dressed up for a Queen's fashion parade. She was wearing well-polished black covered high heel shoes. Only fashion addicts like Kandji knew how to keep the balance from the artificial height of high-heeled boots.

What had brought her? Maahtou was worried. What was their far-off neighbour's daughter-in-law, who lives in Douala, doing in her school? Was she coming from her parents in the village? Maahtou x-rayed her face for hints. Did she have some bad news? A new kind of fear began erupting in her. Kandji's presence in the absence of an immediate family member was unwarranted.

If she had bad news, why would she be smiling? Maahtou kept wondering. Yet Kandji kept exposing sparkling teeth as white as baby's milk. Maahtou wanted to smile back, but the fear of the unknown froze her lips. If only the fire of Kandji's red-polished mouth could light up the wet log of wood that Maahtou had become on that cold Friday morning, she would relax.

There were no clouds, but the sun seemed to be hesitating to reveal itself.

"Maahtou, how are you doing?" Kandji asked for the third time.

"Fine, thank you." She could not wait to hear the news.

Finally, Kandji started speaking but was stammering and searching for her words. She even fumbled around with her wrapper, untied it, and took her time to wrap it around and folded in the edge to her right side. Had she forgotten her cue? Maahtou was getting bored. She bent down her head to politely accord Kandji the time she needed, though, at the same time, she was impatient.

"I've come to see you for Tazor," she finally began her story.

Maahtou's heart almost dropped. Tazor was the younger brother of Kandji's husband. Having completed primary school two years before Maahtou's eldest brother, he moved to Douala to live with his Uncle. Eventually, he became a specialist in metal works. Villagers commonly referred to him as a Tinker.

Maahtou could not believe her ears. Was she having a nightmare or in a trance? Or maybe she had not heard Kandji well.

"He likes you a lot," Kandji went on.

Maahtou raised her head and stole a glance into Kandji's face. To her surprise, there was a trickle of sweat on Kandji's jaws, and that for a cold morning! Kandji was anxiously waiting for Maahtou's response as she uneasily turned away her pretty, round, fair face. Was she consulting Macbeth's witch behind her for fresh promptings? Maahtou wondered. Macbeth was a play that Maahtou's class had just begun studying. She did not know what to say, much less did she feel any urge to answer. Nevertheless, she was shocked, embarrassed, upset, and feeling lost.

How was she going to react to a proposal that had no place in her life? So, Kandji had put on her royal robes to impress her? Maahtou felt a surge of anger coming up from her belly, which gave her a new perspective of her guest. Kandji's expensive costume suddenly became, in her eyes, like the Moukouta rag often used to mop the floor. Like Youla, Kandji was trying to use material wealth to shift her focus from her raison d'être in college into a world charged with emotional currents. So, Kandji was attempting to force her onto the very threshold of betrothal? How on earth did she hatch the idea that Maahtou could be the subject or object of marriage, at that critical time, and to Tazor? That was equivalent to mental rape.

By overall village standards, Maahtou's analysis of Kandji was too harsh. Most men and women would have sworn that Kandji was doing her a favour. Villagers were fond of referring to a certain woman as a "chronic spinster." As a young woman, she had chosen college over a marriage proposal. Those villagers also condemned two other women for being childless because they got married after their 'fertile' years, all due to further education.

Despite those clear cases, Maahtou did not think that she was anywhere close to marriage, much less having children. She felt obliged to defend herself, but she lacked the words, especially for an unpalatable subject. She continued listening to Kandji only out of sheer politeness, hoping that she would soon see the futility of her mission. Maahtou bent down her head. Well-brought-up girls did not look adults in their faces when discussing serious matters, especially if they disagreed. Maahtou kept digging in her heels in a struggle to behave herself. Good breeding did not warrant her either to wear out Kandji's patience.

Kandji quietly stared at Maahtou, waiting for her response. Instead, Maahtou was infuriated. Anger rendered her as good as dumb. She was caught in her thoughts. They were broiling up inside her like a hot pot of cocoyams placed on Baba's typically blazing flames and making a "touro, touro touro" sound. Though her classmates had rated her among the naïve girls, she was sure that there was no room at that moment for gullibility.

"*Aee-eh* Maahtou. What do you say?" Kandji tried to pressure Maahtou.

She knew girls in the village who would have jumped at her offer.

"What did you say?" Maahtou asked with a renewed trembling that was building up in my stomach.

"He will like you to come and live with him in Douala," she said, smiling seductively, and displaying a crack through her red, heavily polished lips.

In those days, Douala, the economic capital of Cameroon, was the most modern fashion city. A student with relatives, working and living there, was considered genuinely privileged. Spending a weekend or a holiday in Douala turned a student into a star, to whom others campaigned for friendship.

"With Tazor? How is that?" Maahtou's mouth mumbled. Though she was totally against Kandji's proposal, her innate curiosity got the better of her. It lent her a measure of boldness that startled her.

"Of course, you know that Tazor works in Douala, right?" she said, smiling dryly.

Maahtou wanted to ask her, "and so what?" How could Kandji openly undermine the importance of college? Kandji herself was a college drop-out. She was often quick to remind everyone in the village, whenever the occasion presented itself, that she had been to college, and proudly so. She was conscious that she had squandered her opportunity. Yet her proposal was an indication that she had not stayed in college long enough to grasp the importance of higher learning.

From that point onwards, Maahtou realized that whatever she would advance to push off Kandji would fall on deaf ears. No matter how valid, it would not fit into Kandji's script. Thus, Maahtou became more upset.

"If you accept, I will take you with me," Kandji dared. "Tazor is preparing a lot of things for you," she spewed out.

"But I'm in school," her voice was barely audible while struggling to push down the ball of anger in her throat, choking her.

"Yes, I know. That's why I came right here. If you accept, I'll take you with me," Kandji proposed.

Boom! Maahtou's heart was almost dropping into her stomach. It felt like Kandji had pushed a brick wall over her. She would not allow it to crush her. Kandji deserved a thrashing from Mr. Molongos's cane, not only for lying about her identity but also for imagining that she could talk her into eloping by proxy.

Maahtou realized that Tazor had not been brave enough to show up to make his degrading proposal.

"Go talk to my parents," Maahtou spoke up and turned around quickly. Her eyes fell on the long flight of stairs, and she began running towards it. Kandji called out, but she did not look back. Instantly, Maahtou felt a sense of victory. She had succeeded in foiling Kandji's vile piece of drama wherein she had lied her way onto the stage. She had tried hard to usurp the role of a heroine, but her prey had turned into the genuine heroine.

The distance between them now required Kandji to shout out if she insisted on keeping her drama going, a risk she could not take. Thus, her only choice was to exit the stage. Maahtou's escape from her seducing claws silenced her. All that Maahtou heard as she ran along the veranda was the sound of neighing horses grazing in the nearby hill, in a rising crescendo. A funny thought came to her mind— even animals were contesting Kandji's stinking proposal.

Finally, Maahtou reached her class. She stopped at the door and tried to catch her breath with her eyes quickly glancing behind her. Kandji was already out of sight. Her trembling hands gently opened the door. A triumphant feeling enshrouded her being. It felt like she had just escaped the attack of a hyena.

Maahtou imagined the unsullied innocence that was still lingering on most of them in class. They were like green oranges steadily clinging onto their respective nourishing, protective branches. Not even the wind could detach them. Nature's quiet and gentle promise of approaching adolescence was still to wean them from lingering childhood. No one needed to tell her that, like a growing fruit, she was still hanging onto the branch, waiting its turn to be fully formed, from inside out.

The class was almost at the end. Sister Maureen was giving out homework. If only the beautiful Irish woman knew that one of her best students had just survived an unwarranted process of osmosis, she would blush or maybe faint. Her pretty, navy blue veil would turn sky blue from the bleaching of a highly concentrated solution concocted from a seductress' proposition.

At the end of the class, Maahtou signalled to the other Four Rocks. They stood by waiting for the other students to leave. It was urgent for her to unburden. "What?" they all shouted out in dismay. "That woman deserves a beating," said Nubodem. "Yes," the rest concurred. "You should have reported her to the discipline master," said Eposi. Maahtou shook her head and took in a deep breath. "How about the principal?" asked Ngwe. Maahtou shook her head several times.

It was time to leave the class and rush to the refectory.

That Tuesday, Maahtou's favourite meal, rice-and-beans, was served for lunch. The refectory was busy with dozens of vapor-laden loaded trays arriving from the kitchen, in an unbroken chain. Maahtou fidgeted at her seat at table number 6. She gobbled down every grain of brown kidney beans and white rice, somewhat mechanically because her very own thoughts were consuming her.

There and then, her delicious mouthfuls of rice and beans felt like she was chewing raw *cocoyams*. Her jaws were itching to pour out everything to her parents during the holidays.

That night it was difficult for Maahtou to sleep. She desperately needed to tell her parents about the elopement attempt. Unfortunately, it was not possible. She still had up to a month to go before the vacation.

Within a week classes were over, and they began preparing for exams. The other Four Rocks tried to console her. She finally put it off and focused on her revision. When the exams were over, she had more time to revisit the elopement attempt with her friends.

At last, it was the morning of the debut of college vacation! Maahtou woke up early and stayed in bed, mulling over Kandji's marriage proposal. She was still upset. What an attempt to equate her to a numskull! Kandji should instead have brought along the tinkered, palm-sized, rectangular black rat trap and attached a *mbonga* (dried fish) head to it. Then, instead of trying to persuade her, she should have placed it in the gutters at Virgin Mother's College. After releasing the snap wire spoke grip, it would have caught the necks of several rats. Otherwise, she should have come, armed with her catapult and grains of corn. She would have attracted chicks that stop in mid-flight to grab a morsel of bread, *puff-puff* or whatever.

Outrage soon gave way to an overwhelming sense of victory. Maahtou began chuckling as she thought of Kandji's misadventure consumed by the overflowing joy of success in her exams. Thus, she imagined the bundles of *achu* and *Keuka* or dishes of *maahfe* (potatoes – sweet and Irish), *meukoohné* (beans), *njaarh* (huckleberry leaves) that she was going to relish upon arrival at the village. Only the size of her stomach would limit the quantity she was going to enjoy.

Minutes were ticking away when the countdown to the official farewell ceremony began. Students pulled their luggage from the locker room and heaped them on the verandas, making it difficult for anyone to pass into the dorms. The brightly shining sun warmed the hearts of students soon to be passengers traveling in various directions.

The bell began ringing at 9:45 a.m., inviting students from all four dormitories to start walking towards the terrace assembly.

The principal, as usual, arrived on time, at the top of the hour. She made a brief statement about the just-ended term.

Delightedly she said that collaboration with the principal of RAC had tremendously reduced distraction caused by the transmission of love letters back and forth. She was happy that no student faced such an obstacle to their studies. In reaction, a Form 4 student whispered, "Pigeon."

"Pigeon, Pigeon, Pigeon," students repeated from Form 3 upwards while cracking up.

"Have I said something in Pidgin?" asked the Principal.

Her question instead provoked more laughter because while she was referring to a language, Pidgin English, the girls were hailing the underground mail delivery system code-named "Pigeon."

Of course, Form One and two students were confused. Maahtou seized the opportunity of the spontaneous rowdiness to recall the Kandji incident that had ridiculously marked the term for her.

"That woman caused me to miss the Chemistry class," said Maahtou.

"Imagine, you should have been getting ready to become Mrs. Tazor," said Ngwe.

"Hahaha," Nubodem and Eposi laughed out loud.

"God forbid," said Maahtou.

"Shirrr, Shirrr, Shirrr," the principal called for silence. "Keep up the good behaviour. Don't walk the slippery pathway with boys that would jeopardize your future. I'm pleading with you."

Youla giggled and said in a low tone, "*Club Cent go hear e mami.*" (Club Cent will get tired of me). Luckily, she was standing at the far corner of the double Form 2 rows. The two girls who were standing by her chuckled. However, they quickly closed their mouths with their palms when those in front turned and looked backward.

The principal, who had not noticed Youla's attempt to distract others, went ahead, and reiterated the importance of being disciplined and obedient to parents.

"Spend as much time as you can helping your parents with domestic chores, farming, and whatever business they are doing," she cautioned.

Finally, she congratulated students who passed as well as those with immaculate behaviour, especially those who positively responded to her warnings regarding lewd letters from self-styled boyfriends. All eyes turned towards a Form 3 student, Camille, for having severed links with her RAC boyfriend, on the orders of the principal.

Indeed, unlike other girls who kept communicating with their boyfriends by the underground pigeon mail, Camille went as far as taking the matter to the confessional.

"You are going to become tomorrow's leaders. That is why obeying college rules and studying hard go along together," the principal said.

Maahtou began thinking about Kandji and her proposal. If only the principal knew that Kanji had tried to terminate her education, she would have rewarded her for resisting such terrible temptation.

Chapter 11

Dissecting Unsavoury Marriage Proposals

Dawn was gradually approaching. Birds were chirping on the mango and avocado trees at both sides of the entrance to Maahtou's parent's home. Maahtou was stretching her body in bed to release the lingering strain on her legs from the marathon race of traveling home with her luggage on her head the previous day. She imagined that it was still hours before dawn. Instead, there was a knock on the living room door.

The person at the door spoke up with a small sharp voice that pierced through the windows. Mama recognized it and called out from her room for Abong or Neumour to let her in.

Mama turned round on her bed and sighed. She had overslept; her planned talk with Maahtou may not be possible.

The woman at the door was one of their neighbours, Mami Nchang. Mothers in the village were often called by the name of their first child. Thus, Nchang was her first child and son. Her compound was just across the street. She regularly visited to chat with Mama. Whenever there were some key events, she would come and engage Baba and Mama, either to be enlightened or to hear their point of view. Otherwise, she sought them to help put the occurrence within the right historical context. She was younger than them. At other times, she wanted Mama's exclusive advice on how to deal with her co-wives, or how to prepare appropriately for some village ceremonies.

Mami Nchang came in and greeted Mama loudly while taking a seat in the parlour.

"What has brought you so early?" asked Mama.

"I'm sorry to have disturbed your sleep," said Mami Nchang. I just wanted to catch you all before you leave for the farm. It was almost 7.00 a.m.

"I'm rather grateful that you have woken me up," said Mama.

She had planned to put the *cocoyams* for *achu* on the fire at 5 am, but she fell back into a deep sleep after Baba left as usual to tap his wine.

"What are you doing with a book, Mami Nchang?" asked Mama.

"It is Adzeh's report card." He was the third of her four children.

She wanted Maahtou to tell her if her son had passed or not. Usually, she consulted Baba. However, news of Maahtou's arrival had reached her. The boy's older siblings had said that he passed, but she wanted Maahtou to confirm it as well as give further relevant details.

Mami Nchang stood up and embraced Maahtou when she announced the good news to her. Adzeh had indeed passed.

"Ever since independence came, illiterates like us are like tailless cows," said Mami Nchang.

However, she equally wanted to know what the teacher had written in red ink on the last page.

"People like us are as blind as bats," Mami Nchang said, shrugging.

The two red ink marks were against Geography and Civics. He scored 48 and 37 percent respectively and narrowly escaped in Arithmetic, a compulsory subject. Despite the red dots, Adzeh got a promotion to Class 6.

"*Mbaah kasee?*" (Didn't I tell you?) Mama intoned in celebration.

"*Anwaarneh abong*" (Education is important), Maahtou responded.

Mami Nchang smiled and clapped her hands. Then, she stood up from her seat like a soldier. She stretched out her dry and greyish looking hands towards Mama joyously. Stress and fatigue were betraying wrinkles on her smiling face.

"Go home and make a large cup of tea and drink," said Mama while handing some tea sachets and a piece of bread to Mami Nchang.

She and Mama had been fellow students at the defunct adult literacy class. Unfortunately, the initiator was obliged to close it because the women were often coming late or were simply absent for days.

"Meeya Mama, meeya, Mama," Mami Nchang thanked her host and danced her way right to the street.

Mama immediately invited Maahtou to come and sit on her lap. "Look at a young woman in this modern age, seeking help in the same manner as her mother," Mama said, swinging Maahtou from side to side. "Hold onto your grooming spouse, you hear me?"

"I figured you were going to say that," said Maahtou. Both of them laughed while Maahtou's younger sisters wondered what they were talking about.

"What time is it," asked Mama while looking at the wall clock.

She decided that it was too late to put the *achu cocoyams* on the fire. Instead, Mama called Neumour and asked her to get ready to go to the farm with her. Meanwhile, Abong had to stay home with Afouomama There was laundry to do. Neumour shouted out a big no from her bed.

"Why farming nonstop? Every day, every day, farm, farm, farm," she kept insisting that she was not going to the farm.

Mama yielded to her refusal. Then, she turned around and explained to Maahtou how hard Abong and Neumour had worked on the acres of land that they possessed. So, she proposed that Neumour should instead go to the market square. Thus, Mama went into the back room of the kitchen and opened the pile of dried plantain leaves that were covering something. Most of the green bananas had all turned bright yellow. Mama went out and got a basin and placed the bananas in them.

As for Maahtou, Mama asked her to stay home and rest. Maahtou suggested that Mama stay home too, especially since the rain had fallen all night.

"You ask others to go make a cup of tea and drink, how about yourself?" asked Abong.

"Hahaha," Neumour and Afouomama burst out laughing.

"Let's stay home and clean the house and arrange stuff," proposed Maahtou. "I will also plait your hair."

"Thank you, sister," said Abong and Neumour with a great sigh of relief. Mama accepted Maahtou's proposal but pleaded that they do some weeding in the garden around the house called *Nkaah*. The day was promising to be sunny and bright.

"Can I make some tea?" asked Abong.

Everyone jumped at Abong's offer.

After breakfast, Mama handed over a sweater, some old shirts, and oversized used trousers to Maahtou. She fitted two pairs of pants and decided on the shorter one. Soon, their arms and legs were well covered, protecting them from the grasses that caused itching upon touching the skin. Coffee branches and banana leaves entangled by creeping stems of *Meutouoh* (surface yams) produced a dense shrub that blocked both the sun and the view from penetrating the ground. Without Baba's regular efforts in separating branches with his sharp cutlass, even a thief could hide and spy on all the movements in and out of the house.

Mama chose the east wing of the house, away from the footpath by the house. But for the kola nut tree, hardly any child in the neighbourhood ever trespassed. Besides, the area was equally out of earshot from the house.

Weeds had grown wild. Tree branches were desperate for trimming. Large *achu* cocoyam leaves were yellowing, waiting for harvest. Tree branches at the boundary were overgrown, providing a shield from anyone passing by the road below.

"There are many types of witchcraft in the world," Mama said suddenly, and as soon as she pulled out the first weed.

"Why do you say that?" Maahtou asked.

She had been waiting anxiously for a follow-up on Kandji's marriage proposal. A few months ago, Mama talked about their loud and aggressive neighbour, having referred to Maahtou as "the best wife" for her son. Mama had quickly dismissed it as one of her ceaseless pranks. Now Mama knew better - Tazor's mother had meant it.

"So, Mami Ntchoular and Kandji have weighed you and decided to pair you up with Tazor?"

"Hahaha," Maahtou laughed and clapped her hands. Then, she took a few steps, dragging her body from side to side, supposedly a wife walking by her husband.

"What is the value of an idiot's love?" Mama asked. "Mere outbursts of declarations like drunkards do," she said, as she fumbled around in imitation of startled winebibbers.

Maahtou could not help herself. She bent over, held her stomach, and laughed out loud.

"A Mouxmoux's love is a river that dries up just when you are dehydrating. Do these dull men know that *akonté* (love), aghouté (affection), and irzieh (wisdom) go together?" Mama asked in renewed amazement.

"Mama, *Ndaar Anwarneh* (education) is all I want now."

Mama was not taking it as lightly as Maahtou. Kandji's attempted seduction had tortured Mama's brains all night, like squeezing bitter herbs to prepare *ndolé* (processed vegetable soup). She had tried awfully hard to suppress it while Mami Nchang was visiting.

Suddenly, a kola nut fell from the tree, which Maahtou picked up and placed on the ridge between them.

"Yes, there are *mouxmoux* (stupid) bridegrooms seeking housemaids in the place of wives.

"Maybe he is a good cook like many of the men from our village who live in Douala," said Maahtou. Mama did not answer. She needed to complete her thought.

"Some girls are cheaper than a pound," she went on."

"You are right, Mama."

Maahtou tried to lift her eyes to look at the birds flying overhead, but the sun was shining brighter.

"*Meeya mba? Meeya mba neumour*" (Thank you. Thank you, darling,") said Mama. She stood up and thanked Maahtou in a very formal voice for having turned down Kandji's proposal.

There was silence. Both were weeding with their hoes at a heightened speed. In barely half an hour, Maahtou stood up and caught her breath. She assessed the weeded area, where they had finished six ridges. Mama stood up and cleaned her hoe. Her back was feeling strained, but she wanted to take advantage of Maahtou's presence.

"I'm so thankful to you, my children, for advising me to stay home today," said Mama.

"So, let's hurry and get back to the house. I will do your hair or cook something delicious," said Maahtou.

Maahtou picked up the cutlass to trim some banana leaves, but it was unable to cut through. So, Mama asked her to go to the house and ask Abong for the file to sharpen the cutlass.

Maahtou was singing on her way back from the house. It was a song for *Acharhne* (sending-off the bride). She got close to Mama and noticed that Mama was standing instead of working. Mama clapped her hands several times as if merely pushing off the dirt that was stuck on her palms.

At that moment, a troop of four big brown birds descended just above their heads.

"Have you seen a vulture pouncing over a prey?" Mama asked.

"Why are you saying that?" she asked Maahtou while smiling in expectation.

"I mean that there are wild birds out there," Her extra fair skin betrayed a new redness. It was like feathered chicken dropped into boiling water.

Maahtou bent down, held her stomach, and laughed uncontrollably.

They were both getting hungry. However, Mama began tackling the chronological burden of threats that have taunted her family, one after the other. Her second daughter, Bongshee, did not have the chance to complete secondary school. They could not pay her school fees. So, she moved to Mutengene to live with Mama's brother, Taabong, a Carpenter. There, she enrolled in an institution to study to become a stenographer. Life was like daggers pointed at her. Her Uncle's friends often mocked her determination to succeed. They usually came home and offered her gifts, including money.

Each of them was shocked because Bongshee never accepted any of their offers. Similarly, she turned down their invitations to go to off-licenses to drink and to eat *sawyer* (skewered beef steak). She never forgot Mama's time-tested advice to her children: To fasten their waists with a belt, and to drink water to ward off hunger, rather than accepting food from simpletons or self-conceited people.

When Bongshee kept turning down their invitations, they moved a step higher. They began making marriage proposals.

"*You no like mimbo* (drink), *but you go be na ma woman*," (though you are not the drinking type, you will become my wife), a suitor said in Pidgin, thinking that she would fall for his compliment.

Bongshee hardly knew what to say apart from shaking her head and moving away. Often, they addressed her with breaths laced with alcohol from various brands of locally brewed beer. Those men were almost always tipsy, if not drunk. That is how they often exposed the limits of their promises. It was not uncommon to see one of them in the streets, walking unsteadily and losing his balance from drunkenness.

"One of my friends is truly serious about wanting to get married to you," said Uncle Taabong one evening to Bongshee.

"Which one?" asked Bongshee.

"The one that brought home sawyer last week."

"Hahaha," Bongshee was thrilled. He was referring to the same drunkard of two days ago, whom Boongshee herself had witnessed, stumping away while trying to escape oncoming cars.

"What's wrong with him?" asked Uncle Taabong.

"If a pig makes "oink, oink, oink," will you listen to it?" asked Bongshee. The more Mama revisited past threats to her children's education and career pursuits, the more she got upset with Kandji's story. A tear dropped from her right eye.

"So, you are crying because of Kandji?" asked Maahtou.

Mama was a very courageous woman, but she also cried very quickly. It was as if her whole body contained only water.

Indeed, Mama's children often wondered how she was able to bear the shocks, one after another, and still laugh, celebrate each victory, while showing gratitude for every act of kindness. Maybe it was because she quickly yielded to her feelings, like a tree by the river bowing and swinging according to the direction of the wind. Pain as much as joy seemed to ooze out of her system like melting ice in the mid-afternoon sun. She would put her mind and heart into the situation, as if to hold happiness and sorrow in perfect balance.

Without prior notice, right on the spot, Mama started humming another popular wedding song entitled, *Tarhmenghirne* (Mr. Bridegroom).

"Mr. Bridegroom is anxiously waiting at home,
"Legs suspended above the bed..."

Mama enjoyed singing that song, maybe because she had a house full of girls. Maahtou's hoe instantly escaped her grip. It fell to the ground and rolled two ridges away. Her dancing legs caught up with her mother's midway. With her right hip, she pushed Mama's hips in dancing steps. Their joint laughter sent the perched birds flying away.

"Oh, sorry, sorry, women are surrendering to men as if they would soon vanish," Mama pressed on.

Maahtou burst out laughing. "Where is Eposi, Nubodem, and Ngwe to laugh with me?" The comic relief was timely.

Chapter 12

Kola Nut Gifts

It was a refreshing morning after it had rained the previous night. The gentle morning sun was shining brightly. Maahtou was eager to go to the farm with Mama. She wanted to hear the kola nut story. She was happy because the weather was conducive for outdoor work, but most especially for chatting one-to-one with her mother.

Mama stepped out and looked at the sky. "It is not going to rain until later in the day. Baba, who was just returning from *Ndooh* (wine bush), flung a log of wood on the pile at the back of the kitchen.

"Your mother is right about the rain," he said. "But you better hurry."

As soon as mother and daughter put down their basins on the ridge, Mama spoke up. "My daughter, I want you to promise me," said Mama.

Maahtou was all ears. "Promise me that you are not going to rush into marriage."

Maahtou raised her eyebrows. What did she mean by rushing? Maahtou wondered. She stared at her mother blankly. Instead of elaborating, Mama began fidgeting into the pocket of her *kaba*.

"You know that each of us have natural gifts" Mama went on. She was going to use a metaphor to explain her thesis.

"Yes, Mama, but what is the link between one's natural gifts and marriage?"

Instead of asking Mama what specifically kola nut gifts were, Maahtou rushed to the subject of marriage. "Wait, my daughter. Let me finish." Mama opened her hands and showed Maahtou two kola nuts. The kola nut trees that Baba planted a few years ago had begun yielding fruits.

Maahtou paused for a while. She took a deep breath as if creating mental space to absorb Mama's awaited lecture.

"So, Mama, what has kola nut to do with talents?"

Maahtou had often pondered over the importance that men attach to the weird, bitter fruit, the kola nut. Men always ask for kola nut whenever they are about to drink wine. They say that it is difficult to swallow raffia wine, or any other wine for that matter, without it. People even bow to receive a kola nut from the hands of a noble or an older man. No male-dominated ritual can end without men sharing and eating kola nuts. Some women follow suit, though to a lesser degree.

As for children, they would stand by and observe without any particular interest. After all, kola is bitter.

"Do you see this kola nut?" Mama asked. She was peeling away the white shield covering several nuts. Then she took out one seed from the pod. She gave it to Maahtou. The latter proceeded to peel the beige covering the nut. It was a pinkish violet-coloured nut. Mama took it and pressed it between her thumb and forefinger. It broke open in her palms, and the various cotyledons fell apart. Mama asked Maahtou to count them. There were four of them. Other nuts come with more or less cotyledons, the least being two. Unlike the single-seed bitter kola, foreign to Santa, the locally grown kola nut always has multiple cotyledons.

Also, the cotyledons of kola nuts come in various sizes. One of the two-part seeds may be more significant than the rest, or two may be of the same size. If not, it could be in pairs of equal sizes. Baba often asked his children, including Maahtou, to peel kola nuts for him while drinking raffia wine with his friends.

"Have you noticed that our kola nuts never have a single seed?"

"Yes, but is there a reason?" asked Maahtou.

"As far I am concerned, it is like someone having several innate abilities."

Maahtou paused and looked into Mama's eyes for more clues.

"But most people have only one job," said Maahtou.

"That doesn't mean that they are only capable of doing one thing," explained Mama.

"But if someone is a teacher, a doctor, or a lawyer, isn't that good enough?"

"What you are naming is their main occupation, but not necessarily their talents," said Mama.

Maahtou raised her eyebrows as if to aerate her brain.

"Do you remember your grooming husband?"

"Ndoumnyui," said Maahtou with her face lighting up as she repeated the name.

Thanks to *ndaar nnwarneh* (education), you will know and better use your kola nut gifts," said Mama. "So, let me tell you straight way — your ndaar *anwaarneh* sheds light on Ndoumnyui."

Immediately, Maahtou thought about latency in her physics classes.

"The role of *ndaar nwarneh* is to unveil and train your talents."

Maahtou kept listening intently.

"Some people are lucky to have a *mbongsoon* (a beloved friend) right from their childhood.

Maahtou nodded. She recalled that her father often referred to his *mbongsoon*.

Mama went ahead and explained the difference between *mbongsoon* and a groomsman. While the latter appears only during the wedding, *mbongsoon* is a close friend who knows the strengths and weaknesses of his friend. They tend to be inseparable.

"So, how does *ndaar anwarneh* help the grooming spouse?" asked Maahtou emphatically.

"Like the sun, *ndaar anwarneh* dispels darkness. Also, it polishes and sharpens your kola nut gifts like the filing of a cutlass. Then, your talents begin to *ngwankhe* (shine out).

Maahtou raised her eyebrows.

"If you cherish *ndaar anwarneh*, you will see and understand things that escape the notice of the uneducated.

"*Heybey!*" Maahtou exclaimed. "Does it mean that without schooling, I could not discover my talents?"

'Some people are lucky, but others, no."

"What if someone never does?"

"Such a person may end up living below their level or living someone else's life."

"Really?" "I don't understand, Mama."

"You know your uncle, who lives by the Nkie Custom, who is a soldier?" Mama asked.

Maahtou nodded.

"Though he has money, he has refused to send his children to the regular *ndaar anwarneh* (schools)."

Everyone in the village knew the story of the said uncle. He was fond of subjecting his children to strenuous exercises early in the mornings. He would get them out of bed before 5 am. On the spot, he would ask them to each drink half a litre of water. Then he would order them to run for miles in the cold as if they were recruits into a military academy. He wanted all his children to become soldiers like him, including the girls. Indeed, villagers referred to him as Tata Hyena. He seemed to have retained the fearful qualities of the hyenas that used to parade the village.

"Maybe Tata Hyena's children don't mind."

"Whatever their feelings, they may never find out their right professions," said Mama.

Maahtou shook her head and took in a deep breath.

"Reason with me— how will their *meumoughmetou* (brains) grow without exposure to general ideas?" asked Mama.

Mama picked up one of the cotyledons of the kola nut. She began explaining that the Ngemba people call it *niebieh,* a word that also denotes planting as well as cooked food.

"The act of planting," Maahtou said while dragging the word. Then she paused to ponder over it.

"Yes."

"When does this type of planting stop?" asked Maahtou. "Continuous planting sounds like failing in school and repeating the class."

"No, not that, my daughter. Planting is ongoing because the life cycle must go on."

"Hmmn!" Maahtou exclaimed.

Maahtou was thinking deeply, trying to compare Mama's lecture to her courses in college. If not, what could be the synonyms or similes?

Mama pitched in promptly. "The second meaning of *niebieh*, "done" may be compared to completing your education.

Maahtou opened her mouth wide in amazement.

"The sad thing is that many girls rush to get married without having planted anything nor set anything on the fire, as if a husband replaces their kola nut gifts."

Maahtou laughed out loud and held her waist before probing further.

"So, what happens to the gifts of such girls, then?" asked Maahtou.

"Their kola nut gifts lie fallow, invaded by thorns and thistles." Maahtou clapped her hands and laughed. Mama was sounding like a professor, a specialist. "The women themselves move around without an identity like shadows,' Mama went on.

However, Mama noted that it is never too late to redeem them. Intelligent and kind husbands would eventually create favourable conditions for their wives to retrieve their kola nut gifts.

On the contrary, a selfish and primitive husband would become an obstacle. He would instead frustrate any attempt by his wife to respond to the ever-present urge to pursue her kola nut gifts.

Maahtou began wondering if she could liken women without professional identities to late bloomers. It was a concept she had heard from senior students. "But why do they prevent their wives from making progress?"

"Some husbands are jealous of their wives, unfortunately," said Mama. "A controlling spouse does not want his wife to find her 'grooming spouse.' He impersonates the gift, thus imagines that by cherishing her gift, she is favouring 'him' over him."

"But a profession isn't a person."

"You got it, my daughter. Selfish men are short-sighted," said Mama. Their sole focus is attention which they mistake for loyalty of sorts.``

Maahtou looked at her mother in awe. She took a deep breath, and then smiled.

"So, *Ndaar anwarneh* is like light. Thanks to college, you will be able to light up our quarter," Mama went on.

"How?"

"Didn't Mami Nchang consult you recently about her son's results?"

Maahtou beamed and smiled broadly.

"With higher education, your kola nut gifts could become as many as corn."

Maahtou gaped at her mother. She kept looking at her in total admiration. However, she wanted an application of Mama's theory in practical terms.

"You keep saying you would have become a doctor and a judge. How did you know your gifts without *ndaar anwarneh*?"

"When you spend time alone in a quiet place like the farm, you learn a lot about yourself. Then, when you are with people, you find out more about yourself because of what they say about you," she explained. "At other times, you know your gifts through recurrent requests that others make of you."

"Is that how you knew your gifts?"

"Yes, I began by perceiving their needs, and each time, I had a strong urge to step in and offer advice or to help them."

"Hmmm, Mama, I feel like I'm sitting in a senior class."

"God made us intelligent, so each one must take the time to find out in what area he or she is gifted. Each time I help

106

people in need, they thank me repeatedly and hug me endlessly."

"Do you have an example of someone else who is shining because of his or her kola nut gift?"

"Look at your father. He is not only a farmer, but also a tailor, and a raffia juice tapper."

"Aw, that is so perfect," said Maahtou.

"He is not the only garment maker nor the only one with a raffia farm," said Mama. "But ask yourself, why do people prefer his sewing and his wine?"

Maahtou smiled broadly and embraced her mother. "I want to know why, Mama."

Indeed, Baba was outstanding; his renown was beyond the village. No wonder, he was better known as Baba Tila (Tailor) than by his real name. Younger city dwellers from Douala and Yaoundé usually brought material for their suits to Baba for stitching.

In the same vein, whenever his wine arrived at a bar, people ceased drinking from other suppliers until his jug got empty. At home, guests often stopped by, hoping to savour Baba's raffia juice and or wine.

"But what makes the difference, Mama?" asked Maahtou.

"Discovering one's gift and getting some training is not enough. What makes someone shine is *Alehme zetshirhneh* (pure blood)," explained Mama.

"Your father puts his heart and his mind into his work. Next is *Abongneze tshirnhneh* (wholesome speech), and *abohze tshirnhneh* (a giving, warm hand)."

At that instance, Maahtou realized that there was more to school than just passing exams or obtaining a certificate. She clapped her hands and tenderly hugged Mama for a long while. Mama grinned from ear to ear. She always enjoyed prolonging her embraces.

Maahtou rested her head on Mama's right shoulder. Her face glowed with satisfaction.

"My daughter never forget that your grooming spouse is none other than your *Ndaar Anwarneh* (education)," said Mama while lifting and shaking her right forefinger. "If you listen to him and ask pertinent questions, he will never abandon you."

The more Mama explained, the more it became evident to Maahtou. It was like holding a microscope over small prints.

Mama looked up towards the sky. The sun was suddenly shining brighter.

"Didn't I tell you that the light unveils your kola nut gifts?"

Then, a cool breeze began blowing into their faces. Maahtou breathed in, deeply. Mama stretched her hand and rubbed Maahtou's head. "*Meumoughmeto* (brain), everything is in here."

"Hahaha," Maahtou laughed out loud. Her brain had registered a lot of new lessons from Mama and needed some refreshing.

The leaves of the surrounding cypress trees were shaking. Birds were singing in nearby trees with large branches.

Maahtou's eyes strayed into the faraway hills with greenish and yellowish ridges. She imagined the unknown owners of the abundant dark green crops. Then, she turned around and asked her mother what to do next. Mama stood up, stretched her arms, and declared that their work for the day was over. It was time to get ready to return home.

Maahtou was surprised. She had never seen Mama leaving the farm so early. Rather than being tired, Mama's face was glowing with satisfaction. Her complexion became fairer. What Maahtou did not know was that Mama had deliberately requested the children to stay home. She had hoped to have a tête-à-tête with Maahtou without any distractions. She had effectively used her farm as a natural and fitful conference space. She was all joy.

"Hold him tightly, do you hear me?" urged Mama.

"Who are you referring to?" Maahtou asked, feigning ignorance.

"*Ndoumnyui o*" (your grooming husband).

Maahtou laughed.

"Though I am the one who has introduced you to your Ndoumnyui, soon you will be one telling all kinds of stories about him," said Mama.

Maahtou smiled and walked a few steps away.

Mama moved a few steps and cut some dry banana leaves. She spliced them, a dry end to a fresh end until she made a long, taut rope. Then she used it to fasten Maahtou's Moukouta bag. It was filled with a variety of freshly harvested crops— potatoes, cocoyams, corn, vegetables, pumpkins.

As for Maahtou, the analogy that Mama had used to convey her message remained vivid. Her mind was darting from one possible talent or career to another. Her thoughts were lively like an unfolding movie while they were climbing the hilly road back home.

Finally, they got home. Maahtou dropped her load in front of the kitchen. Without pausing, she rushed into the main house.

"What is it?" asked Mama.

Maahtou soon returned from Baba's wine cellar with something in her hand.

"*Ndoumnyui* a (my grooming husband)," said Maahtou.

Mama looked at her and smiled. She grabbed a bamboo chair and sat down and began peeling the kola nut.

"So, what do you plan to become in future?" asked Mama.

"Let me count the parts of each kola nut before telling you."

Chapter 13

Trouble at Table

On Monday morning, by 9.00 am, students began dozing off, with heads falling on desks. Some fell asleep and began snoring. Teachers who were busy writing on the chalkboard turned around in shock. "What's going on?" asked the biology teacher in Maahtou's class. "Why is everyone sleeping?" asked the Maths teacher in the Form 4 class. "Why are your heads down?" asked Miss Hortensia in Form 1. None was able to say a word as hardly any student could hold up their heads.

So, teachers jumped out of their classes and met others in the corridors throwing their hands in the air, bewildered. While one reported the early-morning napping incident in his or her class, the others complained about the same. They realized that every class was affected. Helpless and at a loss as to what might have caused the apparent mystery, they rushed to the principal's office. She came out, went into the first class, then, the next, and the scene was the same.

Shocked and confused, she struggled to maintain her composure. Maybe fresh air could help, or so she thought. So, she requested the teachers to return to their various classrooms. Each of them asked students to open the windows even though it was a cold morning. Next, the teachers drilled students in body-stretching exercises.

Other teachers encouraged students to go get potable water. Almost everyone stepped out. Students soon returned to class. As the minutes rolled away, they began regaining their full consciousness. Things seemed normal again.

Nothing happened the next day and during the rest of the week. The principal and staff were more relaxed though they still had to solve the mystery.

The following Monday, the spell returned. Like the previous week, the next day students were as agile as usual. Nothing happened for the rest of the week.

On the third Monday, the somniferous condition recurred.

"We have been saying that it's the *puff-puff*," insisted a few students of Forms 3, 4, and 5. Others concurred, blaming the collective hypnosis on the delicious balls of the fried bread looking like dumplings or doughnuts. They were served for breakfast exclusively on Mondays.

"But how come it never happened before?" retorted other students.

"Whenever I eat oily food in the morning, I become sleepy," insisted those who often shunned the Monday breakfast menu.

The principal held an emergency meeting with teachers. They were all convinced that it was the Monday breakfast. They could not say why it was happening only after two years of serving *puff-puff* in the morning. Nevertheless, they decided to replace it with bread.

The emergency measure was immediately welcomed. However, weeks went by without authorities making mention of the Monday morning collective drowsiness.

"No more dozing off and snoring this morning?" Sister Maureen asked as soon as she stepped into the Form 2 class. She taught the second course on Mondays. As their Chemistry teacher, they seized the opportunity to confront her.

"Well, we have been guinea pigs for three long weeks," said Nubodem.

"Where is the scientific proof that *puff-puff* is the problem?" asked Maahtou.

"It's not enough to just stop serving *puff-puff*," added Rose and Grace.

"So, what else can the authorities do?" Sister Maureen asked.

"Find out what exactly went wrong," insisted Nubodem.

"That's it," concurred the whole class.

"What if it's the oil as some students say?" asked Odile.

"Who knows if it's not the flour," Judith added.

"Or maybe the yeast," said Eposi.

"I'm happy you are raising questions. Rest assured, the school authorities are seeking answers," said Sister Maureen. "But for now, let's continue with our lesson."

Students sighed and shook their heads. What if truly the problem was due to the imported flour and yeast, or the locally made palm oil? They were disappointed that their teacher had not asked for *puff-puff* samples for testing at the school laboratory.

"*Wen na black man, they go say no worry,*" (When it concerns blacks, they dismiss the issue with "don't worry), said some senior students who were not happy with the lackadaisical attitude of the authorities.

"Had it been one of them, they would have rushed her to the hospital," another, Margaret, added.

"No city authorities in charge of food and health has shown up on campus," said Grace.

"So they decided to sacrifice Aunty Paulina?" said Therese. She was referring to the caterer. Supplying *puff-puff* to Virgin Mother's college was the largest chunk of her business. "What about primary school children who stop by her roadside kitchen daily to buy *puff-puff*? What about other restaurants, homes, or hotels using the same flour, yeast, or oil?," she went on.

"*Weah*! Aunty is going to face hard times," said Anna, a Form 3 student and niece of the Monday morning caterer. How was the single mother going to care for her family? She would no longer be able to sponsor her son, daughter, and nephew in college. The *puff-puff* business has been her sole occupation for fifteen years since completing primary school.

As far as the general student population was concerned, the absence of *puff-puff* was already causing problems. Some of the meals served at the refectory were not palatable. Students who used to substitute dreaded meals with the excess supply of *puff-*

puff were at a loss. Starvation was their lot. Usher in a sudden rise in begging for snacks. Besides, were the administration thinking about the effect of hunger on the performance of students?

Barely two weeks after the authorities suspended *puff-puff*, an incident took place at the refectory. A Form 2 student, Florence, became the victim of complaints about the quantity of food served. On Monday, she frowned during dinner. Later, she complained to friends that the Form 4 student in charge of serving at her table had given her the smallest share. Unfortunately, Florence's friend disclosed the matter to her Big. The latter requested the Form 5 student at her table to ensure that her Small was not disfavoured. The talebearers meant well, but the consequence was far from the solution they had expected.

On Thursday evening after dinner, the Form 5 student at Florence's table, Miss Hambug (nuisance), ordered her to wait, without disclosing the reason. Florence stood in an empty refectory waiting when a female cook arrived with two hipped bowls of rice and beans.

Immediately, Florence beamed, supposing that Miss Hambug had requested extra food for sharing among them. Within minutes, Miss Hambug, who had been speaking in low tones outside with the Form 4 student in charge of serving, Miss Cunny (pidgin for cunning), came in and joined Florence.

"Sit down, Flo," ordered Miss Hambug with a surprisingly harsh tone.

"I hope that you will fill your stomach tonight," said Miss Cunny, while pointing at Florence with her right forefinger.

Florence immediately smelled trouble. The lingering hunger in her instantly disappeared. Then, she said that she had eaten enough. The two senior students, staring at her, shook their heads repeatedly.

"You went gossiping that I gave you the smallest share, right?" asked Miss Cunny.

"No, I didn't. When did I say that?" asked Florence.

"You said on Monday that I cheated you. So, begin to eat," insisted Miss Cunny.

"I only said that the food that day was small, not that you cheated," pleaded Florence.

"Sit down and serve yourself and begin to eat," howled Miss Hambug.

At Florence's reluctance, Miss Cunny served the first helping of the food onto the clean plate before her. They ordered her to eat. She stared into their faces for mercy, but there was none. So, she began eating. Halfway through, she said she was satisfied, but they ordered her to finish it. She picked up the spoon and resumed the dreaded dining solitaire race. After forcing down some ten scoops, she said she could not anymore.

Instead of leaving it at that, both senior students started screaming at her. Florence began crying and saying that she was sorry. They asked her to shut her mouth and continue eating. She took two more scoops, but the third remained suspended in her hand while she sealed her mouth. Suddenly, she dropped the spoon and held her stomach.

The two disciplinarians would not hear of it; they ordered her to keep eating.

Tears began rolling down on the victim's cheeks. It was impossible for her to finish all the food, even if she had starved for a whole week. Luckily for Florence, the cook was about to close the kitchen. So, she came to recover the dishes. As soon as the senior students saw the cook, they looked at each other awkwardly. Immediately, they ordered Florence to stand up quickly and disappear through the door.

Florence arrived late in class that night for prep. Endless rivers of tears were flowing on her face. Her classmates were shocked.

"What is the problem?" asked the classmates at the front desk.

Florence was unable to speak. Those who saw her first, stood up and began patting her on the back. Finally, Florence managed to recount details of her ordeal while crying.

"I'm just lucky, then," said Maahtou.

"Me too," added Ngwe. Rice-and-beans was a favourite dish for most students. The intense mouth-watering longing for it often lessened their focus in class on Tuesdays and Thursdays. Besides, of all the meals, rice-and-beans was also the best-prepared.

Meanwhile, the Form 2 students kept whispering about Florence's nightmare throughout the campus. From that day onwards, the Form 1s understood the danger of complaining about senior students.

Despite the attempt to silence hunger complaints, poor nutrition was hitting the stomachs of students like an epidemic. The ban on *puff-puff* had exposed the true condition of the girls. Prior to the Monday morning collective nap, some students had been campaigning for one more day of *puff-puff*. Their reasoning was clear. Half a loaf of French baguette was too light to sustain them right through to lunch time. Barely two of Aunty Paulina's *puff-puff* supplied the needed energy. Besides, unlike the baguette, which dried up like a piece of wood by the following morning, *puff-puff* remained palatable.

Each morning at the refectory, most students regretted they were not at home, where they could eat whatever they wanted for breakfast. Who doesn't know that a lot of leftover dinner often tastes better the next day?

In the absence of any nutrition reforms in sight, students began wishing their skirts had been designed with belts that they could tighten to keep hunger in check.

Chapter 14

Initiatives and Inventions

It was Saturday. Laundry and manual labour were already over. In barely half an hour it will be lunch time. It was also the beginning of collective frowning and sighing time. No other moment during the week registered more discontent than the early afternoon. The menu for lunch consisted of two boiled, skinny plantains with a tiny piece of meat swimming in a 'stew' of reddish coagulated palm oil suspended over a brown liquid.

"*We eh wusai I go take pear for chop ma garri eh*? (From where do I get avocado for my garri?), complained Susan.

"*Ya own better say you even get garri*" (You are better off having garri), answered Gwendoline.

"*Me I wan me na sugar oh*," (As for me, what I need is sugar), said Mary.

In each dormitory, students were desperate for a replacement meal for the sad Saturday lunch. It was the day when students actually experienced starvation.

Over the years, students had complained both to the cooks and the authorities, but nothing had changed. The size of the single slice of meat on each plate, which was just big enough to stick in-between the teeth, remained the same. Dissatisfaction with food was mostly felt as from the middle of the term. That was when most would have run out of *cold water garri*, the most popular snack.

In a last ditch effort, a group of students called Chop Fellows approached the new Cookery Class teacher, Mrs. Tom. Though they knew full well that she was just a part-time teacher, they wanted to give it a try. Chop Fellows hoped that she would use her international experience to influence the administration. She had lived in France and in the UK.

Initially, Mrs. Tom said that she had no say over the college menu. That notwithstanding, Chop Fellows insisted, pleading with her to speak about their plight to the principal. They wanted more delicious meals, even if the quantity remained unchanged.

Students were still waiting for Mrs. Tom to act when another group of students called Aroma Girls started mocking the Chop Fellows.

"Why do you trouble Mrs. Tom?" asked the Aroma Girls. "Ma Aggi does the trick for every meal as long as you sprinkle it."

Aroma Girls were among students who always brought along, to the refectory, the popular bottle of an imported brown liquid with the brand name of Ma Aggi. It was quite common in homes in the city. The miracle liquid instantly changed an insipid dish into a tasty meal. They cherished it so much that not a drop would they give to any student who could not afford it.

As for the Four Rocks, they were among the disadvantaged two-thirds of the student population that contented themselves with the meals served. In comparing situations at each of their homes, each of them said that their father was more or less addicted to Ma Aggi. As for Maahtou's father, though he always ensured that Ma Aggi was at home, the attitude of the Aroma Girls reminded her of her father's stronger attachment to cayenne pepper.

Aroma Girls failed woefully to promote Ma Aggi. Chop Fellows quickly dismissed them and pursued their quest. For the second time, they went to Mrs. Tom's office, which was in a separate building reserved for Domestic Science. They wanted to persuade her to take a stand for them. This time around, two Aroma Girls joined them, however armed with their Ma Aggi bottles.

As before, Mrs. Tom had no concrete answer to give them. She was rather evasive. Thus, the Aroma Girls seized the moment to flaunt their use of Ma Aggi. To the surprise of everyone, Mrs. Tom's eyes light up. She began speaking out the loudest they had ever heard, as if she had been waiting for the occasion.

"This isn't good for your health," said Mrs. Tom.

"What, what did you say, Madam?" one of the Aroma Girls asked in shock.

"Ma Aggi consists mainly of concentrated cow's blood."

"And what is wrong with that?" asked the shocked girl.

"But it tastes so good," said the other Aroma Girl.

"Me too, I used to sprinkle it over whatever I ate," said Mrs. Tom.

Quickly Mrs. Tom stood up while speaking. She moved to the board and grabbed a piece of chalk and began writing. She was sharing the results of research studies that had been carried out in the USA on the Ma Aggi, both solid and liquid. It had been determined that it was one of the causes of high blood pressure.

"Yeah," all the students exclaimed.

No one knew that Mrs. Tom was so eloquent.

The reactions to Miss Tom's disclosure were varied. One of the Aroma Girls was thankful for the information. She vowed never again to use Ma Aggi. The other girl was disappointed and upset.

"First of all, I don't believe, and secondly, I don't care," said the dismayed student. She explained that she grew up with it. Her parents have been eating it ever since she was a child, and they were in perfect health.

Meanwhile, the Chop Fellows rushed with the bad news to tell other students.

"That is why the Cookery Teacher should be the one to oversee the college menu," senior students began clamouring.

"Instead, the Cookery classes have been reduced to making cake and blancmange," other upset students said.

"Who is to blame for our plight?" students asked, throwing their hands in the air helplessly.

"We can't blame Miss Tom," a senior student retorted. "Show me the Cookbooks that your mothers have written," added Rosa, the Form 5 student.

Meanwhile, Rosa had recently dropped Cookery from her list of GCE subjects. Her reason was that the recipes taught were out of touch with the culture and traditions of her people.

"Can't she teach us how to prepare our meals like *achu, fufu, kokki, ekwang, egusi pudding, maccara,* and the like?" Rosa went on. "Why should GCE be about foreign recipes?"

"She teaches only what the authorities ask her to teach," said Therese, a top Cookery class student. "Besides, everyone knows how to prepare our local dishes," she argued.

"Even if she had to teach how to prepare local dishes, where are the standardized recipes?" asked Rosa.

Rosa began commenting on the college menu. She went as far as recalling the *puff-puff* incident. She did not commend the authorities for eliminating *puff-puff*. Rather, she pointed out the lack of a variety of breakfast recipes based on local meals.

Thanks to the spontaneous debate, Chop Fellows kept hoping for a solution to the Saturday lunch disaster. They went on brainstorming from dorm to dorm.

One day, Mangwi, a Form 3 student from Ave Maria dormitory had an idea. After Sunday mass at the Cathedral, she exposed the plight of students to her aunt, Agatha.

Promptly, the following Saturday, Agatha made a surprising move. She arrived at Virgin Mother's College at 9 am. She positioned herself at the boundary line beyond the barbed wire bordering Ave Maria dormitory. Students who were out in the yard doing their laundry spotted her and informed Mangwi. Agatha handed her a bag over the barbed wire fence. It was warm and upon opening it, vapor was still coming out.

"*Egusi* pudding, *egusi* pudding," Mangwi chanted while lifting her bag and running into her dormitory, Imma-Concept. It was a bag of steamed pumpkin seed pudding. The bundles were still hot. Each of the plantain-leaf-wrapped packages was going for 50 francs.

The girls outside left their laundry and ran after her into the hostel. Mangwi's classmates as well as those she had hinted in advance, rushed to her bedside. "Hmmn, *bread ih go cry ih mami today!*" (all the bread will be consumed today) the first girl who tasted it exclaimed. She rushed for her bread, opened it and sandwiched *egusi* pudding into it. Oh, how delicious! Some grabbed a second bundle. Within minutes news reached the other three dormitories. It did not take fifteen minutes before all the thirty bundles were gone. Luckily for the Four Rocks, Ngwe bought two bundles. They could have shared it among themselves right there, but Nubodem advised that they keep it for the following morning's meal. They had already eaten their breakfast. A few other girls reserved theirs as a supplement for lunch.

Soon, girls started paying in advance for their expected *egusi* pudding bundles. Within weeks, the supply tripled and later quadrupled while the bundle sizes reduced in favour of bigger ones for 100 francs.

Nevertheless, endless sighs over the red oil suspension stew for lunch still roared throughout the refectory more than the sound of cutlery. Students who had alternative sources offered their plates to other students. Saturday hunger kept rumbling in the stomachs of students. Their grumbling also rang through each dormitory until another Chop Fellow, a Form 3 student in Assumption dormitory, Sirri, came up with a solution. Her invention brought colour, a feeling of being at home, and, most notably, the flare of victory within the student ranks.

Sirri's brilliant idea was based on a popular local tradition. It was inspired by Chemistry and prompted by sheer need. She got the idea during laboratory experiments. She witnessed a chemical reaction in which mixed substances turned into a new solution.

Since then, she began developing her idea. While doing a chore or sitting quietly in her bed or standing alone by a window in class, she would often imagine how chemistry could be the answer to their Saturday lunch woes. Next, she began visualizing her mother in place of the chemistry teacher whenever her class was in the laboratory.

Sirri's mother, Madam Siche, owned a renowned restaurant downtown Mankon. The highly frequented eatery was called "Siche Delights." Siche had prepared *achu* for so many years that she finally succeeded in standardizing her recipe. Her customers kept increasing because of the distinctive taste of her *achu* soup. Over the years, she found out the type of wood that produces ash for *ndjaah niekki* (the liquid essence of ash) with the required level of alkalinity. Whenever she mixed it with palm oil, she obtained the golden-yellow frothy *achu* soup.

Sirri conjured up her mother in her kitchen, stirring her soup with increasing velocity. She recalled how her customers ate *achu* and leaked their fingers and produced a *touc* sound. She began imagining herself chasing away the Saturday lunchtime frowns and replacing them with smiles.

The hoped-for benefits were worth the try. First, she ordered an indispensable component of her mother's mouth-watering *achu* soup. *Ndjaah niekki* was never absent from any house within the communities of Mankon, Bafut, and Mbatu in Bamenda. *Ndjaah niekki* was a potash (crude potassium carbonate, obtained from wood ash). The alternative to it was *kanwa* (the natural water-soluble crystalline version of it).

For her initial delivery, Sirri received a 75cl bottle of *ndjaah niekki*. Her mother handed the bottle over to her after Sunday mass at the Cathedral. She received the package with both hands as if it were a rare treasure. Her face shone with a glow. She instantly imagined the extent to which the gem in her hands could serve as a challenge to the indifferent school authorities. If it worked, it would also mock the cooks. Best of all, it will send students smiling and begging for a double share of stew to transform into *achu* soup.

On Saturday, a little after midday, Sirri was the first to enter the refectory. She grabbed her plate while it was still hot. She scooped a spoonful from her plate and tasted it. The temperature was exactly right. Then, she carefully opened the blue plastic bag she had brought along.

She poured a teaspoon of *ndjaah niekki* into her plate. Instantly, the spot where the first drop landed on her plate became yellowish-brown. She started stirring. The more she increased the speed, the lighter the liquid. She stopped and tasted it. She shook her head and picked up the bottle from under the table and poured another spoonful of the alchemy liquid.

As soon as the second spoon of *ndjaah niekki* hit the stew on her plate, "bang!" It turned yellow. She stood up and raised her hands in screams of wild, triumphant laughter. The girls next to her, who had been watching carefully, picked up the chorus and began screaming. Those who were still on their way to the refectory started running.

"Eureka," "Eureka," "Eureka," shouted another group that saw Sirri's created soup.

Meanwhile, the news spread throughout the campus. Those who often abandoned their plates heard about the discovery and rushed to the refectory.

Never had such a large number of girls been present at the refectory for Saturday lunch. Sirri's soup was light yellow compared to her mother's golden yellow. Nonetheless, the taste of *achu* soup immediately increased the appetite. At last, she had turned a sad lunch into an appetizing meal. It was so delicious that everyone wanted more. Henceforth, the girls who used to ignore as well as those who used to give away their lunch began looking up to Sirri's *ndjaah niekki*.

Since that Saturday, Sirri's titration formula has been sought after by all students. She was obliged to send a request home for more *ndjaah niekki*.

Before long, her mother could not keep up with the demand. So, all the girls whose families lived in the town and its environs sent requests to their respective homes. Nubodem was one of them. She became the supplier for the Four Rocks.

"Sirri has discovered one of her Kola nut gifts," said Maahtou to the other Four Rocks after lunch.

"Oh, yes," Nubodem and Ngwe responded.

"Now I understand what you mean by kola nut gifts," said Eposi.

"We could also say that Mangwi found one of hers too," said Nubodem.

"Hmmm," Maahtou began thinking while the rest were looking at her for confirmation.

"Of course," said Eposi. "Oh, how delicious is egusi pudding!"

"How is that?" asked Ngwe.

"She knows how to find solutions," said Nubodem.

"That right," Maahtou lifted her right thumb.

After Sirri's success with achu soup made in the college, each student promised to bring along litres of *ndjaah niekki* and or *kanwa* rocks for the next term. Henceforth, they will become critical items in their bag of food supplements. Many more students planned to also bring along egusi pudding. The only problem was that it could not last for more than two days.

Though students were more satisfied with Saturday lunch, Maahtou was still showing signs of nutritional deficiency. She kept losing weight. By the end of the first month of every term, she always lost substantial kilograms. The grip of her skirt was two inches wider than her waist. She was obliged to use safety pins to keep it from moving around her waist.

However, she was not aware that she was as lean as a walking scarecrow. Even when Mama had screamed upon seeing her when she arrived home from the previous vacation, Maahtou thought that she was exaggerating. She only became conscious of her exact condition the day when she became the target of a deriding delirium, involving the whole school. Her leanness on the group photos taken by Chico, the college photographer, was too much to stomach. That photo stood out among the three hundred or so photographs which Chico brought that Saturday.

The more students exclaimed, the more others wanted to see it. After an unbearable degree of laughter at the entrance terrace, two senior students seized the photograph and ran to the dormitories to alert others. Immediately, star jesters did spontaneous marathons of the campus in search of the one transformed into a skeleton by the eye of the camera. The mass laughter attracted those from secret reading spots on the trees by the school boundary.

Indeed, it sent fellow students into a laughing frenzy. The mass exercise lasted for something like an hour, which seemed like a lifetime to Maahtou. She stood still with folded arms while students kept dragging her from side to side. Others were staring into her face and bending over to ease their aching ribs. At first, Maahtou's eyes brimmed with tears, but how odd to be sorry for herself amid such a crack-up! She thought how unkind it would be to cry —it would spoil the stress-relieving mirthfulness. So, instead of frowning, she was content to have caused so much entertainment.

Girls kept on laughing and giggling, thereby turning her into a movable star statue that was visually granting liberty to everyone to test their laughing capacity. Some girls cracked up to the point of shedding tears. Others held their aching sides and squatted on the gravel yard to ease their splitting ribs. They fell on her feet, pulling her arms as if in a struggle to conjure up a liberating release from ecstasy. Eyes kept popping out at her. Maahtou remained unmoved, watching as if she had become an alien.

However, from time to time, she felt a strong urge to seize the photo and either escape with it or destroy it on the spot, but she could not. What authority had a Form 2 student, a "semi-fox"? For the first time, the whole campus got into a comic relief session, powerful enough to heal a sore heart. Whatever happened to that photo, it never came back to her, though she was one of its rightful owners.

However, days after the laughing delirium, some girls still giggled upon setting eyes on Maahtou. She just laughed along with them, as if she had become laughter personified. While the other Four Rocks considered it quite embarrassing, she wondered what else was there to be ashamed of after the scanning of her bones.

She could not wait for the vacation. She desperately needed to return home and enjoy an abundance of delicious food.

Chapter 15

Talents and Skills

Maahtou woke up on Monday morning and began organizing herself to study instead of bracing herself up for some farming tasks with Mama. Upon arrival on Friday, she had informed her parents of her academic challenges. She had brought along books from school. Already she had rummaged in the old, abandoned suitcases of her older brothers for textbooks. After skimming through, she marked out interesting chapters.

Her first farming day with Mama was Wednesday. The main job was the harvesting of corn and beans. So, Mama promised that they were going to return by 1.00 p.m.

"And you believe her?" interjected Baba.

"She said so," explained Maahtou.

Mama took along two hoes. She wanted them to weed and till the soil for the planting of the late-season *njama-njama*.

After working for about three hours in different sections, Mama came over and met Maahtou. It was time to stop, take a good rest, eat, and do some harvesting before taking on the hilly road back home.

Instead of doing just that, Mama held Maahtou's hand in hers, without saying a word except, "come." As they passed by Mama's portion, Maahtou noticed that smoke was coming up at the other end where Mama had been working. She had made a fire.

They went on, wading their way for about one hundred meters through the stretch of corn whose leaves were still green, but bearing ears and waiting to mature in weeks. Then, they crossed into the area with tall grass and wiggled their way through with Mama's cutlass and Maahtou's stick, beating into the turf. Maahtou had no clue as to where Mama was leading her, but it didn't matter.

"For how long has Baba owned this piece of land?" asked Maahtou.

"Since his youth. As a member of the pioneers that arrived in Santa from Akum, the Chief assigned him his portion. Though he was the youngest, he was agile and always ready to help others. His mother was very proud of him," said Mama.

"Oh, how I wish I had known the woman who brought up such a fine man!" regretted Maahtou.

"She was a strong woman, a *Nsaahlaah* (a Judge) who stood side by side with men," said Mama.

"Wonderful!" exclaimed Maahtou. "May her legacy live on for generations to come!"

"Come with me, let's go over there by the flowing river that takes its source from the waterfall. Maybe the huge plantain I saw last month is ready for your father to harvest ," said Mama.

The plantain had not yet grown into full size; it was going to be ready only in about two weeks. Mama pruned the dozens of dry leaves still hanging around its stem.

Mother and daughter returned to their workstation for the day. Was that it? Maahtou was certain that Mama had a piece of advice or a safeguard against the pitfalls in life. She was certain that Mama would soon start a new subject or chapter.

When lunch was over, Maahtou picked up the jerrican. She was going to the spring for drinkable water. Mama stood up and began harvesting corn from the nearby ridges. Within minutes, the basin and the *Moukouta* bag were full.

Maahtou stared at Mama without saying a word. Mama glimpsed at the sky. Her eyes fell back to the ground. "*Abo nyoum akorne*" (The hand of the sun has turned). Mama used the length of her shadow to determine that they were already in the early afternoon. It was time to go back home. Mama began fastening their bags. She placed them into respective basins. Maahtou helped Mama to position her load on her head. Then, she lifted her basin right to her knees. Mama lowered herself from the top of the higher ridge, stretched her right hand, and both carried Maahtou's pan and placed it on her head.

The two began climbing the hill slowly. They knew, like everyone else, that the way to cope with the heavy weight of loads on their heads was to direct their thoughts away from the sheer weight on their necks to something else. That is why in such instances two was always better than one.

Maahtou started a light conversation. She recalled the early morning visit of Mama Sirneh, who wanted to know the age of her son. Baba's date recording- diary was of great help to villagers. Illiterate parents come calling whenever they guess that their child has reached school age.

Next, Mama started a new topic. When Moonshee and Bongshee reached their teenage years, everyone expected them to get married. Other families admired the girls for their excellent characters. They hailed them for their respect for elders, upright morals, home management, and farming skills. Indeed, all the families with boys of marriage age longed to have Moonshee and Bongshee as daughters-in-law.

However, academic incompatibility stood out as a significant barrier. Boys who had only the First School Leaving Certificate did not dare gaze into the faces of college girls. Similarly, each time that the parents of those boys met Moonshee and Bongshee, they sighed and shook their heads.

Despite their conversation, the weight of their loads was becoming unbearable. Mama could carry on until they got home, but she did not want Maahtou to expend her energy on that first trip. So, midway on the steep climb, Mama requested that they stop and take a rest. Her proposal was so timely because Maahtou's neck was hurting badly.

"That pear tree over there is the best place; we can put down our loads, and take a good rest," said Mama.

Mama let go of her walking stick. Then, she instructed Maahtou to wedge her basin against the trunk of the big pear tree before gradually lowering it down. Maahtou hadn't quite mastered the technique. Mama stretched out her right hand

and held the edge of Maahtou's pan to protect it from toppling over. Instead, the edge of the basin clung onto a wedge on the trunk. That was only as far as they could go. Maahtou began feeling some relief, with the basin partially off her head. She tightened her fists and managed to push the basin forward. Now the basin was suspended between the truck and her chest.

"*Ndah mbah*" (sorry), Mama said, while looking around. Luckily for them, they sighted three people coming from a distance. It was a man, his wife, and their son. Mama recognized them. They were going to their farm. Without saying a word, they were able to perceive their need from a distance. The man and his teenage boy began running towards them. The boy singlehandedly lifted Maahtou's basin and placed it under the tree. It was like lifting a feather. Everyone burst out laughing. Meanwhile, his father helped Mama to bring down her basin.

"What a relief!" exclaimed Maahtou while placing her palms around her neck and stretching it from side to side.

"I'm so sorry that I allowed you to overload that basin," said Mama. "After all, when was the last time that you carried such a heavy load?"

"Why did you and Baba choose such a strenuous occupation?" asked Maahtou.

"Your father's real occupation was sewing. He took up farming on a full time basis only after he moved from the city to the village."

"I have heard that he quit the city to care for his ailing mother in the village."

"Not really," explained Mama.

They finally got home. It was 2:30. Almost two hours later than Mama had promised. Nonetheless, Maahtou was happy to have helped her mother. Not only had they prepared the ridges for vegetables, but Mama had returned from the farm earlier than her usual time, close to sunset.

During their fireside discussion that evening, Mama asked Maahtou in the presence of her father and siblings what she was planning to become in the future. Ever since Mama's exposé on kola nut gifts, she was eager to know what was in her daughter's mind.

"Tell us, what will you become?"

Maahtou remained silent for a while; the question was not unexpected. However, she had not yet made up her mind.

"If I had gone to a school like you, I would have become a judge and a medical doctor," said Mama, a declaration that she had made countless times.

"I wish I could become a doctor too."

"That would be great," responded Mama and Baba in chorus.

"Not the type who heals the sick but the one who prevents illnesses," said Maahtou.

"Wonderful," said Baba.

"But what stops you?" asked Mama.

"Where would I find such a school? They don't exist," explained Maahtou.

Baba laughed while Mama was waiting to hear more.

"Why are you laughing?" asked Mama.

"If such schools existed, who would give money to doctors?" asked Baba.

"That notwithstanding, there is so much that we don't understand, my daughter," said Mama. "What precisely are you studying in school?"

Maahtou began naming all the subjects while Mama was trying to repeat after her. Maahtou's younger siblings were laughing and mocking Mama's pronunciation. She kept stumbling on Geography. Baba tried to help her, dragging the syllables, but her mouth was not able to form the right sound. Mama gave up. Yet, she wanted to know the meaning of the subject. Baba reminded her of Maahtou's books in which he had shown her the snow as well as people dressed in thick clothes.

"Do you know that in other countries everyone knows when the sun will shine and also when the rain will fall days before it happens?" asked Maahtou. She intended to give her parents and siblings a better grasp of the importance of Geography.

"Really?" asked Baba. "Over the years, your senior sisters and brothers were the one that brought back the information from school when planting season was about to start."

"More than knowing in advance whether it will rain or not, those countries know how cold or how hot each day will be," added Maahtou.

"How do they know, my daughter?" asked Mama.

"They measure it, just like the doctor taking the level of heat on someone who has a fever," explained Maahtou.

"*Anwaarneh bela Ndoumyui,*" ("education is the way of God" or "education is the divine husband"), said Mama.

"*Mbaah ka seet!*" (didn't I tell you), Neumour, and Afouomama responded in chorus.

While Baba and the children agreed that education was God's way, Mama and Maahtou looked at each other and smiled. To them, the second interpretation was more appropriate: education is the divine husband, and better still the grooming spouse.

"*Ndaar Anwaarneh* helps you to discover your kola nut gifts," said Mama.

"What do you mean?" asked Baba.

"Let me complete my statement first," said Mama.

"My daughter, if you allow your *Ndaar Anwaarneh* (education) to sharpen your kola nut gifts, then you are already in agreement with your first husband."

Baba was frowning, obviously lost. Mama looked at him and went on elaborating.

"You, the men, you keep eating kola nuts, without knowing its educational value."

"What do you mean?" asked Baba

"Let Maahtou explain to you," said Mama.

Maahtou recalled how Mama had drawn a parallel between multiple talents and the cotyledons of the kola nut. Then, she explained the importance of exploiting them even if they did not feature on the school curricula. Baba was thrilled when Maahtou used him as the perfect example of someone who has fully exploited his talents.

"*Chaah* (search), *tshwang* (sharpen)," Abong spoke up, using two words to summarize the procedure of discovering one's talents.

"A woman with sound knowledge will always find a man who respects her," concluded Maahtou as Mama's student.

"I agree, my daughter," said Baba.

"And you, the young children, do you understand what your elder sister is explaining?" asked Mama.

"I understand," said Abong. Neumour nodded.

"How about you? Are you taking *Ndaar Anwaarneh* seriously?" asked Mama to her son, Afouomama, the youngest child.

"Yes, Mama. My teacher says that she likes me because I always do my homework," responded Afouomama.

Mama was still keen on understanding what exactly Maahtou was studying in school; Maahtou attempted to explain the subjects in the local language. Cookery and Needlework were the easiest to explain for obvious reasons. As a Domestic Science teacher, their eldest sister, Moonshee, had demonstrated the importance of those subjects. Apart from cooking rare and delicious meals, she made some of the best clothes, especially for toddlers. She was the one who made most of the embroidered tablecloths at home as well as designing and making the collars of their church dresses.

Mama's inquisitive questions became an eye-opener for Maahtou. Unschooled parents experience frustration resulting from the knowledge gap existing between them and their children. How sad that they were sponsoring their children without any ability to measure the worth of their education!

Spontaneously, the following day, Maahtou took a book and began writing out the meanings of each subject she was studying in college. By the end of the week, she successfully came up with a basic content or objective for each of them. It was equally going to help her younger siblings. An idea came to mind: she would display it. It could help them to begin to acquaint themselves with college subjects long before they reach that age. She searched around the house and found a white cardboard paper. She copied the hints or contents of each subject on it:

Mathematics is counting, measuring for proof, to instil honesty with records.

Language chooses the right words to link the world, North to the South Pole

Biology uncovers self, in awe to behold organs locked up in the body.

Chemistry mixes liquids and solids for food, medicine, and fun.

Physics is light, heat, and sound that bring harmony, if not discord.

History remembers how, when, and why we got here, stating where.

Geography manages matter and space in time as it hosts creatures

While air, heat, light, water, and the ground take their rightful place

Literature is imitating, creating to pen the power of words for effect.

Art is seeing reality by design, switching angles in search of accords.

Religious Knowledge peeps into the invisible, linking the seen to the unseen

Cookery, Needlework, Physical Education, are bonuses for fitness and beauty.

Maahtou entitled her writeup "The Language of Subjects." She hung it up on the concrete wall in the living room, next to Baba's Tilley lamp. She hoped that her younger siblings as well as other visiting youths would glean the meaning of some of the courses before post-primary education.

In the meantime, Baba continued learning from her used textbooks. Then, during each vacation, she and him would review key topics in her books, usually in Mama's presence.

134

Chapter 16

A Friend in Need

On Sunday, around 1.00 p.m., two stately cars, a black Mercedes and a forest green Land Rover, arrived on campus, one immediately following the other. One driver came out and motioned to two girls who were coming out of the refectory. They rushed back to the dining hall. Within minutes, four girls came out running towards the cars. Distinctively, they were all children of VIPs - Minister, Ambassador, General Manager, and Banker. They were part of what students fondly called Up-town.

The drivers opened their cars. The trunks and seats were filled with cartons and bags of food. The girls excitedly began off-loading them. They concerted among themselves and agreed as usual to take them to Ave Maria dorm. Two of the girls were from that residence hall.

Later in the evening, an hour before dinner, the four girls invited their wealthy friends for a sumptuous dinner. It was already becoming a tradition. Each time one of their parents brought or sent food through drivers, they came together and feasted.

That day, there were pots and large bowls. They were full of stewed meat, fried fish, fried chicken, steamed rice, cakes, amidst other delicacies.

However, none of the Up-town members realized that one of them had secretly given part of the food to a Down-town girl. The kind-hearted girl was Bih, while the unknown beneficiary was Maahtou. It soon became a habit. Each time Bih would discreetly share her food with Maahtou before presenting it to her Up-town friends.

As for Maahtou, she did not know precisely why Bih had picked her out for such an extraordinary favour. Although they were classmates, the most time they spent together was during homework time. Bih admired Maahtou's brilliance in Chemistry, her prized subject. She and Maahtou were struggling with Maths and Physics like most students, but the latter was always willing to discuss. Bih appreciated that openness.

So, while the Up-towns were dining in the hallway, Maahtou and the Four Rocks, all Down-town girls, were equally relishing the same meal. They were discreetly having a good time at the well-liked "mopping" (studying) spot under one of the mango trees by the border of the campus.

"Hey, she gave you all of this?" asked Nubodem.

There were four hefty pieces of beef, two large chunks of chicken, and two pieces of fish, altogether with stewed rice.

"Oh, my goodness, it smells so good," remarked Eposi.

"Bih treasures you, Maahtou," said Ngwe.

Bih had wanted to add a slice of the carrot cake, but Maahtou had refused, preferring her to leave it intact.

That evening, much like the Uptowns, the Downtowns were so satisfied that they gave out their refectory dinner to other friends.

Three weeks afterward, Wednesday afternoon, Maahtou and her friends were revising towards the upcoming end-of-year exams. Students were dispersed all over the campus, studying in little groups, in pairs, or individually. However, most students were unable to focus because the easily digestible *fufu* and *njama njama* lunch had only served as an appetizer. They were already craving for more food, barely an hour after the meal.

Hunger was always the first battle to overcome during the examination period. Maahtou recalled Mama's advice to drink water and tighten a wrapper around her waist during those moments. By then, girls had plucked all the mangoes that had matured, yet to ripen.

Suddenly, a fourth-year student, some fifty meters away, began calling Maahtou and waving her hand. Maahtou promptly descended from the tree where she and Eposi were occupying the strong topmost branches. The student pointed to the barbed wire fence. A woman was waiting for her on the other side. Maahtou rushed towards the woman, wondering if the student had not made a mistake.

However, barely two steps away from the boundary, Maahtou began smiling. It was Nghekwii, daughter of Tata (successor). Baba's half-sister, a lot younger than him, she was living in Mankon town. Maahtou hadn't seen her for years. It was also the first time ever that she was visiting Virgin Mother's College. So, Maahtou started to wonder what business had brought her. All she could think of was the village. Maybe she had some news from her parents.

"How are you doing, Maahtou?" Nghekwii asked.

Before Maahtou had time to answer, she made a quick announcement.

"I have brought something for you," she said. Maahtou could not believe her ears. What could it be?

Nghekwii handed over a bag to Maahtou. Maahtou opened it right there and saw three big bundles of *kokki* beans and yellow yams. Indeed, the bag was still hot. Maahtou could not believe her eyes. Tears of joy immediately filled them. She wanted so badly to embrace Nghekwii, but there was barbed wire between them. She tried to kneel to express her gratitude, but they were standing amidst offshoots of spear grass.

"How did you know?" asked an overwhelmed Maahtou.

"I know that you are writing your exams," Nghekwii responded

Maahtou laughed out loud because Nghekwii had pre-emptively completed her question, "… that I was starving?" and then answered it correctly.

"*Meeya, meeya, meeya mba,*" Maahtou thanked Nghekwii until she was beyond earshot.

Immediately, Maahtou began waving her hand as she skidded back towards their reading spot. She invited the Four Rocks, two other classmates, and the students that were studying close by. A total of nine students gulped down the *kokki*.

The following week, on Tuesday, three days to the end of exams, Maahtou received another invitation to go to the barbed wire fence. At the same spot, she found Nghekwii waiting for her with another bag. This time around, she brought three big bundles of a different type of *kokki*. It was made from fresh corn.

"She is an angel," Ngwe commented, looking at Maahtou and the other Four Rocks in amazement.

"This is a miracle," said Maahtou.

"Why?" the others asked.

"Though we are neighbours in the village, my mother and hers will be amazed," explained Maahtou.

"So, she is a saviour," Nubodem said.

"This is the type of unexpected kindness from unlikely persons that my mother refers to as "city love," Maahtou commented.

"Indifferent neighbours in the village spontaneously become friends in the city, right?" concurred Eposi with a nod.

Curiously, in the village, other women distanced themselves from Nghekwii's mother because she was a destitute woman. Even children avoided her.

Maahtou and the Four Rocks voraciously ate two on the spot. They decided to reserve the third package of the *kokki* for their Bigs.

"If everyone were so kind, and each act was a star, their number would have endless zeros," said Nubodem.

"Maybe that's why there are so many stars in the sky," said Eposi.

"Stars like Nghekwii and Bih may not be recognized by many, but they keep shining," said Maahtou.

"Yet, some people have so much, but their throats are deep like the gorges that our Geography teacher talked about," said Ngwe.

Chapter 17

Crossing Boundaries

Friday was like a day on which prisoners are set free after a long jail term. Finally, exams were over. The Four Rocks sat on the stairs comparing their performances in each subject.

"Oh, well, let's hope that we will all pass," said Nubodem.

"My head is hot, but how wonderful to be feeling so relieved!" exclaimed Ngwe.

"I'm getting excited already just thinking about Outing tomorrow," said Eposi.

"You bet," said Maahtou.

All four girls were planning to go out together.

"What did you say to Stella that made her look so sad?" asked Ngwe.

Stella had approached Maahtou immediately after they handed over the last test paper. She invited Maahtou to accompany her to town for Outing, but Maahtou turned down her invitation.

"I'm sorry for her," said Nubodem.

"Maybe you should have gone with her, and then we could arrange to meet you later," said Ngwe.

"I don't understand why someone is so rich yet enjoys taking advantage of others," said Eposi while shaking her head.

Immediately, Maahtou recalled an experience she once had with Stella. It was during their second Outing Day. Stella requested her to accompany her shopping downtown. Following a prior arrangement, the two girls stopped by Stella's aunt's dress-making shop where her mother was waiting for her. All three of them went from one store to another, shopping for Stella's needs.

Maahtou was thrilled watching Stella choosing among brands. At one point, Stella's mother picked up a body cream, but Stella rejected it. When Stella kept fussing about her preferred make, Maahtou just gulped down air and looked on as if she was an unaffected spectator.

Soon, the basket began filling to the brim with a variety of items. They included different types of bathing soap, a giant toothpaste tube, two packages of cabin biscuits, one large-size margarine tin, eight cans of sardine, two body lotions and creams.

Maahtou began wondering why Stella's mother had not offered her even a token during her shopping spree. Did the woman assume that she already had enough for herself? Whatever, Maahtou thought she was a stingy person.

Buying was not yet over. Stella's mother pulled her by the hand into the store for underwear though Stella insisted that she was satisfied.

"Please, bring out the small braziers," said Stella's mother to the store owner.

"No, no, mother," retorted Stella while turning away her face and looking outside. Stella's breasts were barely coming out. They were just about the size of berries. She declined, but her mother persuaded her. Maahtou could not help laughing because her breasts were twice bigger than Stella's. She could understand Stella because barely one day of trying on a brazier made her dizzy.

On their return trip to the campus, Stella and Maahtou hired a taxicab. Had Maahtou been with any of the Four Rocks or other friends, they would have walked back to the college. Stella did not offer to pay for her though her purse was full of banknotes and coins. When they arrived, Stella was unable to carry all of her three bags to her dorm, Imma-Concept, located at the far end from Maahtou's. The latter gave her a helping hand.

Later in the evening, Stella invited her friends, including two from Maahtou's hostel for dinner by her bedside.

Ever since that outing, Maahtou resolved never to go downtown with Stella again. The Four Rocks, who were listening intently, shook their heads and sighed. Two of them clapped their hands in shock.

"Now you understand why I refused to go out with Camille last month," said Eposi.

"Now I know better," said Ngwe. "I don't blame you, Maahtou."

"Those proud Glows already know me," said Nubodem. "I don't have their time."

The following day, Saturday, was Outing Day. It was going to be the most relaxing outing because it came after the exams. As usual, the Four Rocks were preparing to go together, though sometimes they travel in twos. Just minutes before departure, Bih approached Maahtou and asked her if she could go out with them.

"Are you not going out with your group?" Maahtou asked. Both understood what "your group" meant.

"No," said Bih, shaking her head several times without disclosing her reasons. For the first time, Bih turned down the usual ride in one of the vehicles sent by two of the wealthy parents to accompany their daughters for shopping. She took advantage of the fact that none of the two cars belonged to her father.

"You are welcome, but you don't have to dress like us," warned Maahtou.

"What do you mean?" Bih asked.

"We are wearing bathing slippers," Maahtou said.

"And what's wrong with that?" Bih asked.

" Come on Bih, you mean you can wear this to town?" Maahtou asked while pointing at her yellow rubber, striped bathing slippers.

"Of course, I will!" Bih said.

Maahtou laughed out loud and embraced her. While Bih rushed to replace her marron leather shoes, Maahtou quickly informed the other Four Rocks that Bih was coming along.

"Are you for real?" asked Ngwe.

"Hahaha," the rest of the girls laughed.

They were pleasantly surprised while wondering what the other affluent girls would say.

The Four Rocks stood by the entrance to the school, waiting for Bih. Within minutes, she appeared in her pink, two-rope rubber flip-flops. However, Bih did not know why the Four Rocks had chosen to wear bathing slippers. They were 'economizing' their dressy shoes from wear and tear. They could equally have put on *Dschang* (rubber) shoes, but that would have given the wrong signal— lack of sophistication. Flip-flops portrayed the extreme, bordering on a crazy choice. Theirs was an act of courage. Perhaps they could as well be setting a new fashionable standard.

Spontaneously, the girls began laughing before Bih got to where they were standing. Bih walked with agility, happy to be enjoying a new sense of freedom.

Meanwhile, the Four Rocks promised to take special care of their delicate 'guest.' Before they all set out, the Four Rocks warned Bih about the risks involved. She had to be careful because of the pebbles on the road. The weather could suddenly become windy and render the roads dusty. Some roads were strewn with potholes.

"You must be careful with your soft baby toes," Nubodem added.

Bih laughed again and reassured them that she would be okay.

"Don't worry, if you slide, I will *baba* you," said Ngwe, the tallest of the Four Rocks. She meant that she was going to give Bih a piggyback ride.

"Or if you get too tired of walking, we will go slowly," suggested Maahtou.

Bih burst out laughing; the rest joined. The girls kept cracking jokes and practically laughing their way to town. Bih was having more fun than she had expected.

Finally, the girls arrived in town. It took them about half an hour. They promptly informed Bih that they preferred buying in the open market. To allay her fears, they offered to accompany her to her favourite store afterward.

"Don't you worry," said Bih. "The supermarket can wait, at least, for today. So, just take me wherever you are going because I don't need anything."

The girls stopped and bought a few items from the roadside vendors. Then, they went to the area of the market known as Back Market. There, traders were selling *okrieka* (used clothing). Each of them bought an article, from braziers, blouses to handbags, but for Bih.

Next, they went to the Food Market. There was an endless variety of fruits, nuts, and fried foods displayed in large basins, buckets, and trays.

"Wow! Didn't I tell you girls?" said Bih. "You can't find things like this in the supermarket."

"*Tekam, tastam, ma pikin*," repeated the lady selling berries. She was offering them to the girls for tasting.

"Hmmn," exclaimed Bih. "Who will allow you to taste anything in the supermarket before buying?" Her face beamed with excitement. "Besides, there is nothing like this out there.

"So, you've never eaten this?" asked Nubodem.

"Not only this but that too," said Bih pointing to the kernels in a basin.

Bih had not intended to buy anything. Spontaneously and quickly, she opened her bag and took out her purse. She wanted to purchase all that the Four Rocks were buying: Adam fruit, passion fruit, *mbanga, make-me-well, ndjakatou, kouli-kouli, moungwin,* guavas, and parched-corn-and-groundnuts.

After shopping, Nubodem reminded the girls of her special family duty. She had arranged to meet her younger brother, who was schooling at Rock of Ages College. So, the rest of the girls accompanied her to Tee junction. Everyone guessed that she had a message or a letter for him, but they were all wrong.

To their greatest surprise, Nubodem searched into her purse and took out a 500 francs note plus three coins, a total of 750 francs. The little brother curtsied, almost going down on his knees to receive it.

When her little brother left, Nubodem explained to the girls that her younger brother was going to buy a pair of trousers for himself. The girls exclaimed with admiration. They complimented Nubodem for her high sense of responsibility.

What an Outing Day! The girls had accomplished a lot. They were all happy, especially with their purchases. They all started on their return trip.

However, on the way, Bih made a request. She invited them to come to the bakery shop by the roadside. They stepped in timidly. Instantly, the mouth-watering fragrances of pastry hit them. The Four Rocks couldn't afford any of the items. So, they stood by the side and waited for Bih to place her orders. Instead, she turned around and asked them what they wanted. The Four Rocks looked at each other in dismay, and were pleasantly surprised at Bih's kindness. They consulted each other in low tones.

"Choose something for us," said Maahtou. "You know that we are not used to shopping here.'

"Yes, whatever you choose, we will appreciate it," Ngwe added.

Eposi and Nubodem nodded when Bih turned around and looked at them inquiringly. Bih placed orders. She requested a separate package for each girl. Also, she bought a round cake for the road, for all of them.

"Are we not taking a taxi?" asked Bih.

"No, we are not far away from the campus," reassured Maahtou.

"That will be a waste of money," said Nubodem.

"Just let me know whenever you get tired," said Ngwe. "Look at my strong back."

All the girls, including Bih, burst out laughing.

"Maybe the hill will be too much for her," suggested Eposi.

"One day, you will come to our village and see how children and old women walk to the farm," added Nubodem.

"Okay, I will try. I'm keeping my eyes on Ngwe's back," said Bih.

"Hahaha," the girls burst out laughing.

So, instead of walking briskly, the girls strolled back to the college campus, while munching their cake and chatting along happily.

A good number of taxicabs bypassed them on the way. Each time one came close to them, student passengers turned around and looked at them with keener interest than usual. The Four Rocks knew that Bih was the one attracting all the attention.

Anyhow, before long, they had climbed the hill without anyone feeling tired. Neither did Bih complain.

"Are you sure your feet are not hurting?" asked Maahtou.

"I can't complain seeing what you have done for me," said Bih. "How can I thank you all for having taken me to another 'country' and given me such care and fun?"

"Your kindness is legendary," said Ngwe.

"It must be one of her kola nut gifts," said Maahtou.

"What do you mean?" the others asked.

Instead of going to their respective dormitories, they sat on the stairs leading to the academic block. They still had more than an hour before dinner. There, they sat and listened to Maahtou. She explained the meaning of kola nut gifts and the intricate link between it and their education. The girls could not contain themselves when Maahtou referred to *Ndoumyui* as each of their grooming spouses.

That same evening, news of Bih's outing with the Four Rocks spread around the dormitories. Girls clapped their hands and lifted their eyebrows in surprise. Most of them found it odd. "Don't roses and thorns come out of the same plant?" asked Grace, Bih's dorm captain.

"Down-town renders Up-town delicious," Angela, a Form 4 student said. Others chimed in and began singing, "Down-town spices," then the others responded, " Up-town delicious."

"Thank you, Grace," said Collette. You've taught us something new."

"Shakespeare equally reminds us that "there is no art to find the mind's construction in the face," said Joyce, a Form 5 student. "Those girls whose company Bih preferred to riding in a luxury car are not weaklings. They are hard crystals at the core."

Everyone turned around and scanned the Four Rocks, standing by Bih's bed, with renewed interest.

Chapter 18

Narrow Escape from Rape

The second part of Maahtou's vacation was the unfolding of the unknown in a known place. Unexpectedly, her elder sister invited her to their home in Victoria. Maahtou had lived there during her elementary school days with her second elder sister, Bongshee, who had then relocated to Douala.

The first nice surprise was the beautiful and modern house at the northern end of the city. It was one of the plush neighbourhoods, perched on a hill.

The telephone rang just when the family stepped into the house. It was as if to welcome Maahtou into a new lifestyle. It was the first time she was going to live in a home equipped with a landline telephone.

As soon as Maahtou placed her luggage in the room, she began exploring the house. One of the first things that caught her attention was the board on which was posted notices. One was in the corridor and the other was in the kitchen. She stopped and began reading. They were timetables and daily agendas with the assignment of duties to the younger occupants. Indeed, the following morning, Maahtou was pleasantly surprised when Moonshee invited her to help in drawing up the domestic task schedule and menu for the week.

Within a space of ten days, three other holidaymakers arrived in the house to spend some weeks. Two of them were the niece and nephew of Meuma, Moonshee's husband. The third was the daughter of a family friend. As soon as Moonshee welcomed each of the young people, she promptly integrated them into the daily running of her house. She equally advised each of them to draw up their separate schedules to include playtime as well as time for rest or siesta.

Beyond assigned chores, Maahtou was eager to do more. Indeed, among the holidaymakers, she was the only one interested in Moonshee's regular afternoon programs. She was either sewing or baking. Moonshee was a certified domestic science professional.

Whenever Moonshee was about to start a new project, Maahtou would cut short her playtime and rush back home. She would leave behind the boys either playing football or riding bikes. Or the girls playing rope-jumping or some other game. The real test of her determination was the day when the boys offered to teach the girls how to ride a bicycle. The boys contributed 200 francs per hour each evening except for rainy days. Maahtou's younger sister, Adziendoum was one of the four girls, among a dozen boys who took turns on the two bikes rented from the Ibo bike repairer.

"You still have almost twenty minutes on your playtime," insisted Moonshee.

"I know, but I want to see how you design the pattern, and trace it," said Maahtou.

At first, Moonshee regretted that Maahtou was depriving herself of a lot of fun. However, with time, she began appreciating Maahtou's assistance. She was providing the extra hand that her elder sister needed. Maahtou will hold the edges of papers or the materials when she is aligning patterns to the material and cutting it. Maahtou equally helped in tacking, hemming, and stitching buttons.

None of the college-student holiday makers were interested in Moonshee's hobbies. Neither were they involved in the outdoor games. Apart from Maahtou and her younger sister, almost all those in the field were primary school children.

Paradoxically, the college students were keen on going to the cinema and nightclubs, none of which crossed Maahtou's mind. As soon as lunch was over, they began getting ready for the tea-time or night club dances. They were the most popular gatherings for college students in town.

"Maahtou, are you not coming with us," asked Lizzy one evening while ironing her dress for the upcoming dance party.

Maahtou shook her head and continued reading the newspaper. Meuma had brought in from work the previous day a copy of Cameroon Times.

"Why didn't you invite Maahtou?" asked Henry while they were already out of the house.

"I did, but she did not show any interest," explained Lizzy.

"She is somehow queer," said Comfort. "I also tried, but she said she was not coming with us."

"I would be bored to death sitting home for so long," remarked Henry.

"I hope she will soon realize what she is missing," added Lizzy.

When Moonshee noticed that Maahtou kept staying home while all the others were gone, she became curious.

"What happened? You didn't want to go with them?" asked Moonshee.

"No, I find sewing, baking and reading quite interesting," Maahtou answered.

With her younger sister's declaration, Moonshee made it a habit to inform Maahtou in advance of any domestic project. How exciting for Maahtou to learn how to interpret recipes from cookbooks and use the various measuring cups!

Concurrently, Maahtou was exploring the home library. It was equipped with a variety of books, from detective novels, biographies, the inspirational, trades, history, adventures to religion. Meuma was an avid reader. After thumbing through them on the first day, she selected half a dozen interesting ones. She placed them at her bedside table, hoping to read them before the end of her stay.

Henceforth, she did each domestic chore with much more speed. Often she would be reading two books simultaneously, one during the day, and another in the night. It was not unusual for her to wake up before anyone else to read her daytime book.

"Maahtou, what are you doing there all alone?" asked Meuma one morning when he found Maahtou sitting by a window, facing outside. The rest of the holiday makers were still asleep.

"Good morning, brother," answered Maahtou while turning around 90 degrees.

"Wonderful," Meuma said while nodding after recognizing the book in her hand.

Maahtou began walking around the house with a book in hand. Sometimes, while waiting for the pot of soup to simmer, she would be completing a chapter. As for her night-time book, she would begin reading after dinner.

One day Maahtou read something intriguing. It was about a conflict involving a police officer that almost cost him his life. Later, in the evening, she struck up a conversation with Meuma regarding discipline within the army.

"What if the subordinate is afraid to take on a dangerous assignment? Is there a limit to the orders of the boss?" asked Maahtou. There was silence. Meuma had not expected Maahtou to take interest in his career. "What if the officer thinks that the superior is asking for too much?" Maahtou pressed on.

Meuma smiled, took a deep breath, and invited Maahtou to come sit by him on the long couch in the living room. Moonshee, who was sewing, stopped the machine to listen to Meuma's answer.

"From time to time, the commanding officer is obliged to make tough decisions," said Meuma.

"But there are also times when the police shoots and kills even when the culprit doesn't constitute any danger to him," Maahtou went on.

"Unfortunately, there are errors committed within our corps," responded Meuma. "However, our objective is to help reform criminals and not to kill them."

"That's it," said Moonshee with a nod.

"Do some kill because they know that the criminal is ready for the worst if caught?"

"Do you remember Neufang, the fearless burglar code-named Terror N°1, for short, Tee One, who terrorized this whole region last year?"

"The man for whom you risked your life," interjected Moonshee.

"That's right," answered Meuma. "Though I finally caught him after others had tried and failed, it was also because he surrendered himself to me."

"What?" Maahtou screamed out in surprise.

"He bowed to me, saying that I was a kind man."

Meuma further disclosed that Neufang had cautioned him that by running after him in the forest, Meuma was exposing himself to a double jeopardy. There was the ever lurking danger of falling into the hands of more vicious criminals.

Maahtou recalled how Moonshee used to be anxious for her husband. Whenever he set out into the forest in pursuit of Tee One, who had escaped the umpteenth time, she would be anxious and restless until he returned home.

Ever since that interrogation, Meuma began looking forward to conversing with Maahtou. Their discussions were not limited to any topic. They included social issues and general knowledge sometimes related to the life application of theories Maahtou had learned in college. Otherwise, Meuma was thrilled each time Maahtou advanced arguments inspired by what she read in Meuma's books. More importantly, Maahtou would seize every occasion to bounce her ideas culled from her college lessons on Meuma. Often their discussion became so exciting that time would not permit them to dig deeper. Though Meuma spent a lot of after work hours in his office counselling citizens in trouble or mediating in conflicts, he seemed to be missing Maahtou. No matter how late he returned home, he would unfailingly ask if Maahtou was at home. In the affirmative, he would go straight to her room to check if she was already sleeping or not.

Eventually, Meuma began inviting Maahtou to accompany him during some of his daytime business trips to the headquarters in Buea. Indeed, it was during one of those outings on a bright sunny day that Meuma and Maahtou noticed a reflection ahead of the car. It was just above the tar looking like a transparent film of glass.

"Do you know what that is?" asked Meuma.

"Mirage," answered Maahtou without hesitating.

Meuma was impressed. Though he was driving, he turned to his right and looked at Maahtou inquisitively. Perceiving his surprise, she disclosed to him that they had been taught mirages during a Physics lesson.

One day they travelled together to Douala. It was her first visit to that economic hub. Maahtou saw traffic lights for the first time. She began asking a ton of questions. Meuma explained its usefulness. By controlling heavy traffic, it reduced accidents too.

Within a fortnight of her stay, Meuma invited Maahtou to the local tennis club. He was a member of the Senior Service section. The following week, he again asked her to accompany him to Buea in the evening. He often played snooker with his cousin, Mr. Ndang as well as with Chief Ewusi.

As if those two outings were not enough, and despite her young age, one evening, Meuma invited Maahtou to accompany him to a party. Moonshee was indisposed. Upon arrival, a lady stopped to greet them. She embraced Maahtou while referring to her as Moonshee.

"Madam, how come you are looking so young?"

Maahtou was on the point of revealing her identity. Quickly, Meuma shook his head. Maahtou understood. She was Moonshee's former classmate. The lady spoke briefly with Meuma and walked away without realizing that it was Moonshee's younger sister.

Soon, the other holiday makers at home became envious of Maahtou. Meuma derided them for their indifference to his person.

"I am sure you came here only to meet your friends," he said.

None of them refuted his claim. Indeed, they were behaving like independent residents. None of them ever sought permission before going out. They lacked even the courtesy to make known their whereabouts to Meuma or Moonshee. More importantly, Meuma returned home some days in the night and noticed that some of them were still out of the house.

"Go and look up the meaning of "discrimination" and "favouritism," said Meuma to the grumbling holidaymakers.

Nevertheless, his behaviour toward Maahtou did not change. Instead, he began caring more for Maahtou. Meuma would eat and share his meat, the scarcest food item, with her, whenever there was not enough meat in the dish. In like manner, he offered a part of the drink reserved for him to Maahtou.

The climax of it all was when one Thursday evening, Meuma returned from the tennis club. Incidentally, all the holiday makers were at home. He took off his hat and placed it on Maahtou's head. All the four other holidaymakers at home were lost for words. Each of them had admired that khaki-coloured green thin-reamed hat when they first saw it. In reaction, murmuring and grumbling immediately roared through the house.

"I have now realized that you treat some of us like *bobbylongo* (woman without a bra)," said one of the three girls, who promptly stood up and isolated herself into the room.

Maahtou was lost for words. She just stared at her.

Not long after that momentary tension, a terrible thing happened. It was so bad that it almost obstructed the growing connection between Maahtou and her hosts.

One night, everyone was fast asleep. It was the dead of night. Suddenly, Maahtou was unable to turn around in bed. She realized that there was no wiggle room. It felt like the bed she was sharing with Adziendoum had become tighter. There was a lot of pressure on her left side.

Gradually, she became more conscious. She held her breath and listened intently. Then, she heard deep breathing. It was too deep to be Adziendoum's. Within seconds, she felt a steady hand coming over her body. She stretched out her left hand and tried to feel it. Then she realized that it was not Adziendoom's hand. It was too big and very rough. Next, she stretched out her right hand to the other side. Effectively, Adziendoum was deep asleep in her rightful place, close to the wall.

For a while, she remained quiet. She was trying to convince herself that she was not dreaming. Then, the firm hand to her left side started moving over her body. Gently it was sliding down towards her stomach. Was she dreaming? No. No. The hand kept progressing. It passed over her belly. It kept moving down towards her legs. No, no, something was wrong. Maahtou cried out and pushed it away. Apparently, no one in the house had heard her.

Then she pressed the person firmly with both hands. Suddenly the body to her left became still. She moved her left hand over the body. She felt some coarse hair. She felt beards, pimpled jaws. Her hands moved across the body. She felt strong, massive muscles. It was clear that it was a male person. He had drifted into their bed. She was certain that her imagination was not tricking her. Who was it? Was it Henry, the male holidaymaker? He was supposed to be sleeping in another room.

Maahtou moved from thinking to action. She forcefully turned her body around and, with all her might. She pushed the obtrusive mass away with both hands.

"Toum," she heard someone falling to the floor. He must have been clinging at the edge, seeing that he fell so easily. Maahtou opened her eyes, but the room was very dark. Neither Adziendoum nor Mbongmoone, her nephew, who was sleeping on the other bed, budged. They were fast asleep, like everyone else in the house.

Maahtou could no longer sleep. Neither did she have an idea what time it was. For fear of falling asleep, she stood up and almost stepped on the motionless body on the floor. She turned on the light for a few seconds and realized that it was Mulluh, the older boy who was Meuma's relative. He was in charge of doing jobs like washing the car or splitting the wood. Mulluh had dropped out of school in class 4. His teacher got tired of promoting him to the next class. He had come to stay with his half-brother in order to learn a trade.

Maahtou felt an upsurge of anger that caused her to tremble. She was not the type to disturb the peace of others. Mama always emphasized on the importance of sleep. She always advised her children never to disturb someone's sleep, especially at its onset. The house was quiet and peaceful. So, she returned to the bed. She just laid down without saying a word to the violator. Sleep was gone. Maahtou laid in bed, troubled. She began thinking about Mama's sex education home classes. She had just experienced first-hand how easily an adult male could abuse a girl. How was she going to deal with it? Her mind went through a lengthy torture session until dawn finally came.

In the morning, she and Adziendoum began their morning duty. They began with washing the dishes. She recounted everything to her. Adziendoum instantly lost her composure. She immediately stepped out into the yard where Mulluh was splitting wood behind the kitchen. She started yelling at him, threatening to report to Meuma.

Immediately, as if controlled by an electric current, Mulluh fell on his knees on the spot. He held both palms together as if in prayer. He pleaded with Adziendoum not to tell on him. Then, he tried to explain that he had slipped from their bed while in deep sleep, but mistakenly climbed into the wrong bed.

Maahtou was enraged. She joined Adziendoum to yell at him. He pleaded more with outstretched hands, saying, "I beg, I beg," promising that he would never try it again.

Meanwhile, Meuma was having his shower. He overheard voices in discord. He looked through the bathroom window. He saw Mulluh on his knees before young girls. He knew that something was seriously wrong. As an experienced detective, Meuma knew for sure that there was trouble in his own home. For years, he had intervened and mediated in countless domestic conflicts, some of which sounded almost unbelievable until he had listened to both parties. He called out to Moonshee. She was completing a dress in the living room. He alerted her.

Maahtou came and started telling her the story. Mulluh rushed in and tried to argue. Maahtou became upset. How could Mulluh try to twist the facts to discredit her report? Tears began flowing on Maahtou's face. Had it not been for the Deus Ex Machina that woke her up from sleep; had she not been woken up by his rough hand, Mulluh would have pursued his tragic drama. Where would she be now? She had narrowly escaped the bite of a hound.

Finally, an infuriated Meuma came out of the bathroom. He joined Moonshee to comfort Maahtou. He stared at Mulluh until his eyes became red, shot with blood.

"Are you a dog?" He yelled out at Mulluh.

Maahtou could not help imagining what would have happened to her.

"Do you want to return to your vomit?" Meuma went on. He raised his right hand over Mulluh, but Moonshee jumped up and held them.

As for Mulluh, he would prefer to be punished and forgiven than sent back to the village. He fell on his knees and started crying out loud. Meuma asked him to shut up. He was going to be late for work. So, he walked away while roaring with anger right to his car. With his departure, Mulluh rushed towards Moonshee. He bent over in front of her. He stretched out his arms and was crying, "please, Mami, tell Papa that I will never again attempt it."

Instead, Moonshee's eyes began filling up with tears. She was trembling with anger. She was horrified. How could a birdbrain like Mulluh imagine such a dishonest act? The situation was grievous. At once, she was relieved that Mulluh had not succeeded in violating her younger sister under her roof. Yet she wondered what decision her husband would take.

She was in a quandary. If her husband threw out Mulluh, her in-laws would blame her. As for her own family, her parents, primarily Mama, would blame her too. Why did she allow Mulluh to sleep in the same room with the girls? Ever since childhood, her parents never let the children sleep in the same room with strangers, despite visits by countless guests in the village. Mama would not even let her sons sleep on a separate bed in the same room with her daughters.

What would Moonshee's friends say if they heard the story? Indeed, a close family friend had mocked her and her husband's domestic equality policy. "Why do they try to treat each one equally?" she wondered aloud. Moonshee would try to argue. "Is a houseboy equal to your son," Mrs. Tanyong was fond of saying.

Later in the evening, Meuma returned from work, still upset with Mulluh. He had not had enough time in the morning to express his anger. At first, he did not say a word, and his silence scared Mulluh even more.

As the minutes ticked away, Mulluh feared that he would lose the only opportunity he had from his kind half-brother to learn a trade.

Meuma and Moonshee retired to their room immediately after dinner. Soon, Meuma came back out and ordered Mulluh to stand in front of him. Mulluh came out trembling and stood before Meuma. Both of his hands were glued onto his laps. Instead of speaking, Meuma stared at Mulluh from head to toe for a long while until Mulluh started shivering.

"Go and remove whatever belongs to you from that room," Meuma ordered.

Upon his return, Meuma pointed to a corner of the living room.

"Never again step your foot into that room nor any other room," Meuma spoke out with a loud voice, though he looked exhausted.

The following morning, Meuma gave Mulluh money and ordered him to repair the broken door of the boy's quarter behind the house. It was commonly called *ndah edjoumtsimtsim* (Bric à brac house). He had to buy wood to make a bed for himself.

"Thank you, thank you," Mulluh kept saying while receiving the money on bended knee.

Chapter 19

Teatime Dance

Excitement was gripping the village over the biggest upcoming gathering ever of students.

Some of Maahtou's friends from other schools came visiting on Friday, a day before the party. They wanted to get preparation tips for the dance. Her brother, Moonbih, was the scheduled Master of Ceremonies for the ground-breaking dance party.

"Chaii, Maahtou! I see that you are getting your dress ready for tomorrow," remarked Irene.

Irene was referring to the laundry that Maahtou had hung up on the line to dry.

"What is the colour of the shoes that you got?" asked Brigitte.

"Black," Maahtou said as if she was speaking to the gentle breeze that was tapering off the effect of the hot sunshine. She did not want the excitement in their eyes to tempt her. Neither did she want to discourage them. She had thought about attending it but changed her mind.

"Maahtou, why do you sound as if it's an ordinary party?" asked Irene.

"If I were in your place," said Brigitte, "with my brother as the MC, this whole village will hear about me." She was stunned about the eagerness of those girls. They had gone as far as buying new pairs of shoes for the party.

Though their zealousness was like a strong wind, it was the type of wind to which she would not bend.

"Do you know what the program is like?" asked Brigitte.

"Drinking, dancing, drinking, dancing until whenever," said Maahtou.

Irene and Brigitte listened with rapt interest. They jumped up and gave her high five after she had made the disclosure.

They had no idea that Maahtou was barely making a good guess.

On the day of the party, Maahtou got up early to pursue her plans for the day. Mama had bought half a bag of raw fresh groundnuts for her to retail that same Saturday because it was the village market day. Her younger sister, Adziendoum, the gifted marketer of the family, was absent. She was in Victoria, where she was living with Moonshee and her family.

Promptly, Maahtou washed the basin of fresh groundnuts. By 9.00 a.m., she was already on her way to the market square. Vapor was still coming out of it. She stopped on the way three times to serve buyers. Soon after, she met one of her college friends on the way.

"Chaii, Maahtou, *ya own don too much*!" (you are too much) exclaimed Caro.

"What's wrong?" asked Maahtou.

"Or are you going to leave the groundnuts with your small sister or your small brother?"

"No."

"What?" Screamed Caro. "You mean that you may not attend the party?"

"It's not about may," said Maahtou. "I'm not going to attend."

"Strange." Caro clapped her hands and joined a friend who was going to buy pins for her hair.

Maahtou moved on, feeling hurt. Her queerness was not just the act of retailing a food item. By carrying the basin on her head in a public place, Maahtou was breaking an unwritten college student code of self-importance.

Finally, she got to the groundnut line and set up a stool for her basin. There were already three village women and two Hausa girls in place. Apart from groundnuts, other young girls and two boys were selling *macara*, *kouli kouli*, sugarcane and avocados. The was a clear difference between them and Maahtou. None of them had seen the walls of a college. So, again, Maahtou broke another unwritten college student code.

By 2.00 p.m., she had sold half of her basin. She was tired of sitting down. So, she stood up and walked around. When she looked up across the street, she couldn't believe her eyes. Practically every college girl and boy in the village had responded positively to the party invitation.

Students from all the neighbouring villages, namely, Pinyin, Allatsou, Chou, Awing, Akum, Akonka, and Ntarre, were in their special outfit. They were gathering in dozens around the hall, one hundred meters away from where Maahtou was selling her groundnuts.

She could have gone home then and prepared for the party. However, she thought that by returning with half of the bowl of unsold groundnuts, her mother would lose her capital. Every grain had to go, or at least, most of it.

Suddenly and from nowhere, two friends of Saint Augustine's College sighted her in the retailer's line. That was their first meeting since the vacation began.

Stella clapped her hands and screamed out Maahtou's name. Then, she started running towards Maahtou. She had a short floral skirt with a bright blue background, split at one end, above her knee. Her red blouse and red handbag matched well.

The other girl, Gertrude, the taller of the two, had on a light green cotton dress with a Vee cut at the neck. Both girls wore high-heeled shoes. They had on conspicuous make-up. Their lips were polished red while their eye shadows were betraying thick layers of black pencil.

"Maahtou, what are you doing here?" asked Gertrude.

Maahtou just looked at her and smiled.

Within minutes, the three were distracted by a group of well-dressed girls and boys who were approaching. They were all heading towards the party hall. The grand teatime dance was taking place at the newly constructed Sam Mofor's Santa Lion club. It was the first-ever storied building in Santa. The party was the occasion to launch the club officially.

One girl in sunglasses just waved and meandered her way on her high heels. Maahtou's stomach churned as she read the looks of pity on her face.

Nevertheless, Maahtou kept a steady gaze and planted herself behind her basin of groundnuts. She could not help seeing herself through the eyes of her friends. How could she be competing for customers, side by side with illiterate Bororo girls? Next, she imagined a scene in which she was trying to steady herself on a four-inch-high heeled shoe. How thrilling that could be! She could not help chuckling.

However, an opposing thought came to her mind. Mama had spent all her pocket money on the groundnuts. Bringing home some precious coins would add up to a litre of palm oil, some kerosene, and even body cream for herself.

Meanwhile, Stella and Gertrude, who were still standing there, whispered something to themselves. They were looking for ways to convince Maahtou to go home and dress up for the party.

"Maahtou, you should have been the first girl in the hall," said Gertrude.

"We hear your brother is the MC. How could you be absent?" asked Stella.

"Should we accompany you home?" proposed Gertrude.

Maahtou shook her head several times. Her mind immediately went through her suitcase. The dress that Irene and Brigitte had seen on the laundry line the day before was Maahtou's casual wear. She did not have a party dress; neither did she have high-heeled shoes. So, she decided that she did not qualify for the party.

Half an hour had passed in their attempt to persuade Maahtou. She was not making a move. Since she refused to budge, the girls sighed and labelled her as "anti-fashion" and moved on.

Maahtou stayed back, and within an hour, she sold half of what she had left in her basin. It was about 4.00 p.m.; the sun was disappearing, and she was feeling cold. She was tired. The music from the club was already blasting at a high pitch. The whole market square was taken over by it. Maahtou decided it was time to return home.

When she stepped in, Mama informed her that several friends had inquired about her. They had come to fetch her for the party. All along, Mama did not know that there was a grand party, the first of its kind. So, she encouraged Maahtou to dress up and follow her friends. Maahtou informed her that she was not interested. Maahtou's explanations failed to convince her. To Maahtou's surprise, Mama was alarmed.

"Maahtou, how come you don't join your friends for fun outings?" she sounded more troubled than inquisitive.

"How can I go when there is so much to do right here?" Maahtou asked, frowning.

"But you can take a break and spend some time with your friends," said Mama, somewhat perplexed.

"Mama, I don't have time to squander like that," said Maahtou. "GCE exams are not that far away."

"But you need a break. You keep staying home. Where shall you have your own husband?" asked Mama.

"Husband? I'm not yet done with my grooming husband, and now you are talking about a legal husband."

Mama looked at Maahtou and shook her head. She wanted to laugh, but she did not think it was funny. She stood there, staring at Maahtou, bemused as to how else to convince Maahtou to change her mind.

"Have you seen them dancing, Mama?" Mama was staring at her. "*Akwarra Mami, Akwarra papa*, (prostitute)" she began singing and dancing while pushing her buttocks from side to side. She repeated the words that are synonymous with the behaviour of a typical fille de joie.

Indeed, her mind brought back a vivid picture of the scanty dresses that some of the partygoers had worn. The popular body-twisting dancing styles emphasizing the protrusion of buttocks put them in direct competition with hookers. She could not help thinking about the slow dance, which boys

163

cherished. The courageous ones would force their bodies onto the girls. The very thought of it made Maahtou shriek. Had the Reverend Sisters of Virgin Mothers been there to separate dancing bodies, she could have dared to go to the club, even out of sheer curiosity.

"So, where will you find your own man, then? Don't tell me in another far-off village or a foreign country," warned Mama.

"Don't worry, Mama," said Maahtou. "I just want to help you as much as I can."

"Well, I thank you for caring about me. But who knows whether while you are still working with your grooming husband, the social or legal husband might show up?" Mama intimated.

"No, Mama, not now. Let him wait."

"Do you realize that so far, you've turned down three suitors, though with our approval?" asked Mama with a heightened tone. The vegetable she was picking dropped out of her hands into the basin.

"If I had said yes to any of them, where would I be now?" asked Maahtou. "I would have already shut out my grooming husband, right?"

"Well, you are right, but what else shall I say?" asked Mama, looking at Maahtou with a mixture of awe and uneasiness. She took a deep breath. There and then, she began wondering whether Maahtou had misunderstood the principle of committing herself first to her grooming husband.

"*Anwaarneh abongeh*," intoned Maahtou.

For the first time since the family education mantra was established, Mama did not answer with the usual "*Mbaah ka see*." Instead, she sighed and shook her head.

"Don't you always say that the time during which I am still working with my grooming husband, is like when the kola nut is still tasting bitter?" asked Maahtou. "So, why are you worried?

"I am not asking you to stop chewing, my daughter. I'm just concerned for your future."

You worry over everything, Mama," said Maahtou with a frown.

"But you must not forget yourself, my daughter," entreated Mama.

"Don't worry, Mama. One day I may even choose to go beyond the kola nut to multiply like the grain of corn," teased Maahtou.

"Hmmn! Do you realize that a woman's womb has a limited fertility span?"

"My mother, don't worry about that. I am not in a rush."

Chapter 20

Social Class Survey

Early in the morning on Tuesday, Fleurette, a girl in the Assumption dormitory, was reported sick. The Health Prefect had woken up at 2.00 a.m. and given her some aspirin from her bedside medicine cabinet. By 7.00 a.m., a Reverend Sister arrived from the Convent and examined her. She returned within thirty minutes with a tray of breakfast for Fleurette. The sick girl refused to eat. The Sister, the dormitory captain, and health prefect pleaded with her to sit up and take her breakfast.

Later, while students were rushing to class, two other Reverend Sisters arrived in a greyish white Renault 4 and packed it close to the dormitory. It was a rare moment that caused students to stop and watch. Within minutes, the Health Perfect came out with Fleurette leaning on her shoulder, assisted by the dormitory captain, into the vehicle.

Girls who were coming out of Assumption hostel exclaimed. Earlier they had seen Fleurette walking by herself to the Locker room, and then to the bathroom, located some 100 meters from the dormitory. That was before the first Sister arrived,

"It seems as if her energy has just evaporated," remarked a student.

Among the girls watching was Eposi, one of the Four Rocks. The Sisters drove Fleurette to the hospital.

As soon as Eposi stepped into class, she whispered to two of the Four Rocks, Nubodem and Ngwe of Regina and Imma-Concept dormitories respectively: "You needed to see the VIP treatment this morning" she said. They both shook their heads. She promised to tell them during break time. As for Maahtou, she had not witnessed the scene. At that moment, she was in Regina repairing the braids of Pam, a Form 4 student.

It was a sunny, cold morning. Students were chatting in class during break. Eposi signalled the Four Rocks to follow her outside. "Hmm, they say some people are born with a silver tooth in their mouth, oh," remarked Eposi. Then, she went ahead and recounted how Fleurette, one of the so-called Silver Tooth Girls, had become an 'egg.' Fleurette came from a wealthy home. Her mother was a minister in the government.

"Hmm, they have silver, but I'm not trading my enamel for anything," interjected Maahtou. The girls burst out laughing.

"Hold on, Maahtou, let her finish," urged Ngwe.

"And guess what?" asked Eposi. The rest were staring at her. "She may not even be sick."

"Really?" asked Ngwe.

"Sometimes they behave like babies," said Nubodem.

"Spoiled girls usually crave special foods and tender treatment," said Maahtou.

"Exactly," said Eposi. "Sister brought her cheese, butter, and eggs from the convent."

"Didn't I tell you?" said Ngwe. "Why should we waste our time talking about them?" asked Ngwe. "We should be thinking about our exams."

"I know, but it hurts. No sister visited me last week when I was sick," Eposi pressed on.

"What about Matilda?" Ngwe asked. "Each month she screams night and day from menstrual pains but none of them have ever come to take her to the hospital."

"Last month was the worst," said Nubodem. She was crying and jumping up and down in her dorm. The news got to the staff members, but none of the sisters came by her bedside.``

"Oh yes, Matilda's case is worse than any other illness," insisted Eposi. "Now I begin to wonder why no Sister has ever taken her to the hospital."

"Do you remember the gospel reading this morning at the Cathedral?" asked Nubodem.

The others were all curious. All eyes were on her.

"Unto to those who have…" she started the verse while waiting for them to fill in the blank.

"More shall be added to it," Ngwe completed the Bible verse

"Really? I didn't hear it." Maahtou responded while shaking her head.

"So, poor ones like us will remain at the bottom of the ladder, is that so?" asked Eposi frowning.

The bell began ringing, and the girls rushed back into class. However, while the lesson was going on, they exchanged notes with one another. They decided to pursue their talk later.

The final bell rang. The Four Rocks signalled each other. They were going to take advantage of the free Friday afternoon. Immediately, they headed to their favourite reading spot at the south end of the campus. They climbed up the biggest mango tree with sturdy branches. There, they sat and began pouring out their woes. The overriding question was, why were students not given equal treatment, even by authorities?

They were determined to get some clarification on the matter. Could they be enlightened by any of their class lessons? For example, in history, they had learned about societies that practice systems with distinct social classes.

"It is as if we are in a Caste system," Nubodem set the ball rolling.

"Indeed, they ignore us as if we are the Untouchables," added Ngwe.

"You mean peasants or Plebs, right?" Maahtou confirmed.

"Exactly," Ngwe responded.

"So, that means right here in college; some students are the bourgeoisie while others the proletariat?" Eposi asked, rhetorically.

"Didn't you hear our teacher talk about the "have alls" and the "have nots?" explained Nubodem.

"Hahaha, repeat it," Eposi laughed and clapped her hands. "This matter is grievous."

"That is why we must do something about it," insisted Nubodem.

"We need paper," suggested Maahtou. "Let's go down to solid ground and make ourselves comfortable."

They jumped down from the tree and sat on the green grass. The sun was getting hotter, but they were determined. They made themselves comfortable under the tree, shielded from the sun and the heat. How were they going to proceed? First, they asked guiding questions. Eposi offered to act as secretary. Was there a clear line of distinction according to social status in their college? Were some students mistreating others just because they belonged to a higher social rank? They went on until the page was full. Then, they began associating value to each item, from 1 to 5. After that, they decided to cancel the irrelevant ones.

The more they discussed, the more it became apparent that they could classify the population of their college into distinct categories. However, the question was, how many groups?

"Two," Nubodem suggested.

"I would say three," said Maahtou

"Why?" Ngwe and Eposi asked.

Each of the proponents explained their view.

Then, Maahtou raised her hand. Eposi urged that they listen to her.

"There is a large group in the middle between the two extremes that we cannot ignore," said Maahtou.

"I agree," said Nubodem.

The other two nodded and lifted their thumbs. It was clear that they could classify the college into three groups. However, how were they going to refer to each of them?

"No derogatory terms, please," Ngwe pleaded.

"Okay, how about "rich" to begin with?" asked Nubodem.

"Who knows whether you are not richer than some of the so-called rich?" asked Maahtou.

"What do you mean?" asked Eposi. "They have money, food, clothes; you name it, but you also have things of value."

"I think that I understand Maahtou," said Nubodem. "The question is, is it their money?"

"Besides, if we call a group "rich," we cannot condemn another with poverty," insisted Ngwe.

"How about "glows"? Eposi suggested.

All the other three girls raised their hands and tapped Eposi in approval. So, the first group will henceforth be called "Glows."

"Who would qualify to become a Glow?" asked Eposi.

"Plump jaws and red lips," said Nubodem.

"Also, a good number of them wear lenses and own wristwatches," said Maahtou.

"A few speak English with a foreign accent, while others have visited big cities and foreign countries," added Ngwe.

The Four Rocks went on elaborating. They agreed that the Glows were favoured or preferred by all others. Everyone seemed to gravitate towards them naturally. Senior students open their teeth and smile from jaw to jaw even before reaching an approaching Glow. For the same reason and more, others always waited to chat with them.

"How about the sweet fragrances of their perfumed bathing soap and body creams?" asked Eposi.

"Also, the quality of their clothing like their soft linen bed sheets," said Ngwe.

"Have you seen Bih's towels trimmed in style, her white silk shimmies, and panties with edges delicately touched with lace?" asked Maahtou.

Indeed!" said Eposi with a nod. Glows were like human catalogues when they wore their silky pants with laced seams. Even their white underwear sparkled.

"So, what shall we call the so-called poor group?" asked Eposi.

"Rocks," suggested Nubodem.

"You mean students like us, right?" asked Maahtou.

"Yeah, but "rock" doesn't say much about status," said Ngwe.

"How about "struggling girls," asked Eposi.

"If we accept that, then we will always be struggling," suggested Maahtou.

"Modesty," suggested Nubodem.

"Sounds better," said Ngwe. "But some wealthy people are modest too."

"Exactly," confirmed Eposi.

There was a long silence. The Four Rocks didn't know exactly how to describe their very own rank.

"Strivers," shouted Ngwe.

The girls went silent again while thinking hard over the latest suggestion.

"I agree," said Nubodem.

"Me too," said Eposi.

"Let's go for it," said Maahtou after scribbling down substitute names and striking them all out.

Finally, they were able to pinpoint their group characteristics. They were among those at the bottom of the college social strata. They thanked Ngwe for it. They liked it because it was an action word, not static like Glows. It gave them the hope to expect a change for the better in the future, even if that would happen only long after graduation.

It was now time for them to substantiate the choice of their hallmarks.

"Strivers are not easy to identify at the beginning of the school term," said Ngwe.

"Hahaha," they broke into laughter.

From the fortnight onwards, Strivers began looking somewhat haggard, revealing scaly skin and scarred lips. Also, their faces got pale while their jaws started sinking in sync with their drooping skirts.

"Talk to me," Maahtou was almost screaming, with her right hand up. She was among the girls who required a safety pin to hold their skirt in place around the waist.

Other features of Strivers stood out during special days when casual dresses replaced the uniform. Strivers tended to wear poorly stitched dresses. "We are the champions of *cutam-nailam* (roughly stitched gowns), and *okriekas* (hand-me-downs)," said Nubodem.

"Say that again," said Ngwe.

"So, Glows are stars, then," said Eposi.

"I hope they are happy to have us admire their imported ready-made dresses," said Maahtou.

"If they were smart, they would be very kind towards us," said Eposi.

"Right?" the rest answered and gave her high fives.

Talking about strivers, Ngwe stood up and asked, "do you want to see my panty?"

"Sit down," said Eposi. "Which of us doesn't know that?"

Strivers wore cheap panties and locally sewn waist-slips, exposing the rough finishing with or without low-quality lace. Their innerwear readily absorbed tainting particles in the water, thus turning them into beige sooner than desired.

It was now time to name the third and middle class. Everyone was thinking hard; it was challenging to come up with an appropriate appellation.

"Average," suggested Ngwe.

Everyone shook their heads.

"Moderates," Nubodem suggested.

"That sounds more political," cautioned Eposi.

Meanwhile, Maahtou was silent, and thinking extremely hard. She was the one who had convinced the others of a third group. She began writing names on the last page of her exercise book. They included "sustainables," "unbeatables," "suppliers," and "merchants."

The rest debated on Maahtou's proposals.

"Sustainable" is too familiar. Let's come up with our term," suggested Nubodem.

"Unbeatables" sounds like fighters in the Bakweri elephant dance," said Eposi.

The girls burst out laughing and threw their heads on Eposi's shoulders.

"Suppliers" and "Merchants" could refer to any businessperson in town," said Ngwe.

There was silence. Everyone was thinking hard.

"Okay, I have a good idea," shouted Maahtou. "Let's call them Brickwall girls."

"What?" the rest asked with enquiring frowns on their faces.

"Let me explain," said Maahtou. "It combines all the rejected names, and besides, it is original."

"How?" Nubodem and Eposi asked.

"Brick walls are resistant in all seasons though not as sturdy as concrete," said Maahtou. The other three laughed until tears rolled down Nubodem's cheeks.

"They remain strong, even when the sting of hunger is biting everyone," Maahtou explained further.

Finally, the other three accepted the name. However, they decided to shorten it to "Bricks."

Maahtou recalled that her parents had moved out of a mud house twice. She elaborated on the justification for "Bricks." There was a vast difference between mud houses and baked brick ones. Unlike basic mud houses in villages, Virgin Mother's College was built with baked bricks. The walls were solid, unshakable, and pleasing to the sight. Thus, the most distinctive characteristic of the Bricks was their steady supply of snacks throughout the whole term.

The others became inspired. Each began providing more details unique to the middle class.

"Bricks are fatter and maintain their weight throughout," said Nubodem.

"Yes, of course," said Ngwe. "They have enough ammunition to keep hunger at bay."

"Though they don't look like, smell like or sound like Glows, they are sure of themselves, right?" asked Eposi.

Nubodem gave her a pat on the back while the rest applauded. Talking about their looks, even when a Brick did not have the famous ready-made dresses, their home or locally made clothes had excellent finishing. Their shoes were neither *Dschang* shoes nor imported, but they were reliable and beautified their feet.

"Those girls are also like wholesalers," said Maahtou. Everyone stared at her to elaborate. They bring along *mbiarre*, groundnuts, *garri* like us but they never run out."

"Hahaha," each one laughed.

"We bring small quantities like *minndjanga* (crayfish), right?" asked Eposi.

"There you go," said Ngwe.

For example, most Bricks brought along two packages of sugar compared to counted cubes wrapped up in brown carton paper by Strivers. When the avocado of Bricks were all consumed, they proceeded to open their cans of margarine and liquid chocolate. Though they could not afford the foreign biscuits or rich cakes of Glows, they armed themselves with two or more boxes of Cabin biscuits and a heavy bag of chin-chin. Meanwhile, Bricks from the coastal areas had coconut sweets filled in plastic bottles.

The Four Rocks were thrilled at their ability to map out the various social classes in their college. They stood up and gave each other high fives and laughed out loud. The differences were becoming more evident. If a guest walked into a dormitory, he or she could not determine who was who if each bed were covered by a counterpane. However, as soon as the bed covers were removed, one could determine which bed belonged to which social class.

At the end of the exercise, the Four Rocks held their hands together. It was as if they had viewed their school with a magnifying glass. They were satisfied with what they had accomplished.

"We accept our place," said Eposi. "The only thing that hurts me is when some of them treat us as if we were their housemaids."

At that, they bent down their heads, held onto each other to push back their tears. There and then, they took a firm resolve to focus on their studies. Maahtou took advantage of their resolution to emphasize the importance of paying careful attention to each one's grooming spouse. Though they counted themselves lucky to have passed from elementary to secondary school, they regretted that discrimination existing between social classes was a reality.

They were about to round off when some past acts of discrimination resurfaced. Thus, they decided to stay back and just maybe an idea would spring up on how to fight back.

"Imagine Sisters rushing from the convent to care for Fleurette when none came to my bedside when I was sick," said Eposi.

"It's sad, but we have to be strong," proposed Nubodem.

"You're right," said Maahtou. "My mother says that while you are still eating the kola nut, it is bitter, but it gets sweet once you drink water. The bitter reality is there, yes, but let's rather focus on our homework."

"All those who think that they are better than others are fooling themselves," said Ngwe.

"Some of them bully us, but they are just as good as bulls," said Eposi.

"That means that their tails are longer and more damaging than those of foxes," said Maahtou.

"Hahaha," they all laughed out loud.

Despite the evident woes, they had each other's interest at heart.

"Have you realized that our Religious Knowledge teacher keeps repeating a statement that hits directly at us?" Nubodem introduced the subject.

"What does she say?" The other three asked in chorus with widely opened eyes.

"That poverty is a sin," Nubodem reminded them.

Indeed, the first time that Miss Tantoh made that statement in class, students exclaimed in bewilderment.

"That day, I shivered," said Maahtou.

"It was like Miss Tantoh was obliging those from poorer families to gobble down a cup of bitter herb juice," said Ngwe.

It was perplexing.

Is Miss Tantoh insisting on her theory because her father was a popular rich man in town?" asked Ngwe.

"Shouldn't a Religious Knowledge teacher be the one to close the status gap?" asked Nubodem.

The questions kept flowing. Were diligence in studies and character not more critical than the amount of extra cash in a student's pocket? Did she realize how much of a sacrifice low-income families were making to sponsor a girl in a renowned college? If Miss Tantoh was right, why was the church not promoting riches as the proper credentials for heaven? If so, why did priests every Sunday qualify offerings as wealth stored up in heaven?

Their unanswered questions brought back some sad memories. Some of them were unfairly treated during tail-cutting. For example, senior students withdrew Maahtou's Seraphims status, while excluding Nubodem.

"I wish they could just be happy with their money and leave us alone," regretted Nubodem. "Have they forgotten that God added value to the widow's mite?"

"No, they think that we are beasts of burden like donkeys or *Nguenakohs* (shepherds)," said Maahtou.

The girls burst out laughing, though it was not a laughing matter.

Whether their situation was going to evolve or not, there was no way of telling on the spot. Their greatest need was for tactics to deal with difficult circumstances created by arrogant and callous students.

Thus, it became imperative for them to be proactive. Instantly, the Four Rocks had an idea. How about consulting their history teacher? Maybe he could help them find a solution. Quickly, they left their cosy place and rushed towards the administrative building. The history teacher was at the library.

"Hahaha," Mr. Adzie Mbom laughed out in his characteristic manner. He folded his arms and listened to them one after the other without interrupting them.

"So, you girls want to change society?" he asked.

"Yes, if possible," the girls answered in chorus while nodding their heads.

"So, where do you want to place yourself, on top or below?"

Each one of the Four Rocks giggled and laughed until their sides ached. He had taken them by surprise. Mr. Adzie Mbom leaned back on the wall and watched them holding each other and laughing and staring at him. In the end, none of them answered his question.

Instead, there was a long pause. Finally, Eposi, while hiding behind the others, said: "on top."

"Yes," agreed Maahtou.

He waited for the other two to express their views, but they were keener on listening to him.

"Okay, I see," he responded. "You have been able to apply the history lesson on the various classes in society to the college. I applaud you for such a great job."

The girls smiled and continued listening intently.

"Secondly, I want you to henceforth watch out for one vital thing," they all looked up, and their eyes were on his lips.

"One: distinctive appearance, and two: behaviour. Whether a student is on top, below, or in the middle, that's all that matters."

They listened while absorbing every word and trying to dissect them.

"But sir, one of our teachers keeps saying that poor students are sinners," Ngwe explained. Eposi concurred.

"What would you say about that?" asked Nubodem.

"That is the real problem we are having," Maahtou pressed on.

"Your teacher may be right or wrong," said Mr. Adzie Mbom, "But you must realize that even Science makes mistakes, and sometimes it only corrects itself years later. So, don't let that bother you," he reassured them.

They kept fixing their eyes on their teacher's face. They wanted more.

"Finally, study hard and do your best. Keep smiling, and even when you are feeling sad, always keep a smile close to your lips. You know why?"

"No," answered the Four Rocks while shaking their heads.

"It is a rose that beautifies your face, and it remains fresh."

The girls giggled and laughed in amazement. Their faces glowed.

"Didn't I tell you? If each of you could see the radiance on your face as you smiled, even millions can't buy that," said Mr. Adzie Mbom.

"But, sir, a smile is not money," said Eposi.

"One day, you will understand," said the teacher.

"Thank you, sir, for listening to us," said Maahtou.

"And now for the road," said Mr. Adzie Mbom while lifting his right forefinger, a reflex action whenever he was ending his lesson. "Endeavour to be nice to others," he said, pausing and staring into their faces. "You tell me, can money buy that self-made perfume called Smiling and Niceness?" he asked while fixing them, one after the other.

They all stood by, nodding in awe, and looking at him with admiration.

Chapter 21

Parents' Day

By 12:30 p.m., the whole campus was full. Students were running with excitement in all directions, greeting and falling into the open arms of their parents. The variety of colours of outfits was endless— from George wax to cotton *wrappers*, and *kabbas* for women while men were in *jumpas*, *Aguadas*, or simple shirts and trousers. The college campus had no more standing space. From the entrance, dormitories, refectory, terraces to the handball court, it was full. Hug after hug as well as lively chatting were going on.

The guests swelled up the head count to at least five hundred, more than double the student population. There was also a multiplicity of bags and boxes of food, visible everywhere. It was Parent's Day. What an explosion of joy! What a burst of bright sunshine to highlight every happy face and a multiplicity of teeth-displaying laughter!

Maahtou spotted Mama among groups of parents searching for their daughters. Heartily, Mama hugged her, holding her close to her chest for almost five minutes. Then, Mama introduced her to a father and a mother, with whom she had travelled from Santa. They were the parents of fourth and third year students, respectively. The two students and Maahtou warmed up to each other as they never had. It was a new connection established among them.

"She is your small sister," Mama said to the two students.

"That's right, Mama," they answered with broad smiles.

"That is why Parent's Day is good," the father of the Form 4 student said.

"Otherwise, they will continue behaving like strangers to each other," concurred the mother of the second student.

On that note, the three parents agreed to meet each other at the end of the activities.

Maahtou's eyes began searching into the snack bag Mama had brought. There and then, Mama recalled that she had brought a bundle of snacks for another student, Esther, who was in Form 1. Although her parents were younger than Baba and Mama, they did not come. Whatever prevented them from coming, they were known to be self-effacing, often shying away from public places. That notwithstanding, Esther's mother had brought a bag of snacks the previous evening for Mama to take along to her daughter.

Like the other students, Maahtou guided her mother amidst endless hugs and handshakes to her dormitory, Ave Maria. They sat on her bed. There and then, Mama opened the bag and pulled out several bundles of goodies. They included garri, avocado, *miyiondo* (fermented cassava rolls), *mbiare* (dried sweet potatoes), and roasted groundnuts. Then, there was a rectangular bundle of the length of an adult's palm. It was wrapped in a heated plantain leaf and tied up with a banana leaf rope. Mama began unwrapping the double layer while Maahtou was all eyes. She opened the second leaf and held it out to Maahtou. "Hahaha!" Maahtou laughed merrily. It was a chunk of cooked dried meat that Baba had cut out specifically for Maahtou the previous week.

"You like it?" Mama was smiling broadly. "Baba kept this for me?" Mama was pleased to make her feel at home. The delighted daughter picked it up and took the time to scan through the brownish strands of the Santa delicious beef. She pulled out two strands and ate. It was like eating a work of art.

"Tell Baba that I treasure the meat in the same way that he and his friends enjoy kola nut."

Then, she hugged her mother. She went on quietly chewing the pulp, moving it from jaw to jaw like chewing gum.

"This is six times the size that we have here," said Maahtou.

"Munch it," said Mama.

Instead Maahtou folded the bundle. She was preserving it to share with her friends, the other members of the Four

182

Rocks. There was a distinctive delicious taste to meat from Santa.

Mama started to unwrap the other bigger bundles. The *garri* looked so inviting with its typical pale-yellow colour— the result of mixing drops of palm oil with grated white cassava in the hot steel frying basin. Maahtou dipped in her fingers and carried a handful in her right palm. Quickly, Mama made an apology. "Neumour (my darling), I didn't have money to buy some cubes of sugar for you. Eat your garri with groundnuts and pear."

"Hey, Mama, with all this food that you've brought for me, how can I complain?" It was a timely rescue. All that Maahtou had left was half a cup of garri.

Having said and done the essentials, Mama requested Maahtou to go search for Esther. Maahtou rushed to Regina dormitory.

Esther and Maahtou ran all the way back to her dorm. Esther smiled and fell into Mama's opened arms.

"Your mother and father asked me to greet you."

"Are they doing well, Mama?"

"Yes, only that there is too much work," Mama said. "I guess that's why they were not able to come," she explained.

"My father will never show up at events like this, so too, my mother," said Esther with a sad tone.

Mama understood Esther's discontent. Her father was a polygamist who was always busy working on his tomato farm miles away from home. As for her mother, her lack of formal education always made her feel inferior. Mama hugged Esther again and comforted her.

"Your mother sent something for you," said Mama.

Then she picked up a large package and handed it to her. Esther's face lit up. She smiled and stood up and curtsied to Mama while saying repeatedly, *"meeya, meeya,* Mama" (thank you).

The bell began ringing. Dormitory captains and prefects started going from group to group requesting students to accompany their parents to the school hall. The staging of William Shakespeare's *Macbeth* by senior students, the main event of the day, was coming up soon. The actors, drawn from Form 3 to 5, had been seriously rehearsing for the past weeks. Maahtou's class had already begun studying it too.

Soon, the hall was full. Apart from the actresses, each student was sitting by their parent(s). The Four Rocks had arranged for their families to sit next to each other. Ngwe's mother, Nubodem's mother, Eposi's uncle were all sitting on the fifth bench from the front. Mama asked Maahtou to look out for Esther and bring her to sit by them. Maahtou, who was sitting at the edge by the aisle stood up and tried to go out of the hall, but it was near impossible as parents were flocking in.

When the hostess came with a pile of the playbill, Maahtou signalled her to skip her mother. Without understanding what Maahtou was explaining, Mama quickly stretched out her hand as soon as she noticed that other parents were stretching out their hands. She got a copy for herself. She promptly began reading. She was moving her lips oddly, all to show off her 'literacy.'

Maahtou quickly noticed what was going on and asked Mama to tell her what was written on the bill. Mama looked at her and smiled. So, Maahtou stretched her neck and peeped into Mama's bill. What did she see? Mama had been reading it upside down. Maahtou began laughing. Of course, Mama suspected that something was amiss.

"What's wrong, my daughter?

"Even myself, I can't read it like that."

"How can that be, my daughter? Is the language too strong for you?"

"See, Mama, the head is facing downwards."

Mama quickly flipped around the playbill. She and Maahtou laughed it out.

"*Mbaah kasee*? (didn't I tell you?)" Mama intoned.

"*Anwaarneh Ateirhnne*" (book is tough), Maahtou responded in place of the usual "education is good."

"*Meeya mba, Neumour na*," (thank you very much, my Mommy), Mama said while turning around her seat to hug Maahtou.

Soon after, the lights went out. The opening scene began. Lightening amidst smoke as well as the sound of thunder filled the stage. The first characters walked onto the stage. For the next one-half hour or more, Maahtou was interpreting for Mama.

Beginning from the prologue, she gave her an idea of what was going to happen. "This is a serious story, Mama. Strong people struggle for power and they do terrible things."

"Like what? Fighting?"

"Yes, that and more;"

"So, where are these people coming from?"

"It is just acting. All the actors are students. Let's just watch them"

Then, Maahtou kept up the explanation, scene after scene in a low tone. Promptly, as a new act opened, she introduced the characters, their titles, and how they were related to one another. Of course, some meanings were not easy to convey in the Ngemba language. Maahtou kept going as best as she could while the drama unfolded line after line. Scene after scene, the play moved from the battlefront to the street, the woods, and the bedroom. The rising and falling tone in various speeches, coupled with tensions and actions. They all created a pathos in the audience that exclaimed or clapped from time to time.

It was evident that most of them were seeing a staged play for the first time. However, most of them could link the scene with witches to some of the rituals in their respective villages.

Finally, the staging of Shakespeare's *Macbeth* was over. All the actresses came back on stage. The lights turned on. Their colourful costumes were displayed for all to see, even as the soldiers turned their swords around for effect. Together, they bowed their heads. The thunder of applause seemed endless.

Mama was most probably the only one who did not clap. She just sat still staring at them in a disinterested manner.

Instead, she was looking around inquiringly as if wondering why everyone was so excited. Then, Mama twisted her mouth, threw her body back into her seat, and sighed.

Maahtou was disappointed though she did not understand what was going on in Mama's mind. She asked Mama if she had not enjoyed it.

"Enjoy what?" Mama asked with disgust.

"But the actresses did such a good job, mother," Maahtou insisted.

"Can someone enjoy listening to witches? Or should I clap for people killing others?"

"No, but at least from this, we learn to be vigilant," Maahtou pressed on.

"Ok, fine, but will that stop witches and wizards from beating your father each night?"

Maahtou realized that unlike other parents who had let go for the moment, Mama was linking the play to real life in a more personal way.

Nevertheless, she did not want Mama to be sad on such an exceptional day, set aside for light-hearted issues. So, Maahtou quickly changed the topic. "How are Abong, Neumour, Afouomama, and Baba doing?" Since Mama's arrival, both had not yet had the chance to talk about her siblings.

"They are all fine, my daughter."

Parents and students began moving out of the hall. Hand in hand, Maahtou took her mother back to her dormitory. They sat on her bed. Mama gave her more details about how everyone back home was doing. When Mama finished, she asked Maahtou to stand up and face her. Mama scanned Maahtou from head to toe. Then, she pulled up her beige blouse and got hold of her red skirt at the waist. Except for the safety pin that Maahtou had gathered it with, it would have dropped.

Mama removed the safety pin and placed her forefinger along the width of the fold like a measuring tape. She shook her head from side to side and clapped her hands in disgust.

Without saying a word, Mama took a deep breath and tightened her lips. Then she looked into Maahtou's blinking eyes. In desperation, she stretched out her right hand and cupped Maahtou's face into her right palm. Then, she pulled back and clapped her hands again and exclaimed, "*lah abeh lah-lir*? (so that's how it is)? For a while, she could not speak; neither could Maahtou. Both were struggling to hold back tears.

Mama bent her head down as if looking at her feet. Maahtou's eyes followed. Mama's black sandals had gathered a lot of light-brownish dust. Maahtou hoped no one was witnessing their moment of despair.

Luckily, the other students also had a tête-à-tête with their parents. A dozen or so were seated in the middle and at the other end of the dormitory. Eposi was in the yard with her uncle, who had come to represent her parents. Men were not allowed to enter any of the dormitories.

Mama moaned. After a while, she recollected herself, raised her head, and looked straight into Maahtou's eyes. Though Mama tried to smile, her fair complexion exposed a redness over her face and especially around her eyelids. Then without notice, she stood up and asked Maahtou to remain seated on the bed. With her back turned towards the other students, she raised both hands and placed them over Maahtou's head.

"May the God of our ancestors, who guided our fathers, preserve you from all attacks, even the stings of hunger! May he who has been a shield for humankind, strengthen you and keep you! May he who makes the sunshine, light up your pathway, and make you wise!"

When she ended her prayer, she sat down again. Her face brightened up; she smiled and hugged Maahtou.

"My daughter, don't worry," she said in English.

"Of course, Mama, my grooming husband must have his way despite the hard times."

Mama was thrilled. She nodded in approval. "You will pass in all your exams until you finish."

Mama's blessings ended on time as the first bell began ringing. It was the signal for the wrap-up. In a little while, the second bell was going to ring, and that would be it for Parents' Day.

Mama picked up her handbag, and Maahtou invited her for sightseeing before leaving. They descended the stairs that led to the back of the dormitory. They paused and looked at a dozen or so twine ropes fastened onto iron poles for the drying of laundry. From there, they could see the three other dormitories, horizontal buildings parallel to Ave Maria, with the refectory perpendicular to them.

They kept moving forward and walked past by the flower garden bordering Ave Maria dormitory. Maahtou pointed to the barbed wire demarcating the boundary. A gentle breeze caused the mango tree branches to shake from side to side as if they were waving at them. They were in bloom. Mama said she was happy that the fruit trees were within the campus. Maahtou concurred, reassuring her that, indeed, they were permitted to harvest them when they got ripe.

However, she added that ever since she was on that campus, no one has seen a ripe mango fall off the tree.

"I don't understand," Mama said, looking inquiringly at Maahtou.

"Mama, students begin harvesting as soon as the fruits have grown to full size."

"You don't mean it."

"Since we climb into them to study during the exam period, girls begin touching them weeks before they ripen," Maahtou explained.

"Well, what shall I say, if it wards off hunger and if you don't get sick," Mama said and continued exclaiming.

They were now going towards the gate. Or better still, the solid line beyond which it was out of bounds. Mama once more asked Maahtou to go search for Esther. Maahtou rushed towards her dormitory while the parents of the other two Santa girls were waving to Mama from a retreating crowd.

Maahtou returned within minutes. Mama embraced Esther first. "Stay well and study hard," Mama said to both girls.

"Please, do greet my mother for me," said Esther.

"I will," said Mama while gently rubbing Esther's back. "Do you have any message for them?"

"Tell my mother not to work too hard. She should take good care of herself," pleaded Esther.

Mama looked at Esther and smiled warmly. "Don't let any worries distract you from your schoolwork, you hear me?"

Esther nodded, thanked Mama, and wished her a safe trip back home.

Meanwhile, the other Santa mother who was less than a hundred meters away was equally bidding adieu with her daughter. As for the father, he had already crossed the boundary line and was patiently waiting for both mothers.

Maahtou reminded Mama that it was time out already. Mama opened her arms and pressed her daughter on her bosom for a long while. Esther stared at them and chuckled. It was time to go. Mama waved to both girls and crossed the boundary line and turned back. Then she turned around and started going downhill to meet the other parents who were waiting for her. With every step, Mama turned back and waved. Maahtou stood there, struggling to manage mixed emotions of joy and sadness until Mama was out of sight.

Meanwhile, Esther had excused herself and rushed to her dormitory. She had soaked a bowl of *garri* from the bundle that Mama had brought to her. Her mother was an expert *garri* maker. Indeed, her mother and uncle were jointly sponsoring her in college, thanks to money from the sale of *garri*.

As for Maahtou, instead of returning to her dormitory, she took the stairs leading behind it, where she and Mama had passed. Her mind began playing back Mama's reassuring words. It was like listening to a tape recorder. Then she recalled the parting blessings her parents gave her the first time she was leaving Santa for college. It was the usual departing ritual. With a cup of water in hand, Mama had spoken words of success and victory and in rhythm with the sprinkling of the water on her feet. Then, she kept repeating the mantra, "If you hit a stone with these feet…"

"Let the stone shatter into bits and pieces," Baba's baritone voice stood out in the chorus of voices of Mahma (grandma) and Maahtou's younger siblings.

Maahtou recalled that Mama had pleaded with Baba in vain to conduct the parting ritual. "What's wrong if you are the one who leads out?" Baba often asked.

"So, why are you the head of the family?" Mama would ask.

"Just go ahead and do it, we are all together," Baba would entreat Mama.

Maahtou smiled as she thought of her father as a man of action rather than a man of words. Just like he always ceded the priestly ritual to Mama, so too, he must have decided that Mama's presence at Parent's Day would be more useful than his more formal ways.

Maahtou was not disheartened by his absence. If only one of them had to come, Mama was the better choice. Baba would probably have refused to carry the snacks. He would have said that the college oversaw providing food for students. Secondly, he would not have had the chance to enter the dormitory, much less sit on Maahtou's bed. Thirdly, he would not have noticed that Maahtou had lost so much weight. And fourthly, Maahtou wondered what his reaction would have been in seeing *Macbeth*'s witches. She had no way of guessing.

Maahtou's thoughts carried her away until the stem of the flower called Christ's thorn scratched her foot. She bent down and examined the itching and hurting skin. She touched it and pressed it, but no blood was coming out. She was relieved.

It was only then that she also noticed that the sun had already set. She began moving faster. The end of the long wall of her dormitory was right before her. She followed the leftward curve and rushed up through the stairs leading into the back entrance of the residence.

It was time for supper; yet no student was budging. There was excitement in the dormitory. Most students were more interested in showing off and sharing the various food items their parents had brought. Who was going to bother to go to the refectory, anyway? Surely only girls whose parents live in far-off cities, including those who did not have an aunt or uncle living in Bamenda or its vicinity. Not only they but equally girls who did not receive a cooked meal from visiting male relatives.

Nevertheless, a treat was waiting for those who would go to the refectory. On Parent's Day, cooks prepared a smaller meal. It was more delicious. Above everything else, the meat pieces were four times larger than usual.

Meanwhile, Maahtou and Eposi went to Imma-Concept, Ngwe's dormitory, where Nubodem had preceded them. Ngwe's mother had brought the most comprehensive meal, *achu*. It was accompanied by steamed *ndjama-ndjama* (huckleberry leaves), roasted eggplant, and mushroom. With Maahtou's two pieces of meat, each of the girls had enough meat to eat that evening, to their satisfaction.

In addition to *garri* that each of them had received from home, Nubodem's mother had brought groundnut pudding and *miyiondo*. The girls were going to eat those for the next two days as a complement to their lunch. Eposi's uncle had brought some coconut sweet, two packages of sugar, biscuits, and chocolate paste. For at least two weeks, the Four Rocks were going to enjoy themselves like the Bricks.

Chapter 22

Tinkered Beauty

Two weeks to the national youth day celebration, students began sharing ideas on how to resurrect their buried beauty. Their common desire was tantamount to rebelling against a recent law. According to the injunction, authorities forbade anyone from wearing their hair longer than two inches. Students had complained to no avail. Ever since then, instead of plaiting the traditional *Pass-Pass*, *Parking*, *Motoboor*, Follow-Me, *Begoudis*, or braiding *Bakala* (cornrows), Rasta, or adding extensions, every style was loosened, cut off and reduced to trash.

Infuriated students mourned for weeks, blaming those who had abused the freedom they hitherto enjoyed. Indeed, some girls usually skipped classes or prep time, feigning illness to plait their hair. Meanwhile, others carried around old hairdos speckled with dandruff, which they kept scratching in class. Worse still, some pulled off loose braids during class sessions.

Besides, the more extravagant students wasted their pocket money on unnecessary hair products. Those were later obliged to borrow essential items like bathing soap, laundry soap, body creams, and pens. In extreme cases, girls were torn between making a fashion statement and concentrating on their studies. A few found themselves obliged to start undisclosed relationships with men. Those men were either less educated shop owners or wealthy married men. Gradually, they acquired beauty implements. Those included hairbrushes, black eye-pencils, make-up kits with multi-colour talc, dark powders with accompanying foundation creams, various sizes of combs, and especially the hot comb.

Though parents were in support of the strict measures discouraging any undue attachment to the physical appearance of students, students never stopped imagining themselves in all forms of styled hair. They wasted no time in the search for creative ways to circumvent the law.

With the beginning of the countdown to youth day, students began to mobilize support for the campaign to regain their beauty. "I will see how Orpah will stop us," was the quiet defiance that was rumbling through all the dorms.

"If there are no flowers, what will attract bees?" asked Monica of Imma-Concept.

"Hahaha," girls in the dormitory roared with laughter.

"Once a rose has budded, who can stop it from blossoming?" asked Cecilia.

"No one," responded Agnes.

On the 11th of February, some girls woke up as early as 5.00 a.m. It was the day to regain their lost glory. It was the day on which to display their regained beauty while mingling with hundreds of students from other colleges.

Little charcoal fires in pressing irons began lighting up outside one block to the other and dispelling the darkness. All those with hot combs brought them out. The process of stretching each other's hair to crispness started immediately after the early morning bath.

Then, they proceeded to twist and weave hair towards artful directions. The step-by-step maquillage process followed. It began with the application of foundation and powder. Then, the tracing of the under-eye with black eyeliners and the application of a bright colour eye-pencil to the upper eyelid. Next was the darkening or reddening of the lips. A few went as far as attaching artificial eyelashes.

"Are you going to Hollywood?" asked Miranda?

"You only die once, so let's live fully today," responded Regina. Indeed, the unusual looks created could have competed with stars on international magazine covers.

Soon, the names of specialists skilful with placing or propping eyelashes, colouring eyelids and lips received a special mention from dormitory to dormitory. "Wait until you see

Glory, Julie, Christine or Camille?" They had successfully painted up their faces to a perfect finish. Thus, other girls started lining up before the experts, pleading for their delicate touches. "*Abeg, make me up too*," was everyone's request. What an art to behold! Their tender hands were like a gentle breeze blowing over surrendered faces, in a desperate attempt to redeem their Eden-inspired attractiveness.

However, in all the excitement to define and redefine their congenial contours and uncover their innate exquisite perfection, a few girls chose to keep it simple. They were the so-called natural girls, who were satisfied with their rustic charms. Among the dozen bizarre girls were the Four Rocks. Vogue promoters became curious. Didn't they care about their image?

"What's wrong with you?" asked Mary, their classmate.

"Wrong?" asked Nubodem.

"How else can you enhance bright eyes like mine?" asked Maahtou.

"Please, leave those primitive girls alone," said Youla. They did not mind standing out by their oddness.

"You can use my makeup kit," said Stella to Maahtou.

"No thanks," answered Maahtou. "Preserve it for someone else."

Of course, the fashion simpletons were the first to get dressed and ready for the outing. With extra time in hand, six of the peculiar girls, including the Four Rocks, became observers of the all-absorbing make-up sessions. They were going from one hotspot to another and from one dormitory to another. In the end, some of them changed their minds, not Maahtou and Nubodem. The new recruits quickly rushed for their eye-pencils with which they began imitating the contouring styles in display. In their struggle, they received help from stand-by experts.

By then, almost all students were lined up at the entrance, waiting for the whistle to signal their departure. Faces were sparkling beyond the captivating contrast of red skirts and beige blouses.

The college prefect came out and clapped her hands for attention. Then, she announced that in fifteen minutes, students should begin marching down the hill.

Suddenly, three girls, Maahtou's Big, Bertha, and two other Form 4 students, Julie and Adeline, kindly invited her to the back of the dormitory for a hairdo. She did not want it, but she could not resist their gentleness.

When they got there, they asked her to sit on a stool while one of them rekindled the smothering coals in a pressing iron. Immediately, her Big damped her hair, and multiple hands began rubbing it.

Meanwhile, Julie rushed to her dormitory and grabbed Vaseline from her shower bag. Next, with the help of a tiny-toothed comb, they pulled out strands of hair into sections. Then, they hand-pressed the hair from side to side. After that, they carved Maahtou's strands at the front into contours downwards towards her face though some of the partitions were resisting redirection. Adeline wetted her hands further and damped that portion. Then she proceeded to press the first bunch of hair from her luxuriant hair towards her face. Within minutes, they finished the job. Each stepped backward and began admiring Maahtou's new and striking look.

"You see how beautiful you are?" celebrated Julie.

"*See me some fine girl, oh!*" (Look at this pretty girl!) Adeline exclaimed in Pidgin English while Bertha clapped in amazement. Then, Bertha took out her pocket mirror and held it in front of Maahtou.

"Yeah, thank you," Maahtou exclaimed as she beheld a glowing ornate look of herself. She smiled and thanked them repeatedly. Her heart began beating faster as they escorted her back to the line. All eyes were on her face; classmates came and crowded around her.

"Maahtou, you look so cute," Eposi commented.

"I tell you Maahtou, boys will hover around you like bees," remarked Youla.

"Leave her alone," said Ngwe, whose hair was too short for treatment. She contented herself with her black eyeliner as well a slight touch of powder on her face without foundation.

"Why is Youla saying that?" asked Nubodem. "If someone looks good, is it only to attract boys?" Nubodem was a thoroughly natural girl, who did not even own an eye pencil.

The more they admired Maahtou, the more she felt awkward. Had she suddenly become a photo on the wall, succumbing to the standard prescription?

"You are okay, Maahtou," reassured Bih. "Your make-up is not as exaggerated as others."

Instead of feeling happy and triumphant like the fashion queens, Maahtou felt enfeebled as if her Make-up Artists had underestimated her self-worth. To her, wearing make-up was like being pretentious. Why try to promote a dummy version of her real self, particularly with the intent to capture someone's attention?

Maahtou hoped that no boy would give her special attention as Youla had suggested. She was convinced that one's self-assuredness should be more alluring than a painted face. Similarly, if a girl already had a boyfriend, why prop up her face to maintain him or show proof of deserving him? Even if the make-up sculptors were conforming to nature's order wherein plants with nectars attract bees, Maahtou decided that she was not ready for pollination.

"Who wants a superficial boy who is enticed by make-up?"

"Indeed," said Maahtou.

"Make-up beauty is evanescent," said Bih.

"Can you imagine a boy falling in love with my picture, and not me?" asked Maahtou.

"I totally agree with you," said Ngwe.

Maahtou soon passed to action. Halfway to the stadium, she discreetly lifted her right hand towards her hair and began rearranging it in random movements. Like a hen, she scattered the arranged furrows on her hair, in a desperate search to return to her original looks. Wasn't her smile and gentle manner enough to charm any intelligent boy?

After all, with the rising temperature, heavy make-up would disappear with a little sweat and a slight touch of the handkerchief, leaving a distorted shade of colours on the face. Maquillage on hot days could become an embarrassment to a conceited girl, causing her to lose balance.

"Glory, glory, alleluia, Glory, glory, alleluia," the distracted Maahtou joined others in singing the refrain of the marching song with more confidence. The first houses beyond the road leading downtown from campus were already visible.

However, Maahtou was still upset. She compared herself to a hen. She decided that she alone had the sole duty to protect her eggs from any suggestion of premature exposure. She did not want to impress a Rock of Ages College student, though they were considered the most handsome, intelligent, and eligible guys of all the colleges in the city.

Finally, Virgin Mother's College students reached the town and were already crossing the Tee-junction. They were less than ten minutes away from the stadium. At the entrance, ushers were pointing to spots carved out for each school. Hundreds of pupils and students from dozens of academic institutions in the city were flocking in and taking their assigned places.

Within minutes, the Governor of the province arrived and took his place at the grandstand. Immediately, the Coordinator gave the signal for the official ceremony to begin. He ushered in an official who conducted the singing of the national anthem with the police band.

The second item on the program was the recognition of some newly appointed officials. Next, the Master of Ceremonies announced the debut of marching, beginning with officers, workers, and the national constituted corps. Then, it was the turn of schools, colleges, public institutions, and social groups.

The parade was over after some two hours of marching. The award of prizes for best performance in various categories received a lot of applause. The Governor and the personalities at the grandstand stood up, waved goodbye, and returned to their waiting cars.

After that, the pupils and students left their lines and began mingling with friends and family. Those whose parents or relatives were living in town, went straight home.

Nubodem's home was less than five hundred meters away. In accordance with the plan of the Four Rocks, Maahtou accompanied Nubodem home. Meanwhile, Ngwe invited Eposi to come along to her aunt's place at Azire. Other students remained at the stadium, hugging friends from other colleges and gradually dispersing in various directions. Joy was overflowing amidst the noise of a sea of voices. While some girls were excitedly chatting with boys, others seemed lost in the ocean of pupils and students.

"Wey, eh, what will I do?" wondered Sophie, a Form 3 student.

"Don't worry, if you don't meet any boy today, you will surely meet one next week," consoled Monica, her friend.

Sophie was anxious because she had been looking forward to getting a boyfriend in readiness for the upcoming annual dormitory feast day.

"So, it means that some girls turn themselves into parcels, hoping to meet a boy who will gladly accept them?" asked Maahtou.

"Let them get out," answered Nubodem. "Some of them criticize girls like me, forgetting that it's not the main reason why we are in college."

So, while the anxious girls were worried that they might end up not attracting any boy, Maahtou and Nubodem were rather grateful to have been left alone.

By the time they returned to college later in the evening, the campus was as noisy as a grand bazaar. The only subject on every lip was, which girl had been "campaigned" by which

Rock of Ages guy? Some of Maahtou's classmates ran to her, hoping to get some pleasantly surprising news, but they were disappointed.

"For how long will you continue to live in utopia?" asked Collette.

"Why did you undo your hairstyle?" asked Linda?

"What would you do when biology finally kicks in?" asked Bertha, her Big.

"No boyfriends before graduation," Maahtou answered while shaking her forefinger in the air.

"Really?" Her Big said, shaking her head jocularly. "Wait until when you can no longer ignore chemistry."

Maahtou listened without saying a word. She was not sure of what her Big meant by chemistry.

"When a handsome guy will stare at you, Maahtou, I will see how you will resist," her Big went on. All the girls around burst out laughing. "Though you are speaking boldly now, when that feeling gets hold of you, you will be digging your heels into the ground, with your head bent down," added Adeline.

"At that moment, if anyone tries to stop you, you would be quick to insist that there is chemistry between the two of you," her Big explained.

"Hahaha," her classmates who were listening all burst out laughing, giggling and clapping their hands. They were aware that Bertha was equally sending a message to each of them.

"Wait, before you realize, it will hit you like lightning," Youla insisted.

Maahtou looked on, with no more justification in her self-defence. She knew that her Big was speaking based on experience.

"Why did my Big use chemistry to talk about boys?" asked Maahtou to the other Four Rocks when they extricated themselves from the crowds.

"It's the mixture of the feelings of two people," answered Eposi.

"Also, because chemical reactions are rapid," said Nubodem.

"But what if one element refuses to mix with another?" asked Ngwe.

"Yes, that's what I wish for myself," said Maahtou, skipping up excitedly.

"I don't think you can escape love, especially if it is strong," said Eposi.

"Then, I will have to keep up the suspense until there is proof that there is no infatuation in it," answered Maahtou.

The girls burst out laughing and began walking towards their various dormitories.

Chapter 23

Boys on Campus

It was Imma-Concept dormitory's feast day. Apart from the staff, church, and some city authorities in attendance, only the Rock of Ages College received invitations. Guests from there were mainly their principal, staff, and Forms 4 and 5 students.

The all-day event was in two parts. Students of VMC played games and sports in the morning. The variety included Basketball, Handball, Volleyball, and track sports featuring running and relays. Also, there were fun-filled competitions; among them were Speed Dressing, Fastest Eater, Moukouta Bag Jumping, Bottle Head Balancing, and Egg-in-Spoon racing.

In the early afternoon, sports and games gave way to a special sumptuous lunch for all.

The crowning event of the day was the evening Social Party. Preparation took four hours. Guests and staff withdraw to refresh themselves, and to return, all clad in evening wear.

Students equally dispersed to their various dormitories to get ready. Soon, the smell of burning hair was in the air. Girls spread out dresses on their beds and began trying them on, particularly the Glows and Bricks.

"My dress is too tight," complained Pauline. "What am I going to wear?"

Maahtou and Eposi looked at each other and smiled discreetly. Pauline was a Form 4 Brick.

"Mine is instead loose," said Comfort. "Can someone give me a belt?"

Maahtou and Eposi glanced at each other again. Comfort was a Form 3 Striver.

Meanwhile, girls with make-up kits invited their friends to use whatever they wanted. Bih shared Eau de Colognes and perfumes with her Big and five other Form 4 girls. Agnes borrowed a pair of shoes from her.

Beauty items like hairpins, eye-pencils, lipstick, and perfume were passing from hand to hand, even from dormitory to dormitory. A few borrowed shawls, waist slips, belts, and matter-of-factly shoes. As for the Strivers, most of them were content with their single party dresses and shoes.

The Social night started at 7:00 p.m. The first part of the program was dedicated to a mixture of songs, poetry recitations, and skits. While presenters were entertaining guests, a select number of girls were serving snacks. They consisted of diluted soft drinks and chewables, including chin-chin, roasted groundnuts, and sandwiches.

Each class sang a song, but for the Form Ones who sang two, "This Little Light of Mine", and "Swing Low, Sweet Chariot." Apart from just singing, they acted out their songs. They equally had multiple lead singers. Thus, of all the performances, they received the most considerable applause, and a standing ovation. Some Bigs got so excited that they called out the names of their Smalls. It turned out to be a great chance to discover some of their talents in stage performance.

After thirty minutes, the Mistress of Ceremonies (MC) came forward and announced the debut of dancing time. "Are you ready to shake your body a bit?"

"Oh yes," was the chorus of answers.

"Our dear principals, members of staff, ladies and gentlemen, we are highly honoured by your presence," the MC went on.

The official opening dance was in honour of the authorities. Thus, the principal, staff, other workers, and guests from Rock of Ages College were paired up with Virgin Mother's College principal and staff. Then she signalled the DJ to play the first song.

Since it was the icebreaker, the organizers intentionally chose the song, "Baby Love" by The Supremes. Though the opening dance was formal, it caused a lot of giggling and laughter from the students. Some students were busy scrutinizing every step and move. The rest were singing along. Its gentle repetitive rhythm made for easy and smooth dancing.

"Ladies and gentlemen, it's time to increase the energy level in this hall. Are you ready? If so, let me hear your applause," the MC spoke after the first dance.

Everyone clapped while some students gave the thumbs up.

"The next song is one that everybody likes. So, please, let go, and let's have a good time together." When the acclaim toned down, the MC read the names of all the authorities, this time with a switch of dancing partners. Each of the European members of staff had a Cameroonian partner, be it a teacher or senior student.

As soon as the MC turned around, the DJ pressed the button. Of course, the rhythm was faster. The song was the popular South African tune "Pata Pata," by Miriam Makeba. The Cameroonian dancers jumped to the floor. The Reverends tried to keep up with the rhythm of their dancing partners, but their dancing steps kept going out of rhythm each time the music took on a different pace.

Soon, all eyes were on the feet of the Sisters. They were facing the biggest challenge. Some students began anticipating that they would miss their steps and probably fall, particularly the principal.

"Watch her," said a Form 4 student. "She has lost the rhythm again."

"If it were an examination, the reverends, especially the principal, would have all been dismissed," another Form 4 commented.

Not only were the principal's dancing steps out of tune with the music, but she kept changing her rhythm.

Spontaneously, the commenting Form 4 girl began doing something malicious. They started nodding and humming in sync with the dancing steps of the principal. They were saying repeatedly in pidgin, "*Kouba Kouba dog fowl*," that is, the steps of a scared running duck. Those sitting by her started laughing; some were choking with laughter while covering their mouths with their hands. Of course, they turned their laughing faces behind.

How relieved were the sisters when their song ended! "Ah, finally," one of the sisters said while rushing to her seat.

Next was a special show of Bottle Dance. It was by a select group of girls alongside some boys of Rock of Ages, all dressed in traditional costumes. The boys were wearing uniform *ngwashis* (pieces of cloth wrapped around like shorts) and singlets. As for the girls, they had on knee-length *wrappers* and blouses. The ladies also wore bands on their heads studded with cowries and cha-chas strapped to their ankles to accompany the drum music. The suppleness of their bodies, the speed and flexibility were simply amazing to behold. Thunderous applause filled the hall.

While the Bottle dancers were quitting, the DJ played a High life tune to allow time to cool down. Mostly the Cameroonian staff and a few students from both colleges stood up and danced. After that tune, popular soul music started playing. All the senior students jumped to their feet. However, what was surprising was Maahtou and Youla, both of whom spontaneously jumped up from their seats before the MC invited their class to the floor. "*See me that one them oh!* (Look at those!)" a Form 4 student exclaimed.

Apart from Eposi, the rest of the Four Rocks were not used to dancing like Maahtou. Gradually, everyone else got up on their feet, including Form 1 students.

After that, the DJ played a series of Makossa tunes. The hall became rowdy. Dancers were twisting their bodies freely in whatever direction. Next was Rock and Roll music. The principal of Rock of Ages took the hand of Sister Maureen. Male students who were already dating took advantage of it to pair up with their girlfriends.

Meanwhile, half of the dancers sat down and watched them. Rock and Roll took up all the dancing space. Soon, dancers began sweating and breathing hard. Some girls with high heels bent down and removed them and continued dancing barefooted.

Next, reggae music began playing while previous dancers sat down and fanned themselves. Only a third of the dancers of Makossa stood up.

Everyone was having fun. Students were applauding and singing along joyfully.

However, there was a brand of music, the Blues or Slow music, still awaited, without which the evening would be incomplete. Though there was no law against it, the MC and DJ deliberately kept it for last. Their wish and hope were that the Reverend Sisters would retire before they played them. The minutes were ticking away, but the Sisters refused to budge.

Tired of waiting, the DJ made the bold move and played the first slow song. The MC announced that it was a special dance. She called out the names of all the Sisters, pairing them up with male partners. To the surprise of many, they promptly stood up. Applause accompanied them to the floor. All eyes were on the deck, watching dancers moving from side to side. A few bolder male partners held the hands of the ladies and danced gently in rhythm.

The next Slow music was open to all students. All Rock of Ages boys stood up and invited girls to the floor. Dancing began civilly and with innocent, friendly movements.

Notwithstanding, and gradually so, the words of the songs became obliging, and steam started building up, making dancers bolder. From the touching of hands, some boys began wrapping their hands around the body of the girls. Others leaned over their partners and started getting closer until bodies were rubbing against each other. That instantly provoked an allergic reaction in the nuns.

In the middle of the song, the principal of Virgin Mother's College stood up. Three other Sisters followed suit. Their duty automatically changed from participants to supervisors. The nuns, clad in pretty, pleaded blue-white gowns, and hair concealed under long overflowing veils, began darting about on the dancing floor. They were searching for body-touching dance partners. The touching of body parts, other than hands, was not allowed between boys and girls. They kept on spotting such couples and proceeded to separate them with wide-open hands.

After the first song ended, the Sisters went and sat down. However, more dancers stood up at the second Slow dance. Instead of dancing couples respecting the no-touching order of the principal, dancers decidedly became more daring. They were holding each other and even closing their eyes while dancing.

Shocked, the principal stood up in the middle of the song while all eyes were on her. She walked straight up, pressed the button of the turntable with the force of fury as if she would have ripped off the pin had it not instantly stopped. Then, she proceeded to the microphone and called out on the girls, especially the senior students, to order.

"Girls and our dear guests, I'm sorry for interrupting the fun," said the principal. "We want to ensure that you don't trample upon the high moral values taught in both of our institutions. So, please, don't spoil the fun by allowing your emotions to rule over you."

All the dancers returned to their seats. A long pause followed until the principal lifted her hand high from her seat, authorizing the music and dancing to go on. By then, the DJ had gathered the slow records and placed them at the bottom of the pile of documents.

The music resumed as the DJ began playing soul music and Meringue alternately. Dancing couples returned to the floor, but in the middle of the song, some couples started holding each other rather too tightly, though it was not a blues tune. Those sensual dancers had overstepped their bounds. The principal stood up like a soldier responding to a high command. She walked across the hall to the turntable and turned off the whole system. Then, she asked the DJ to unplug the cables and wrap up the records. There and then, she confiscated the system, parts of which the other sisters picked up.

The abrupt interruption of Social that evening made it a sad ending; students grumbled and complained. Some followed the principal and pleaded, but she turned a deaf ear. She and the others left the hall with the music player in hand, which they took away to the convent.

8:30 p.m. was too early to retire to bed after such an exciting day. There was up to one hour left for the official closing time. Besides, special student guests from Rock of Ages were still around, looking lost. How else could they spend the evening together? All the authorities were gone. So, students began chatting with their boyfriends. The rest were standing mostly in small groups here and there, wasting time.

The sisters had hardly had time to reach the convent, when a new sound of music erupted from the hall. All the students in the corridor rushed back into the hall. They were emanating from unusual dancing instruments: school drums. Everyone was astounded. "My goodness!" exclaimed some guys of Rock of Ages.

"What ingenuity!" other students exclaimed.

And guess who were hitting them— Youla, Odile, and Agnes. The girls had rushed into the store downstairs and triumphantly brought along a large drum and two small ones for a very timely rescue.

They were already playing some soul music. "Inside out," Youla was singing and others responded, "boy you touch me." Some students began dancing. The MC rushed in and signalled to those who were still standing in the corridors. They moved right to the centre of the hall. In full force, they played a piece of famous soul music. The MC requested the drummers to start all over. Spontaneously, a few students who were still outside began singing to Diana Ross' Upside Down. "Boy you turn me," the rest answered while dancing towards the hall.

The number of dancers began growing from fifteen to thirty until most students, including the boys from Rock of Ages, were in the hall dancing and singing along. Agnes began singing too. Many others chimed in. Meanwhile, three more girls rushed out in search of other instruments. Together they formed an orchestra. The Four Rocks and the rest of Youla's classmates stood by watching her. "Club Cent has moved to the campus," commented Maahtou and Eposi. "You bet," other concurred.

Excitement continued building up. Soon, lead singers began mimicking popular songs. As they displayed their ability to sing, requests started coming from the floor. Right on the spot, lead singers motivated other soloists. Meanwhile, singers hummed unknown parts of the lyrics of current songs until they got to the climactic end of it.

"This is an extraordinary party," commented staunch party goers, clapping and happy that it had everything to make for an exciting Social. Indeed, the night turned out to be more entertaining than planned, filled with applause and shout-out compliments.

Better still, that night, students discovered talented musicians among them. More than ten soloists, among whom three boys from Rock of Ages. They were singing traditional music, soul, Makossa, slow and reggae. Both guests and hosts danced to the point of sweating on the dance floor.

Outstanding performers received the most applause. The stars for the evening were in two distinct categories: dancers and singers. The thrilled guests from Rock of Ages were so moved that they expressed their satisfaction. "We will henceforth include drum music in our parties," said the college prefect.

"We can't wait to discover other soloists through drum parties," said their overjoyed social prefect.

In the end, the boys hugged their friends, and waved goodbye to all. They promised to share the inspiring event of the unexpected outcome with their college mates.

As for the happily exhausted girls, they retired to their beds and slept profoundly.

Chapter 24

Love Relaxes Control

Surprisingly, the principal did not scrap Social from college events despite confiscating the record player during the celebration of Imma-Concept dormitory feast day. Instead, the number of Socials increased. Barely a month after the crisis of that evening's Social, a decision by the principal put a smile on student's faces. Dormitory feast day celebrations were going to become more adventurous. Henceforth, students would take part in Socials beyond the campus.

According to the decision, the principal requested prefects to pair each dormitory with another in the most renowned boys' secondary school, Rock of Ages College (RAC). Their campus was at the far end of town. According to the new arrangement, each dormitory would take a turn in partaking in the feast day celebration of 'her brother's dorm' at RAC.

Students shouted with joy and danced on campus upon receiving news of the twining of dormitories. "Who would have imagined this? So, we will have a chance to see the RAC campus," said a Form 3 student.

"So, finally, caged birds would be set free to fly for a whole day," said Delphine, a Form 5 student.

"Yeah, I will see how she will stop us from touching the guys," Rachel, a Form 4 student, said.

However, amidst the joyous shouts of those eager to meet their boyfriends, some students began suffering from anxiety. They were the girls without boyfriends. Those were not ready to flap their emotional wings in flight with boys. Between the two extremes was the neutral group who had brothers, cousins, or other relatives at RAC.

Rather than go with the flow, some students became curious. They kept asking, "What has prompted this radical change?" Another student questioned, "What had moved

Orpah to grant us more liberty?" Orpah was the nickname of the principal. It was inspired by a Bible character. The biblical Orpah was willing to separate from her mother-in-law after her husband died. Similarly, the principal was often criticized for keeping students at arm's length. Unlike Ruth in the Bible, who followed her mother-in-law, Naomi, to her country, after losing her husband, Orpah definitively estranged herself.

The curious girls persisted in their quest of what had caused Orpah to backtrack. Finally, their curiosity caught the attention of more students. They began wondering why their disappointment had changed into an opportunity overnight. Was the principal trying to make amends for the seizing of the record player during the last party?

"Who knows what happened between her and Tata (nickname of the principal of RAC) during the last social?" asked a Form 5 student.

The student who first raised the question, Gladys, a Form 4 student, suggested that a mathematical approach could lead to an answer. Immediately, Elizabeth, a Form 5 concurred. In fact, she called it "an equation to be solved."

Straight away, Elizabeth wrote down an equation: confiscation of the record player + dancing with drums = XXX+girls attending feast days in RAC.

Gladys and Judith, her classmates, went from dormitory to dormitory with the equation to elicit interest as well as obtain further suggestions for their inquiry.

"We believe that something palpable motivated Orpah to officially declare a boogie license," announced the original pollster, Gladys, in each dormitory. "We want to hear what you think must have obliged her to make this decision."

By evening, they succeeded in garnering the interest of students within the ranks of the senior classes of Forms 4 and 5. Later, a dozen more students joined the research team. Guesses made up a basketful of opinions submitted by students. On Sunday after lunch, they gathered at the hall and brainstormed on the best approach to obtain the missing part of the equation.

They began classifying collected ideas, but unfortunately, interest dwindled, causing original adherents to quit. They preferred to focus on their homework. In the end, only Gladys and Judith held on. They sat on the stairs, wondering whether they should also give up. Just then, a Form 3 student, Adelaide, joined them. She was the best algebra student in her class. Besides, Adelaide's classmates fondly called her Miss Curiosity. Gladys and Judith welcomed her with a hug. What caught Adelaide's attention in the quest was the idea of applying Algebra to life. Indeed, she code-named the quest Life Application Algebra (LAA).

"Though the two of us are Form 4 students," said Judith, "your sheer enthusiasm places you above class consideration," noted Gladys.

So, the trio of the boogie license quest resolved to keep building up momentum until they balanced the equation. The tenacity of the three girls led others to henceforth refer to them as Equation Solvers (ES).

The ES began by analysing all the reasons so far submitted. Some of them were blatantly funny like "*Na ndjumba palaver*" (it's a sensual matter); "Slow dancing touched a hidden nerve;" "Is it forbidden for sisters to fall in love?" "I saw how Tata was eyeing Orpah during the opening of the floor;" "Maybe rock and roll created a longing for freedom," and so on.

As for opposers of the quest, some wrote, "do not blaspheme;" "Mind your own business," "the clergy are celibate," "focus on your classwork and leave them alone;" etc.

Of course, the ES put aside the vetoes of the opposing group and concentrated on the endorsements. The most recurrent answers became the basis for their hypothesis: There is romantic chemistry between the two principals, and they have decided to give it a chance.

"Hahaha," students laughed from dormitory to dormitory after the ES announced their hypothesis.

"Are you crazy," declared a senior student in Regina dormitory. "So, you don't know that romance, and much less, intimate relations are forbidden by the church?" It was common knowledge that all Reverend Brothers and Sisters of the Roman Catholic Church had taken the oath of celibacy.

"This sounds like a kola nut gift," said Maahtou to the other Four Rocks when they first heard about the ES quest. Everyone nodded but for one.

"I doubt it," said Nubodem.

"Why?" asked Ngwe and Eposi.

"It's like questioning the morality of the authorities," said Nubodem.

"They are looking for facts," said Ngwe.

"It sounds quite interesting," said Eposi. "I want to know what's going on."

"Above everything else, it's a way of testing theory," said Maahtou.

"Exactly," concurred Eposi and Ngwe.

Nubodem just shook her head in a disinterested manner.

Opposition notwithstanding, the ES started nosing around like hounds for proof to support their hypothesis. On Wednesday evening during prep time, two cars arrived from town. They were a white Volkswagen and a light blue Renault 4, belonging to the principal and another Brother, both of RAC, respectively. Their high speed left behind a trail of dust. They headed for the convent; located some four hundred meters away.

The trio made a note of it. Then, they decided to continue observing from their respective classes. That evening, prep was over when the cars had not yet returned. So, instead of going to the refectory, two ES waited by the terrace. The third went to the refectory and collected their dinner plates. After about half an hour, they heard approaching cars. One ES quickly crossed to the West side of the road. The first car drove past with just one person inside, a brother. The second car followed.

"Did you see what I saw?" said the ES who had crossed the road.

"We did," confirmed the other two.

They had sighted Orpah at the passenger seat of the car of RAC's principal. They carried the news to the students. Upon hearing their assertion, two respected Form 5 students shook their heads in disagreement. Of course, their observation was not conclusive of a relationship between the two.

"Seeing two people in a car is not conclusive," said one of the two respected Form 5s without mincing her words.

That notwithstanding, the ES refused to give up. Next, they kept an investigative eye on the principal's attitude and movements for weeks. One evening, having stayed back in class to catch up with homework, they finally left when it was already night-time. As they walked out of their class, they saw the light reflecting from the principal's office. It was unusual for her to be in her office at that late hour. So, they whispered to each other and tiptoed while passing in front of the academic building in pitch darkness.

Quietly, they approached the principal's office as softly as if they had become as light as cotton balls. When they got there, they stopped and strained their ears. Two people were talking, one of them was undoubtedly a male. Although the voices were not audible enough, they decided that there was a high probability to their guess. Satisfied, they walked away. As soon as they got to the last step, they saw a car parked by the curb.

"Is that not Tata's car?" asked ES1 rhetorically.

"Who is going to deny that something is going on between them?" ES2 stated.

ES3 nodded and smiled, thrilled. The trio moved on, feeling triumphant. They gave each other a high five and rushed to the dormitories to report.

"What's strange about that?" asked the first Form 5 who first heard their report.

They related their findings to other Form 5s.

"It's normal for the heads of two major institutions to have an extended discussion after normal business hours," stated another Form 5.

"Let's not listen to her," cautioned ES3. "Her elder sister is in a convent in Nso."

So far, the overall feedback from senior students was discouraging. So, they began wondering if there was any reason to pursue their search.

"But we have to balance the equation," urged ES3, eager to see her LAA dream come true. It was the encouraging voice they needed to go on.

There was no turning back. The ES kept sharing their findings. Once more, the ES came together during breaktime the following day and brainstormed. If the principal confiscated the music and then woke up one morning and threw the girls back into the arms of boys, then that was tantamount to denouncing her lifelong moral principles. What was the reason for the sudden change? They were determined to find the missing link.

It was a sunny Saturday afternoon. Lunch was over. Most girls were out enjoying both the bright sunshine and the intermittent cool breeze. Others were watching their laundry; they were removing dry clothes from the lines.

Suddenly, they heard approaching cars. Girls turned around and looked, including ES2. Three cars drove past by and went straight up to the convent.

"There must be a party going on at the convent," commented a Form 4 student.

The news spread quickly.

The ES got excited. It was a timely bait. They communicated among themselves and decided to do the most daring thing ever. Each of them, armed with a book in hand agreed to go on an adventure. They went past the first and second terraces right up to the third level. Hardly anyone ever put foot there. It was the closest vantage point from where to view the convent. They pushed away gravel and up-rooted weeds to make a nice seat for themselves.

By then, the sun was cooling down. The sky was still and blue. Birds were chirping away in the nearby bushes. A bird or two flew overhead and headed towards the eucalyptus trees by the valley beyond their classroom. There was total silence at the convent as if the sisters had gone away on vacation.

The whole convent was fenced in by barbed wires. Creeping flowers were all over, shielding it from any direct view from the outside.

However, from their end, there was elephant grass that provided an extra shield.

The ES girls strained to see what was going on inside. For the very first time, they saw a beautiful white mansion with wooden doors and light blue windows with iron protectors. The house was big enough to host at least six families, all of that for five sisters.

The yard had a well-kept lawn with extensive flower beds, bordering a tennis court at the far end.

"Wow! Look at that," whispered ES2.

"I wonder if any of them knows how to play tennis," remarked ES1.

"I wish they built one like that for the students," said ES3.

"Why don't they organize official visits on special days for students?" asked ES1. The convent was out of bounds. Had it not been for their research, they would have graduated and gone away without ever setting eyes on the private residence.

The girls went back to their reading while whispering to each other from time to time.

Suddenly, and after waiting for approximately an hour, the front door opened. Mixed voices of male and female began coming out of the mansion. A car trunk opened and closed. They saw a brother pull out a blue-handled racket. Something unexpected was about to happen.

"I've not played tennis for almost a year," said sister Jane.

Brother Andrew opened and closed the trunk of his car. "I got a new tennis racket early this year when I travelled to Ireland," he said.

The three ES closed their books in unison as if someone had pushed the "close" button on the remote control. With elephant ears, they stretched out their necks to pick up every sound. Luckily, the voices of the players were growing louder. They identified their principal's voice and that of a staff member, Sister Maureen. No student had an idea that the sisters could play tennis. Though they were excited, they remained silent like cats while peeping through and admiring the barbed wire fence adorned by creeping flowers from the inside and invaded by grass from their side, the outside.

With eyes enlarged like an owl's, they saw the hair of the sisters flying in the air. Sister Maureen spoke in her characteristic tender voice, now sounding seductive. Her enchanting beauty came out in its fullness with her unveiled head exposing curly hair flowing beyond her neck. She was the perfection of beauty. Students have often wondered why she chose to become a Reverend Sister. Then without warning, they heard the principal calling out in a friendly, tender, and alluring voice to her play partner. Like a chameleon in a new environment, the stern, formal tone of the principal turned into a soft one, inviting sweetness.

So far, the Reverends have revealed the unsuspecting sides of themselves. The ES could not get over her blushing when the RAC principal served the ball to her.

"Mamamié!" exclaimed ES1 in a low tone.

"Camouflage," said ES2.

Meanwhile, ES3 raised her eyebrows in shock. The ES looked at each other in total dismay. What more evidence did they need? Their lips were itching to take back the news to the rest of the girls.

It was time to go. They began crawling on fours over the gravelled soil until they reached the edge of the terrace. From there, they dropped onto the next terrace. After that, they stood up and ran the rest of the way to the campus.

When they got to the terrace by the entrance, they decided to conclude before taking the news to fellow students.

"After all we saw and heard, is there any more doubt?" asked ES1

"Did we even know that we will stumble on so many facts?" asked ES2

"Wow! So, our equation is solved," shouted ES3 while jumping excitedly and clapping both hands.

"So, what's our conclusion?" asked ES2.

ES1 pulled out the equation paper from her book, and all three of them looked at it and took a deep breath. They looked at each other and smiled. <confiscation of record player + dancing with drums = XXX+attending feast days in RAC>.

ES1 borrowed ES2's pen and asked the other two what they should write in the blank. They exchanged ideas and decided to make it simple and clear. Thus, ES1 took the paper and filled in the blank as follows: <seizure of record player + dancing with drums = Tata and Orpah in an idyllic garden of roses+girls attending feast days in RAC>.

From their findings, they deduced a vital truth; namely, no one can give to another person what they do not have. That was the theory upon which they drew their conclusion. Thanks to their adventure, they had discovered their campus' own Garden of Eden; it was a picturesque sight. Only students who would become Reverend Sisters would one day see the charming spot.

Rather than condemning Tata and Orpah, the Equation Solvers were happy for them.

"After all, is there anything that could bring more joy into one's heart?" asked ES1.

"Not at all," responded ES2 and ES3 in chorus.

It was time for them to go and announce their results. They were going to start with Ave Maria and Imma-Concept, where they had more followers. Then, followed by Regina and Assumption.

"You, doubting Thomases, we will see how you will argue again," said ES1, their Spokesperson.

The dormitory was quiet, and students listened to the persistent and daunting ES.

"The facts are glaring," ES1 went on.

A lot of girls expressed total admiration to the ES for their display of courage. Those were not questioning the validity of their research. The veto girls, the fervently holy students, were broiling in indignation.

"Your so-called research, and unwarranted pursuit, is as good as sinning," said Theresia. She and her supporters argued that by seeking to know too much, the ES were sowing seeds of discord. They feared that the results would cause rebellion against rules regarding boyfriends.

"Girls, let me tell you, you have gone too far," warned Celina, another veto girl.

"Why are you ignoring the rose and picking up on the thorns?" cried out ES2 in retort. The ES refused to be drowned by the menace of the veto girls. The reality was clear. Two people stopped and smelled the roses without fixing on the thorns. Romantic chemistry became the outcome. Without the duo sharing the fragrance of the roses, Orpah would not have granted them more freedom with the boys.

"Have you ever asked why a man gives flowers to the woman with whom he has fallen in love?" asked Elizabeth. All the girls in the dormitory applauded.

Thus, Elizabeth motivated the ES. Despite the heated debate, the researchers continued insisting on the importance of smelling the petals to savour the freedom of love.

The Four Rocks were split on the issue. While Maahtou and Eposi were in support of the ES, Nubodem dismissed it as a distraction. As for Ngwe, she was waiting for the outcome to make up her mind. The only point on which they all agreed was their common concern for the barriers separating students into social classes. How they wished the ES method could be replicated to increase the level of kindness and gentleness on campus.

By the time the ES toured all the dormitories, a Form 4 student, Clara, advanced the strongest arguments to debunk the ES findings.

"You can say what you want, but if you knew how lonely the clergy were, you would not be spying on them," said Clara.

"If they are serving God, what is there to hide?" ES1 retorted.

"It's their private life," Clara added.

"Be there, I hope you join them soon at the convent," said ES2.

Clara stood up without warning and walked away. A good number of students knew about her connections with a European Priest. For the past months, each Sunday after mass at the Cathedral, while students promptly return to campus, Clara would extricate herself with the pretext of greeting her family members.

However, her continuous absence from Sunday lunch started raising eyebrows. Her Small would take her food to the dormitory, but she would return one to two hours later and show no interest in eating. Often, she arrived with a variety of packs of biscuits.

"*Booh* (my friend), is he preaching personal sermons to you or what?" two of her friends once cornered her.

"No, we are just friends," explained Clara.

"Friend?" asked the other friend, a Form 5 student.

Clara nodded and reassured them that there was no problem.

Despite her explanations, students remained perplexed. How could a female student befriend a priest and visit him alone for up to an hour? What could they be discussing or doing during those visits?

Soon, Clara came back into the dormitory with a frown on her face. Students stayed quiet to avoid trouble, but Clara decided to speak out.

"I know what you are thinking about," she told the ES in the presence of the whole dormitory. "Have you ever heard of a platonic relationship?" she asked them with an air of pride.

Onlookers burst out laughing while younger students rushed for their dictionaries.

Meanwhile, Clara continued enjoying her fun-time with the priest week after week until it soon became routine.

"Do you see the extent to which curiosity can push students?" some of Clara's friends said, referring to the ES research. "They pry right into the paradise of Reverend Sisters."

"Where did they have the time?" others wondered.

"Imagine me with one brain trying to memorize science formulae and barely coping with menstrual pains," said Suzie. "You have that much time to waste?"

Whether the ES or Clara was right or not in their respective declarations, Elizabeth, who had come up with the equation, stood up and calmed down the girls. "I don't see any contradiction between ES, Clara, and Celibacy proponents," said Miss Elizabeth. "The ES girls wanted to do Life Application Algebra or LAA for short. They have done it without the intent of hurting anyone. So, don't mistake their motives for the facts staring into our faces. Peace! Peace! Peace!"

Girls applauded. Maahtou and Eposi instantly became fans of the ES. They decided to join Miss Elizabeth to accompany them to the other dormitories. Each time Miss Elizabeth explained, following agitations, they gave her loud applause. However, there was a student at Assumption dormitory who loudly expressed her lack of interest. "I should rather be thinking of what I would wear to RAC," said Mary Magdalene.

Ngwe joined the two members of the Four Rocks when it was time to go to Regina. The ES found out that they had the highest number of veto and uninterested students combined. Nubodem was one of them. She was reading behind the dormitory, as the three members of the Four Rocks later found out.

Surprisingly, the adherents of Regina were equally the loudest. Three senior students stood up and picked up the ES. "You girls are brainboxes," Felicitas, one of the girls said.

"Keep using your inquisitive mind," the second said.

Meanwhile, the third suggested that the ES be rewarded for their efforts. A few girls donated groundnuts and sweets.

"I'm just eager to see if in reality the twinning of dormitories with RAC will hold," said Ngwe.

"Let's wait and see," the other members of the Four Rocks answered.

Chapter 25

A Taste of Romance

Ave Maria dormitory was the first to go to Rock of Ages College (an all-boys institution) to attend their twin dormitory party. One week into the Social, girls began worrying about what dress to wear.

On the eve of the intercollege Social, most girls plaited their hair into *Begoudi*. The plan was to undo it an hour or so before departure. That way, the thread would have formed tight, long-lasting curls. The demand was high. That evening, Maahtou *bigoudied* the hair of up to eight girls. The most difficult ones were those with short and coarse hair. It required pulling the strands several times from their roots to obtain the minimum length for twisting.

At last, the news-making day arrived. It was a sunny Sunday. Departure was scheduled for 10.00 a.m. Taxicabs were invited on campus to transport the girls.

On the way, most students were singing and cracking jokes. Maahtou and Eposi were smiling and making faces at each other. They did not know any student of Rock. Maahtou's brother had graduated the previous year. Meanwhile, the more daring girls were busy guessing which of the nervous girls might be "campaigned" by a boy. A few were rather anxious about the possibility of losing their guy to another girl.

From the minute that the girls entered in through the massive iron gates, it felt like landing on an enchanted planet. Shyness, joy, and excitement were like a perfume mixed to varying degrees of intensity, and then sprayed on each girl's cheeks.

The program opened with a tour of the campus and dormitories. It was a befitting icebreaker. Girls saw for themselves how well or how poorly boys made up their beds. A few guys decorated their beds with flowers and personal photos while others left their sheets twisted and ruffled. It was difficult for the boys to hide their identity as their names were on the beds, safe for those who scribbled instead of writing theirs legibly.

Lunchtime arrived. The boys led the girls into a large hall and got them seated. According to a predetermined plan, sitting was not according to classes. Each table had students from each class. Meanwhile, at least two girls were at each table.

Just before prayers, the college prefect ushered in the principal. What a pleasant surprise for the girls! They had never seen their own principal in their refectory. Everyone stood up at the same time.

Brother Emmanuel greeted the Virgin Mother College's school prefect, Bridget, who was sitting at one end of the rectangular table for eight in the middle of the hall. Then he shook hands with Rock of Ages' school prefect, saying, "be the perfect host," to all the boys." The senior student nodded while the rest responded, "of course," and others, "we will do our best." Their senior prefect, Vincent, re-echoed the principal's entreaty while lifting his right forefinger. Spontaneously, students gave him the thumbs up.

"As the first delegation e-v-er, of g-i-r-ls, to visit our college, I want you to know that we are great-ly honor-ed to have you in our midst," the principal said excitedly in his characteristic friendly tone. He paused, looked and waved at the guests from table to table. The girls applauded. Some of the senior students stood up and curtsied. Then he raised his voice and added, "I hope that you will all have a great time here today." He gave them a gap-toothed smile. The girls responded with "thank you" and gave several rounds of applause. He was a handsome man with an engaging personality. The students of both colleges liked him. Indeed, whenever his car drove past Virgin Mother's College, any girls in sight would greet him from afar off with raised hands. Promptly, the principal waved to them and left the dining hall.

Maahtou and Eposi were seated two tables apart. They were missing the other Four Rocks, but they were lucky to be facing each other. From time to time, they looked at each other and smiled timidly. At one time Eposi discreetly held up her left hand with crossed fingers. Maahtou closed her eyes and smiled.

The smell of onions in the salad as well as that of the tomato stew with ginger, caused mouths to water. Rather than just serving a single meal for everyone, the menu offered choices. It was either rice and beans; rice and stew or *njama njama* and yellow yams. The variety generated table talks which greatly facilitated communication. Girls who had not yet uttered a word began talking about the dishes.

The prefect of Virgin Mother's College clapped her hands in total surprise. "Are boiled yams a regular dish here?" she asked.

"No, not at all, responded the boy to her right.

"You have no idea how many hours we spent in meetings looking for ways to impress you?" said Vincent. The other boys at the table smiled while two others nodded.

"Oh, my goodness!" exclaimed Bridget. "We will never forget that you went the extra mile to make us feel at home."

In the early afternoon, games and sports came next. There was basketball, volleyball, and some track sports. The girls were content to be spectators. Entertainment of the guests reached its peak level. Laughing, clapping, and shouting praises to excellent performers were all in the mix.

After an hour and a half, the games were over. The players were accorded time to refresh themselves while random chatting was going on. After that, the late afternoon dance party, the last event for the day, followed. When the ushers let their guests of honor in, the social activity hall was ready. Everyone took their place. There were over a hundred students.

Immediately, the girls noticed something unusual. Unlike the Virgin Mother's College parties, neither the principals nor staff members were present. The girls began commenting in small groups. "What would be the conduct of students left to themselves?" "The authorities know that we can handle this without any problems," said a Form 5 student who overheard the two girl senior students.

As expected, the party began with refreshments. While they were eating chin-chin, roasted groundnuts, biscuits, and cake, light music was playing. Soon after, it was time for jokes and riddles. They were done successively by three renowned Campus Comedians. The last of them got everyone cracking up with laughter while he exited.

"Bis, bis, one more time, bis," girls began shouting spontaneously from their seats.

"Sorry, no more" said the Master of Ceremonies (MC). "We are reserving it for your next visit," he went on.

Then he turned around and glanced at the DJ. The first song began playing. It was reserved for the opening of the floor. It began with all the Form 5 students, including prefects, some of whom were Form 4 students. The second dance came as a surprise to the girls. It was for the Form 1s; a new and popular disco piece of music by The Hues Corporation.

"We want to welcome our small sisters and brothers in a special way," said the MC. "You are the first batch to attend a party on a boys' campus upon admission into college. Can we put our hands together and clap for them?"

The applause went up with whistling sounds and lots of giggling.

The designated dancers were all looking very shy. Some were even trembling. Youla stood from her seat abruptly, sat down, shook her body, and sat back. As a Mankon resident and someone who had been to popular clubs downtown, a handful of boys knew her. Like her, Maahtou and Eposi wished they were Form 1s. It was a familiar tune to the two friends, who were sitting at a 45% angle on two separate benches.

Promptly, MC requested the Form 1s to raise their hands. He paired them up randomly. There were more boys than girls.

So, he pleaded with the extra boys to hold on for their turn. In the middle of the song, the MC asked for applause to encourage them.

The fourth tune was for everyone. Students could choose their own partners. Apart from girls who were quickly taken by their boyfriends, each girl was waiting for the boys to invite them to the dance floor. It could take only about a third of the total number present. The bold ones as well as senior students stood up first. Dancing started with a mixture of daring and timidity from both boys and girls.

Twenty minutes into dancing, everyone noticed that boys had invited some girls several times while others just sat and watched. "Hey guys, be nice. Don't just invite your sisters, cousins, or friends to the floor," said the MC. "This is your opportunity to make new friends."

"Remember what the principal said this morning?" asked the senior prefect, who stood up to encourage the boys. "Don't let any girl leave this campus today with a frown," he added.

Maahtou and Eposi sat at a corner watching girls with boyfriends enjoying themselves. They were all senior students but for two girls in Form 2.

Meanwhile, a handful of Form 5 students seemed to be more interested in showing off their outfits than dancing. Their dresses were perfectly matched with their shoes.

Before long, three girls began attracting attention to themselves. They were one Form 4 and two Form 3 students. First, they were rowdy, applauding, commenting, and making gestures. Those bold girls who were sitting close to each other stood up, boldly walked across the hall and invited three boys to dance with them during two records. They danced freely from disco music, Makossa to Slow without any effort to create security gaps between partners, as their principal would have advised.

"Look at them," said Celine to her classmate who was sitting next to her. "Those two dancing partners have become Siamese twins."

Orpah can't tolerate this," remarked Pauline, a Form 5 student.

It was clear to everyone that unchecked freedom was like sliding downhill into a deep dark pit.

"Now, you can see the importance of a boarding school," said Pauline.

"You mean single-sex boarding school," stressed Celine.

Pauline nodded.

"Those who often blame Orpah for being too strict can see for themselves," said Celine.

"You bet," answered Pauline.

"Maybe, this new law to grant us more freedom was to let us see for ourselves how far we can push the limits," said Celine.

"I know," answered Pauline.

Maahtou and Eposi who were already in Form 3 did not yet have boyfriends, but they liked dancing. Maahtou could dance well and better than most girls, but her heart was beating extremely fast. Indeed, each time a boy walked across the room towards her angle, her heart began beating even more swiftly. Only about half of her classmates had so far danced. While Maahtou's mind was still straying into the times she used to dance at home, a boy was coming.

He came and extended his hand to Eposi. She was not as nervous as Maahtou. She jumped to her feet and followed the boy. It was a Makossa tune. Eposi let go, dancing and twisting her body. Those who were watching the dancers gave them loud applause.

Maahtou was struggling to regain her composure. Though she naturally grabs the first opportunity for an adventure, dancing with a boy was like venturing into a virgin forest or jumping into a river with swift waves without the ability to swim. She even started imagining that anxiety could cause her to fall on the floor. What a disgrace would that be in the presence of a hundred pairs of eyes! Maahtou began wishing she had not come. She felt so inhibited that she became content with the visit that was filled with many first-time experiences.

It was already the sixth dance since the party started, and the DJ was selecting another record. Maahtou tried to bolster her courage, just in case it was a disco tune, and someone invited her. If it were Makossa, she would accept an invitation but try not to shake her buttocks as fast as some of the girls were doing. If it were rock-and-roll, she hoped that her partner would be gentle enough to give her a chance to enjoy it without missing any steps. However, if it happened to be slow, she would prefer to lend her legs to someone more daring.

Whether Maahtou was dreaming or actively observing, willing or unwilling, a well-polished, sophisticated-looking, light brown, average height guy, quickened his steps towards her direction. As he came closer, she quickly glanced to her right and left, but his legs were barely one step from Maahtou.

"Hello," said the guy, standing right in front of her and opening his stretched-out hands.

"Hi," said Maahtou while stretching her right arm to him.

Maahtou looked at his face and smiled. Immediately, she began thinking about the handsome Darcy in *Pride and Prejudice*, the book they were currently studying in class. "How are you doing," said the Darcy lookalike. She looked up, and said "fine, thank you." Maahtou's heart leaped as he helped her to stand up. He led her close to the centre of the floor, her right hand in his tight grip. It was like Desire meeting Anxiety. Maahtou managed to steal a second glance at his face and noticed that he was indeed handsome. She shuddered at the first step but thanked God that he had not noticed her trembling. He was carried away by the music, singing along, "How Deep is Your Love" by the Bee Gees.

Within minutes, she was surprised that her shaking legs were becoming faster and rendering her body more agile. 'Darcy' and Maahtou were getting closer to the centre of the hall, her hand in his. He was leaving her no time to pause and think whether they were already crossing the principal's Berlin wall or not.

Who could have imagined that her first dance would be a Slow dance? Immediately, 'Darcy's' right hand tenderly held Maahtou around her waist. She could tell by his tender hesitating movements that he was a gentleman. The softness of his hands made Maahtou wonder whether he has ever touched a cutlass, let alone a hoe. She concluded that he was either a Glow or a Brick. In any case, he was well brought up, she thought to herself.

Maahtou's body jerked a little though, so far, she was doing a good job. Those who were watching the dancers began clapping for Maahtou. She thought that maybe the spectators were applauding for someone else, but her mates were pointing at her. She hoped that she would not miss any step. However, she credited the cheers more to her partner's ability to steer her on. 'Darcy' was indeed a good dancer. Maahtou managed to steal another glance at his face. Their eyes met and he smiled. They were having a good time. Maahtou hoped and prayed that she could keep her steps in rhythm to his.

Gradually, Maahtou began having fun. She wanted to relax and enjoy the music, but heat, from nowhere, started building up inside her. She imagined that if she were an ice block, she would have melted before the record ended. Indeed, tiny drops of sweat started collecting on her forehead.

Finally, the music came to a gradual end. 'Darcy' held her hand and accompanied her to her seat. He bowed and smiled. She smiled back timidly and thanked him. Maahtou's heartbeat settled. She began wondering how well she had performed.

"You have a very nice dress," said Rosemary. "And it fits you very well."

The new checked brown, flair dress was made by Moonshee during her last vacation. Maahtou was more grateful to her elder sister. Moonshee had offered her a saving grace. It was the most elegant dress she had.

Maahtou began thinking of her mother. She wanted so badly to tell her she had finally danced with a boy. It was a first-time experience since reaching her teens. Whatever the rating, she was happy to have travelled some long miles on the social terrain. As far as she was concerned, it was a great achievement.

By sunset, the first group of girls got back to the campus. They met the rest of the students crowded at the entrance to hear the highlights of their premier prolonged encounter with boys.

Maahtou was in the third group that was welcomed by noisy groups of overly excited students. Some girls had volunteered to be announcers. They were interviewing the party goers and dishing out headliners at the top of their voices, mimicking broadcasters. As soon as they heard the latest reports, they transmitted it to others. The details were about which girl danced well as well as which was "campaigned," especially in the junior classes.

Dozens of stories and anecdotes kept circulating from group to group, laced with tickling comments.

"Can you believe that no guy, except her cousin, invited Youla to dance," Therese, her classmate whispered.

"Oh yeah, what happened?" asked Vivian.

"Is there anyone who doesn't know her?" asked Therese rhetorically. "Maybe she turned them off by her loud talking, gestures and continuous giggling."

"Sometimes, it's just better to become a Cinderella," said Julie.

"Hahaha!" the girls laughed. "The first shall be the last," they chanted.

During the crisscross of anecdotes, Maahtou's performance hit the top of the charts. Even senior students gathered around her. "We heard that Darcy chose you," said Ngwe.

"We also heard that you danced very well," added Nubodem.

"Let me tell you," said Eposi. Maahtou was the star of the day."

"Yes, indeed." Gwen, a Form 4 student. "Not only was she and the boy a perfect match, but her flare dress was just swinging from left to right as if a gentle breeze was blowing it in rhythm."

Students kept coming to embrace Maahtou. She was pleasantly surprised. Of all the outrageous, daring, and classy performances, how could hers generate such interest? All along, she had no idea that students who had hardly ever spoken to her had been watching her. Notwithstanding, she understood that all the thrill about her was because she did not yet have a boyfriend.

"This is just the beginning," said Rita.

"Everyone is on your case because they know that all your romance talk is just theory," said Eposi. Maahtou enjoyed sharing ideas from the books she read. As for dancing, she was grateful to her elder sister, Bongshee, for often playing music and requesting her to dance at home. It all began with her village traditional girls' dance group, Makongui. Not until she reached the floor, did it become clear that she was ready for a western-styled dance party.

All through the weekend, the RAC party was the main subject of conversation in all the four dormitories. On Monday, fingers were still pointing at Maahtou. Her Big, Bertha, came along with her friends and shook Maahtou's hands after class.

"You remember my chemistry prophecy?" Bertha asked.

Maahtou smiled and giggled.

"These girls think that it is easy to have a boyfriend and still concentrate on studies," said Nubodem when they were by themselves.

"They are obviously speaking from experience," said Eposi.

"Let them excel in GCE, then we will know that they are tough," said Ngwe.

"Some of them are just aiming at obtaining passes in the minimum number of papers," stressed Nubodem.

"I hope that I will not receive a love letter from RAC before this term ends," said Maahtou.

"Hahaha," they girls laughed and gave each other high fives.

Chapter 26

Vocation Week

"In nomine Patris, et Filii, et Spiritus Sancti," (In the name of the Father, the Son, and Holy Spirit), sang Father Donatus in Latin

"Amen," chanted students in response. They were kneeling at the assembly hall. Classes were on suspension for the whole week. It was a peculiar Monday, marking the beginning of the annual vocational week. Everything on campus had become white. Students were wearing white dresses. The dormitories were brimming with white beddings. Spotlessness reflected purity in the surroundings.

The second innovation was at the level of communication. Students were to remain silent and still everywhere throughout the day and night. For six days, conversations between students were reduced to whispers, signs, and gestures like *mouxmouxs* (dump people).

All focus was on the spiritual aspects of their lives. Irrespective of class, all students racked their brains for the examination of their soul. The ultimate objective was to scrutinize one's purpose in life to accept the calling to serve the church for a lifetime. Every student was concerned except the few who were non-Roman-Catholic faithfuls. They could abstain from the activities of the week. However, they, too, were required to wear their white dresses as well as respect the silence code. In any case, they were not allowed to disrupt the vocational week activities by any means.

Two days prior to the opening of Vocational Week, priests and reverend sisters had educated students on the aim of what they called "an exceptional privilege." The focus was only on one calling, namely, becoming a reverend sister.

"So, we are going to eat bitter kola throughout the week," said Maahtou to the Four Rocks. They were returning from the conference hall after a lecture on Monastic Orders. Maahtou was referring to the difference between kola nut with several cotyledons and bitter kola with a single cotyledon.

"What a talent blockade!" responded Eposi.

"Especially at this stage when we've not yet explored our talents," added Ngwe.

"Whatever their intentions, I'm just attending because I have no choice," said Nubodem.

The three speakers of the day had outlined the various professions open to women who have taken public vows. They included charitable works, teaching in boarding schools, religious instruction, medical and social works, and missionary work. Yet, to most students it boiled down to a single career path— the sisterhood.

The Four Rocks continued struggling with the upcoming call to join the sisterhood. The most troubling question was, why were tests not given to those interested as was the case for positions anywhere in the world? "We don't know who might become interested along the way," the principal had explained. The automatic admission was open to all. "Any student who came forward and reported to have heard a divine voice calling her to service would be welcomed with open arms," said Sister Anne.

"What type of work skills are we going to learn during this week?" asked Sandra, a Form 1 student, to her Big.

"These Sisters think that we came here to end up living at the convent," complained Sheila in a low tone to her confused Small.

"Each year, they try to capture us into that cage, but free minds like us cannot be confined," grumbled Youla, though no one asked her opinion.

Despite all the cases of quiet resistance, every student was present in the hall on opening day, even the non-Roman Catholic girls. The program unfolded unperturbed.

Throughout the week, each morning of Vocational Week opened with all students assembling in the hall.

"*Agnoscamus peccata nostra*" (Let's confess our sins), Father Geoffrey introduced the morning dedication session, in Latin.

"*Kyrie eléison*" (Lord, have mercy), Sister Gertrude intoned the plea for God's forgiveness, closely followed by "*Christie eléison*" (Christ, have mercy), with all students chiming in.

Those moments of responsorial psalms and brief singing were the only occasions when students used their voices throughout the day.

The core of the program featured intense studies consisting of readings presented from the Catholic Catechism, a collection from various religious orders, and other theology books. Priests preached sermons on the importance of the church in the lives of the members of each community. The biographies of the various Saints who had dedicated their lives to advance the work of God were shared. Priority was given to females, beginning with the Virgin Mary, the mother of Jesus.

"It is because of the Virgin Mary's purity, humility, and simplicity that she became the mother of God," explained Father Michael.

He pointed out that the Virgin Mary was the holiest woman on earth. Thus, he urged each student to emulate her example. Emphasis was laid on her unique experience, something that no other woman on earth had ever or could ever experience. Thus, Holy Mary was equally known as Our Lady of the Nobility of Suffering, Simplicity, and Sacrifice.

The next speaker was Father Donatus. He focused on the Immaculate Conception of the mother of Baby Jesus. "Take a few minutes and think about the importance of the agony that Jesus Christ endured during the Stations of the Cross," he said softly and slowly while lifting his head and looking towards the ceiling.

New topics were exposed each day. They highlighted historical dates and notable places of the Roman Catholic Church. Excitement gradually built up among most of the students who were novices as far as Catholic theology was concerned. They remarked with regret that they had heard

Mass in their various localities only in Latin. Though they had attended the Roman Catholic Church, in which the priest baptized them at birth, everything seemed so distant to them. Some openly confessed that thanks to the lectures, they could feel an atmosphere of heaven about them, which hitherto had only crossed their imagination.

The priest went ahead and explained that the name Rosary was also closely linked to the place where the Virgin Mary appeared. Thus, students were further encouraged to pray the rosary.

As for Fatima, they explained that it was a holy place in Europe where the Virgin Mary had also appeared to three children. The site, after that, attracted so much attention that people from all over the world travelled there on pilgrimage. The priest reiterated the story of her apparition in France. He dwelled on visions and ghosts, while citing instances of divine callings.

Another name, Bernadette, was brought up. Father stated that she was a young girl to whom the Virgin Mary appeared. Some girls pointed out the impossibility of becoming as holy as Mary. In response, the priest explained that any girl could play minor but essential roles by becoming like Mary of Magdala, whose many sins Jesus forgave after she confessed.

Unlike the majority who were novices, there were four girls or so from highly reputed religious families who kept nodding while the priest was speaking. Indeed, one of them was Benedicta, a Form 2 student. Her parents were not church workers, but the highest authority of the Cathedral held them in high regard due to their contributions towards the construction of the edifice. While Father was speaking, she took notes and later shared them with the girls sitting by her. Indeed, they had figurines of Saints in their home. She talked about some saints, including Saint Augustine, Saint Francis of Assisi, and Joan of Arc, citing the last as her favourite. Also, her parents were fond of talking about Lourdes, the place where the Virgin Mother, Mary, appeared.

The closing session for each day took place after dinner. It was the shortest. It was reserved for girls who had already heard the divine call. The first in the series began on Tuesday. Emphasis was on the primordial importance of answering the call. The principal particularly cautioned against turning down the invitation. She said it would be terrible for anyone to do so.

On Wednesday, a special confessional took place in the afternoon. No sin had to be allowed to stand in the way of hearing the call. "It is the greatest honor to serve the church," authorities took turns to repeat that message in every session. They explained it was the main reason why silence was imposed throughout the campus round the clock. No contrary voice was to be allowed to distract students from the call from heaven. That afternoon, the session was taking place outside of the college. All students had to walk down to the Cathedral quietly.

However, most of the students, irrespective of class, honestly confessed that they were not guilty of any sin, tangible, palpable, or visible. Thus, the shaking of eucalyptus branches on their way allowed them to converse with each other in low tones.

They began by questioning the obligation to go to the confessional.

"What if I have not sinned?" asked Linda?

"I feel the same as you," answered three other students in the chorus.

"What if I'm unable to pinpoint my sin before my turn to stand before Father?

"Hmmn, you know for how long I've been searching my soul for sins to go and confess?" asked Ngwenyui?

"I do have some sins, but they happened a long time ago," confessed Beatrice.

"What are your sins," asked Glory. "Please, can you share one of them with me?" she pleaded.

"Hey, how can you ask for such a thing?" asked Beatrice.

"Yes, *naar* (Of course), what's wrong with that?" retorted Rose.

"You know what, let's make a list of sins and share," suggested Stella.

On that note, they quietly formed a group as they walked downhill. The girls who were familiar with the confessional quickly composed a list of common sins. They included, "owning lost and found items," "using lost and found coins," "bearing false witness, especially to dormitory captains," "disturbing in class," "stealing snacks, especially *garri*," "dishing out more food into one's plate at the refectory," "copying from another student's during exams," "complaining about some staff members," "labelling the principal," "maintaining forbidden relationships with boys," "concealing the identity of lovers by describing them as relatives," "accepting a kiss from a boy," etc.

"This is so good," said Vera, "but let's leave out those concerning authorities. I'm happy that I know what I'm going to confess about."

"Now you agree with me when I insisted that we should make a list, right?" stated Stella.

After members of that group had chosen their preferred sins, the others became curious. So, the list of offenses began circulating from student to student. While a lot of students selected one or two for themselves, the list inspired others to scan their consciences for misdeeds that were until then seemingly buried. Some hitherto latent misdeeds became clear like red ink dots on a plain sheet of white paper. Students got excited and began moving faster. Upon arrival at the Cathedral, the officiating priest gave a sermonette on the importance of confession.

"Make it a habit to confess each week during the confessional hour," said Father Paul. "Can anyone hear the teacher if there is noise in class?" he asked.

"No, Father," students answered in chorus.

"Sin is like noise. You can't hear the clarion call to divine service like Mary, the Mother of God, did," he advised the students.

He went further and stressed on the importance of heeding the conscience. Failing to act promptly on one's conscience, the voice inviting a girl to serve the church would become silent. So, the confessional was of utmost importance in the call. "No student has to return to the campus with unconfessed sins. The confessional is like removing accumulated wax from the ears," said the Catechist in attendance.

"After confession, you will become attentive like the child Samuel in the Bible. He received a call in the night while he was under the pupillage of Eli, his guardian in Shiloh," Father Paul explained.

"*Agnoscamus peccata nostra*" (Let's confess our sins), Father Paul chanted from the altar while raising his right hand. The congregation was made up exclusively of Virgin Mother's College students, apart from the officiating team.

"*Kyrie eléison*" (Lord, have mercy), intoned Felicitas, the music Prefect. She was standing and facing the girls from her front pew seat.

"*Christe eléison*" (Christ, have mercy), the rest of the students sang along.

It was time for each student to go and confess their sins. A Form 5 student, Immaculate, stood and walked towards the Confessional located at the back angle of the church. It was Father Peter who was officiating. He pushed open the window as he heard the approaching steps. He had been waiting in the one-person office, seated on a single chair. His eyes were fixed on the small square window, just big enough to show the face of the sinner. Immaculate moved closer and stopped in front of the wooden wall on which she genuflected. There was silence while she searched her conscience. A chill came over her, and her body began trembling. Immediately, her expression became solemn. She opened her mouth to confess her first sin, but her voice seemed to have disappeared. Father

Peter patiently waited for her to regain her stability. After all, she was the first in the queue, a place that many were too shy to occupy. Immaculate coughed two times to clear her throat. Her voice came back, but it had a treble to it. She began and successfully finished confessing. Father Peter waited again, to give her time to name all the sins that might still be tugging her soul. She had emptied herself. Her conscience was at peace. She blinked and remained quiet.

"Your sins are forgiven," Father Peter said while raising his hand towards Immaculate and making the sign of the cross. She equally raised her right hand and made the sign of the cross. She touched her forehead, her heart, and her left shoulder, followed by her right shoulder. The remaining half of the students followed suit. It was already thirty minutes since the priest opened his window.

It was Maahtou's turn. She was the last of the Four Rocks to rise from the pew, after Nubodem, Ngwe and Eposi. She knelt and began trembling. She tried to regain her composure, but she could not. Suddenly, upsetting thoughts came over her like a cold shower. She paused and recalled the incident where Mercy had heaped insults on her. Her shoulder became heavy as if she were carrying a cross. She equally remembered how Miss Tantoh, the Religious Knowledge teacher, used to refer to less fortunate students as sinners.

Maahtou had been going to the confessional ever since she was in primary school. However, this time around, she would have preferred to face the priest in the company of Miss Tantoh and the students promoting discrimination in college at various levels. Unfortunately, the confessional had no provision for that. She and the other members of the Four Rocks had tried to bring the thorny matter regarding Miss Tantoh's utterances to Mr. Adzie Mbom without any solution. Since Miss Tantoh described sin as poverty, what was the point of confessing if a teacher would continue labelling her as a sinner?

She had prepared two wrongdoings, one from the concocted list of transgressions. She and the other members of the Four Rocks wanted more than a ritualistic reciting of sins. There were untouched grievous sins that were dividing students in groups. They wanted a sweeping change in the whole college. Why hadn't Father Paul called out the bullies, those who discriminated, as well as those who despised others, for whatever reason, to stand up and apologize?

At last, Maahtou decided to give in to the sacrament. Since she and her mates had tried to seek change but had not succeeded, she had no choice but to confess her sins. She began speaking. Her lips were moving, but indeed she was not audible. There she was kneeling in front of a Father, but her mind kept wandering away. Father Peter raised his hand to indicate that she needed to speak loudly, but Maahtou thought that he was asking her to leave. As Maahtou was about to stand up, Father Peter stopped her with a show of his fingers, waving multiple times. Maahtou steadied her knees on the bench. He then started making a circle with his forefinger. Maahtou finally understood that she had to take it all over. So, she started confessing again. Though her voice was louder, Father Peter leaned forward to listen.

Maahtou's time had elapsed. At the end of her confession, Father Peter observed a moment of silence. Then, gently, and robotically, he lifted his hand towards Maahtou. She raised hers too and made the sign of the cross.

Meanwhile, students were looking at each other inquiringly. Maahtou had spent more time at the Confessional than was expected. As she walked away, the rest of the students looked at her and wondered what she must have been telling Father. Some students made grimaces at her. She just remained unmoved. Instead of soothing her, she felt the confessional had opened an old wound.

Student after student knelt and confessed their sins. Finally, the last girl made the sign of the cross and stood up. Father Peter closed the window. It was good riddance. The girls began smiling broadly. The college prefect assembled all of them in front of the Cathedral and instructed them to move back up quietly. They walked back to the campus in little groups.

"Maahtou, why did you take so long," asked Ngwe, one of the members of the Four Rocks.

"Don't you think that Miss Tantoh should have confessed in my place?" asked Maahtou.

"You are right," concurred Eposi.

"I don't understand," said Nubodem.

"By insisting that some of us are sinners, she is the sinner, not us. So, whether we confess or not, nothing will change," explained Maahtou, frowning.

The rest of the Four Rocks shook their heads. The girls walked up the hill without saying a word for a while. Each of them was struggling to personally process the labelling that Miss Tantoh had given to less fortunate students.

"I also hope that Tongsi had confessed to having insulted me before graduating," whispered Maahtou, breaking the silence.

"You are right," said Eposi, who was almost in tears. "All the Sisters who take special care of Glow girls whenever they are sick and yet ignore the rest of us should also confess in our place to the Father.

"That is so true," affirmed Nubodem.

Meanwhile, Ngwe held her lips tightly to prevent tears from coming out of her eyes.

The Four Rocks were lagging behind the rest. The college prefect sent a message. It was transmitted from mouth to mouth, requesting that the girls should move up quickly. It was almost time for dinner. The final lecture for the day would follow the meal.

Before the girls got back to school that evening, there was hot news circulating. Two girls had received the heavenly call. Girls exclaimed and clapped their hands softly. More was still to come.

Chapter 27

Heavenly Call

Later in the evening, Sister Aileen, a Reverend Sister from Ireland, presented an exposé on the topic Listening Techniques. She opened her lecture with an outline of the conditions for listening. Among them was silence, earnest desire, and confession. She was delighted that students were already putting into practice the first and the last of the three requirements. She went ahead and emphasized the fact that an earnest desire was the most critical of the three because the level of determination makes the difference.

Thus, a sincere willingness was a high degree of inclination, a courageous decision made in each heart. A person who earnestly desires something is equally attentive. Therefore, an earnest desire was critical to hearing the call. It meant that someone who does not want the call would not hear it even if it happens.

"In other words," she went ahead, "earnest desire is a prerequisite for active listening because it opens up the ears of the heart." She reiterated the invisible connection between the physical and the spiritual ear, what she described as the "ears of the heart."

"Those with "opened-heart ears" will hear even in the noise. Do you agree, girls?" she asked.

"Yes, that's true," some students answered while others laughed.

Besides, Sister Aileen added that "earnest desire will be shown by those who consider it an honor, the rare privilege to give one's life for service to the church." She stressed that everlasting blessings, more significant than any other, accompanied those who choose that path in life.

On Thursday morning, Sister Kathleen taught the importance of praying the rosary. "That is, asking Mary to pray for each one, as exemplified by her son, Jesus."

Form 1 students had only received their rosaries the past week. They were in a separate section of the hall for a special initiation into the use of the fifty-nine beads of the rosary. Apart from the beads, the presenter carefully explained the crucifix and the metal, "there are three sections of rosary prayers - the introduction, the Decades, and the Conclusion." She kept on until listeners understood how to use their rosary.

The afternoon period, following lunch, was set aside as a critical moment for the beginning of the 'harvest.' Organizers extended the siesta from one to two hours to lengthen the listening time for the divine call. Sister Aileen encouraged students to "sleep in-between their white bedsheets in their spotless white dresses."

The girls did, each lying on their bed without making a sound. It was a one-on-one moment wherein a divine encounter would happen to those listening earnestly. Priests and Sisters pleaded with students to open their hearts or the "ears of their hearts," while waiting in expectation. "A voice is going to speak to you individually and personally, either faintly or vividly, depending on each case," Father Donatus had emphasized on opening day.

Unfortunately, some students ended up sleeping, at least three per dorm. It was like drifting from wakefulness into holy dreaming. It was only thanks to the ringing bell that they woke up suddenly and shaking. Sweet sleep had slipped in like an intruder and shut off their active listening capacity. Quickly, they jumped out of bed and rushed to the lavatory. Each of them splashed cold water on their faces before arriving at the lecture hall for the scheduled pre-dinner testimonies.

Something more grievous happened at the Assumption dormitory involving the captain and two other Form 5s. They simply broke the rule. After exchanging beds with junior students, they began speaking in low tones instead of remaining quiet to listen to the voice from heaven.

"Do I have to be obliged to join the Sisterhood?" asked Violator 1.

"I did not come here to become a Reverend Sister," answered Violator 2.

"I hope we pass the GCE, so we don't go through this anymore," said Violator 3.

"How about the case of those who joined the Sisterhood and later dropped out?" asked Violator 2.

"Who does not know the case of Sister Immaculate?" asked Violator 1.

Immaculate, who graduated three years ago, was in Form 5 when she answered the divine call. Thereafter, she lived in a convent for two years. She was very devoted to the course. Her former classmates often described how her gentleness, soft voice, and abstemiousness naturally predisposed her to her calling.

Indeed, each Sunday, students crowded around her at the Cathedral after mass. Even those who did not know her personally would stand by admiring her beautiful blue robe and white veil. None of them could visualize her in everyday clothes.

Nonetheless, circumstances obliged her to quit the convent. The authorities granted her permission based on family reasons. She was the first of seven children and the most highly educated. Her parents had hoped that she could get a job after her graduation. They desperately needed her support to help her siblings through school. One day during vacation, she instead informed her parents that she had received the heavenly call. It was a hard blow, difficult to stomach. They could not utter a word of disapproval for fear of sinning. For days, they lost their appetites, bit their fingers, and sighed whenever Immaculate was not around. Theirs was a very devoted Christian family.

On Sunday, the priest preached about the privilege of giving one's life to the service of the Lord. For the first time since Immaculate made the announcement, her mother embraced her as soon as she returned from the mass. Her father kept nodding, without a word. How was he going to make his grill-making business flourish? From where would he get extra material, the stamina to produce more, much less plod through the city, hunting for buyers? He had sacrificed most of his youthful energy on the education of Immaculate, and now she was gone.

Despite the impending difficulties awaiting them, Immaculate's parents bowed to the divine appointment. They resolved to increase their efforts in the daily struggle for survival. They endured the first year. Their second child, a son, gave up his studies in Class 5 and joined his father at his workshop. Immaculate's third brother passed into Form 4. Unfortunately, her mother fell ill. The family plunged into abject poverty.

Immaculate received the news and sighed all day. When she visited her family, and saw her mother, she just broke into tears. The convent felt obliged to make an exception. They relieved her of her Sisterly duties and asked her to return home.

"In that case, was Immaculate's case a divine calling, indeed?" asked Violator 2.

"I think that she dishonoured her parents by not respecting the tacit agreement between them," said Violator 3.

"Besides, is caring for your family, not a divine calling?" asked Violator 1.

Despite the logic of their analysis, those three Form 5 students could not openly rebel against the college. It was the end of siesta. They rushed to the hall and joined others who were anxiously waiting to hear the evidence of those that angels had so far called. The hall was dead silent.

Sister Kathleen took the microphone and stepped forward.

"Thank you for your diligence and respect of the rules. The peace and tranquillity of this campus shows that you have opened your hearts, thereby connecting heaven to earth. We are very convinced that you have heard the call. So, our most fervent question to you is, what is your response? I invite you to come out and tell us."

There was silence. Eyes and heads were quietly turning from side to side. The Four Rocks were sitting on the same bench, hand in hand. They were just quietly observing what was going on.

Meanwhile, the team of twelve presenters flanked the principal. They were all sitting at a long table in front. They too were quiet, staring at the girls, blinking, and thinking deeply.

One girl stood up. All eyes turned towards her. She began moving towards the front. A second girl stood up. All eyes again fell on her. By the time she reached the front, a third girl stood up. Spontaneously, the rest of the students began clapping.

"Shiiirr," said Sister Aileen, while placing her right forefinger on her tightly closed lips. A few minutes of silence followed.

"Anyone else?" asked Sister Kathleen.

No one answered, but some students turned and began looking at Clara. Instead, she frowned and bent her head.

The principal's heart almost shrank with disappointment. She whispered to Sister Gertrude, sitting by her, who conveyed her message to one of the priests.

Suddenly, Father Donatus stood up and took the microphone.

"Let me see your hand if you think an angel cannot appear to you," said Father Donatus. No one raised their hand.

"Oh, how easy it is to hear that distinct voice calling you! So, don't be afraid to come forward. It is the most important decision you could make in your life."

No one responded for a while. Suddenly, a Form 1 student stood up and walked to the front. There were exclamations accompanied by clapping. After that, silence ensued. It seemed as if no one else was going to come forward.

So, the principal stood up. She frowned and took a deep breath. Then she began speaking. "The school, in collaboration with our parish, has made enormous sacrifices to organize this vocational week," she regretted. "God is looking out for a more abundant yield," she went on. Suddenly, she stopped. It was as if she was about to cry.

At that point, Sister Kathleen took over. She asked the first three girls to share their experiences with others. The first of them, Helen, said that she was delighted to have heard the call, but added that she was not surprised at all. "I have always wanted to become a Reverend Sister," she ended her speech. Some girls nodded.

Indeed, her characteristically reserved and retiring attitude had led many girls to refer to her as a Reverend Sister.

Next was Martha. She fastened her lips and looked down. She began trembling. Then she placed her right hand over her mouth.

"It's okay, Martha," said Sister Kathleen. "You can step back and wait until you are ready to speak.

The third, Rachel, was the surprise of the evening. She was a girl with a bubbly personality. She was fond of talking about music stars. Indeed, she used every opportunity to make the flashiest make-up. She often wore tight dresses and enjoyed dancing and twisting her body as if her parents raised her in a nightclub.

As soon as she started speaking, girls could not hold back their remarks. "*Ase eh*, even this one?" (Tell me, …). "*Mami Nyanga*" (stylish woman) "Who would discipline her?"

The principal curtly asked the girls to be silent.

"I am not surprised that you are all surprised," said Rachel.

Everyone burst out laughing. Sister Kathleen hushed them.

"What is important is that I have answered the call," said Rachel.

It was the turn of the little-known Form 1 student, Anna. She shook a deep breath. She held her lips tightly and shook her head repeatedly as if she were shaking off a discordant inner voice. "I am happy for my call," she said. Then, she paused. Girls were eager to hear what had prompted her. Some were moving their hands while others were signalling with their moving lips, requesting her to say more. "I know that my mother will be happy." Then, she stepped backward.

The evening program ended, and the principal dismissed the girls, asking them to go to their dorms quietly.

"Wonders shall never end," said Youla, referring to Rachel.

"That one, can she survive the convent for more than a year?" was the question on everyone's lip.

"Hmmn, I'm afraid for the brothers," said Stella, a Form 4 girl who was very outspoken.

Ah no talk?" (Haven't I said it?), whispered Youla.

Girls who were heading towards the bathroom burst out laughing. Nubodem was among the first to rush out of the hall. Ngwe was in the crowd, keenly listening to the comments of others. Meanwhile, Maahtou and Eposi slowly walked to their dormitory without uttering a word.

That night Maahtou lay on her bed recalling the final scene of Vocation Week. The response of Rachel to the divine call reminded her of another reverend Sister in Santa, called Glory. Her family lived a few hundred meters away. She had decided to join the Sisterhood while she was still in primary school. Upon obtaining her First School Leaving Certificate, she promptly moved into the convent. The authorities regularly gave excellent reports about her to her family. Her family was so proud of her choice. Indeed, they felt as unique as the nobility.

However, when Glory turned 17, everyone in the village began wondering whether she had made the right choice. Her attitude during her annual leave raised eyebrows. She would sing and dance to popular, secular songs played on the radio, including romantic ones. Glory went as far as writing out the lyrics, which she spent time memorizing. Her siblings and neighbours were always shocked by her behaviour. Instead, she often regretted that she had not attended a dance party at the

Santa Lion Club before opting to become a Sister. Now it was too late to even come close to it or openly display interest in it.

"Does Mother Superior at the Convent know that she sings secular songs?" asked villagers.

"The only difference between her and other girls of her age is her blue robe and white veil," commented the young men.

Right up to the following day at lunch, Maahtou was still thinking about Glory.

On Saturday evening, the count down to the official closing ceremony of Vocation Week began. The bell was ringing for the final assembly. In less than ten minutes, all the students were in the hall. The silence was notable. True to tradition, the last major item was the sermon. Father Donatus, who was the chair of the extraordinary week, was the speaker.

"Girls, you have been exemplary," said Father Donatus in his opening remarks. "Our message has not fallen on deaf ears."

After that, he handed it over to the principal to invite those selected for the sacred office.

"The call was open to all, but only the dedicated ones heard it," said the principal.

Then, she called the four girls by name, inviting them to come forward. At first, no one made a move. The principal began trembling. What if they had changed their minds? She took a deep breath. "Don't be shy, girls," she said. "You did it before, and marvellously so."

One after the other, they began coming out. There was a girl who had not come out the first time. "Wonderful," the principal said. Her face was glowing. Two other sisters jumped up and clapped.

"I'm sorry I didn't do it the right way," said the principal. "Now I'm inviting the new girls as well as the first set of girls to come forward. Two more new girls left their benches and moved forward. Applause filled the hall.

The principal smiled broadly. The Sisters moved up and took turns to embrace them, one after the other. After that, each of the three girls gave a short testimony. Then, the priest handed out a gift package to each of them while the rest of the students applauded.

As usual, the Four Rocks were sitting next to each other carefully watching. They remarked that the six students who came out represented all the three social classes on campus, namely, three Strivers, two Brick-Wallers, and one Glow. That notwithstanding, they had some common qualities. They were distinguished from the rest of the student population by their quiet disposition, and frugality. Also, they were self-effacing; hardly expressing private opinions on any topical issues.

Unlike them, Rachel always seemed to be bubbling with excitement and speaking her mind freely.

Father Donatus invited Father Geoffrey to make the closing prayer. After that, the Choir Prefect gave the closing song, "Thank you, Lord."

The principal took the microphone, thanked students for their cooperation, and dismissed them.

"I can't wait to go to Rome to see the Pope," said Rachel while heading to her dorm. Meanwhile, the other five girls became more pensive, preferring to whisper to each other. In any case, apart from the Form 1 student who was new, the other four did not seem to have any personal ambitions beyond the convent.

Maahtou listened to all the criticisms levied against Rachel and realized that there were similarities between her and Rachel. The most outstanding was spontaneity, though she did not express herself as loudly as Rachel. To her, it was like she and Rachel were opposite sides of the same coin.

However, neither Maahtou nor any of the Four Rocks regretted not hearing the call. "This doesn't feature in our kola nut gifts, right?" asked Eposi. "You bet," said Ngwe. "Definitely not," added Nubodem. The Four Rocks had had time to share notes and examine their consciences. None of their innate talents was akin to the piety and the stillness that life in the convent required for long hours each day. Ngwe and

Nubodem each had a quiet and reserved demeanour, but they were more like plants waiting for the right season to bloom. Meanwhile, Eposi and Maahtou were too sociable to be confined. Besides, the shared quality of the Four Rocks was their inquisitive minds. They tended to be non-conformist whenever other options were available.

Nevertheless, when the foursome met on Monday during break, they were happy that Vocational Week was behind them.

"Now we can focus on our class notes," said Nubodem.

"I have a lot to revise," said Ngwe.

"Some of the definitions I had mastered have evaporated," said Eposi.

"I know," said Maahtou.

Just like them, those who had not confessed to having heard a voice were experiencing a renewed sense of freedom. "Let me pass my exams and move on," said a Form 5 girl to her friends. Most girls felt like fishes that had been caught, but let off the hook, and thrown back into the Ocean.

During the time for siesta, Maahtou was still pondering over Vocational Week. "Had she missed a golden opportunity?" she wondered. Immediately, her spirit dismissed the thought. Instead, she got into an introspection. Her personality was more attuned to swift waves splashing and towering over rocky obstacles like the waterfall in their farm in the village. She could not align herself with the still currents of life in the convent which seemed more like water trapped in a pond. As far as she was concerned, the protective walls of the convent were inhibitive. Instead, she envisaged herself going through the rough terrains of life, trekking, hiking, falling, bruising her knees, rising again, and taking bumpy rides, even on horse-back.

Though she had not yet settled on a career path, she was grateful that there was still time for her grooming husband to complete his job.

Chapter 28

Bracing Up for the Ultimate Battle

The history teacher was the first to bring past examination questions to class. In and of itself it was a signal to Maahtou and her classmates that they were barely steps away from the battlefront, their raison d'être. After they went through the questions, they began understanding the nature of questions. Both the overall understanding and the details were crucial in passing the GCE (General Certificate of Education).

"Do we have to know all these periods?" asked Prisicilla

"Of course," answered Mr. Adze Mbom

"I'm not good at memorizing dates," said Mary.

"You have no choice," answered Mr. Adze Mbom.

The other teachers soon followed suit ---from Geography, Biology, Chemistry, Physics, to Mathematics. The more questions students were exposed to, the more they began measuring their capability and the ease of grasping a given subject vis-à-vis the difficulty and or the dislike of this or that area of discipline.

Whatever the case, Mathematics and Physics remained shrouded in mystery to all the students in the whole school. Even those who were spending long hours, cracking their brains to solve problems were barely getting by. They were the courageous ones. As for the rest, Mathematics, especially, was daunting. So, they stayed away from it. The best overall scores were just an average pass. It was almost like obtaining a consolatory prize for collapsing at the finishing line.

Unfortunately, it was a compulsory subject for the GCE, along with English and French.

One of the immediate changes that the focus on the certificate exams brought to class was the sense of responsibility as well as that of urgency. A kind of silence, never before felt, descended upon the students. Jokes and distractions in-between classes suddenly disappeared. Oddly enough, Youla was hushed by the changing air of awareness of a harsh reality.

"Even if a pin drops in this class, everyone will hear it," commented Vivian, the new class prefect. Her job had no stress compared to the tenure of each of her two predecessors.

True to the new social climate, no one commented or responded. All heads were down. Students' attitudes were changing in several ways. Some turned passed exam papers into bookmarks. Those of them who had older siblings and family members who had written the GCE were going about with a dozen green examination sheets in their bags.

Abruptly, a few students began making friends with classmates that formerly they barely waved and walked away or even gossiped about. Jackie and Mary, who were Glows, started offering compliments to Nubodem, especially after tests in the sciences. Youla would ask Maahtou to look through her French assignment before she handed it in. Meanwhile, Bih stayed close to Maahtou. The two had often solved Math problems together, and studied French, especially when homework was due.

As anticipated, the Four Rocks kept close to each other. Their past performances over the years revealed the extent to which they complemented each other. Eposi was a champion in Geography and Cookery. Ngwe was an A student in History and English Language. Nubodem topped the class in all the Sciences. Maahtou excelled in Chemistry, Literature and French.

"Have you realized that Birnam wood is moving to Dunsinane?" asked Maahtou during breaktime to her friends. She was paraphrasing Shakespeare's *Macbeth*, while alluding to the new friendships forming in their class.

"Hahaha," laughed the rest.

"Finally, the walls between Glows, Bricks, and Strivers are crashing," answered Eposi.

"Who said the brain is not higher than the mouth?" asked Nubodem.

"Now I see why Mr. Adze Ndom told us that some solutions come only with time," said Ngwe.

"Plus, the Form 5s that called us Hard Crystals chanted that Downtown spices Uptown. Remember?" asked Eposi.

The girls gave each other high fives.

Besides, it was only in Form 4 that Maahtou and her classmates realized the importance of some of the warnings that senior students used to issue. For example, Judgment Day, wherein some of them were treated unfairly, became a lesson book.

"Even I, who used to be lazy to wake up to read, I can't afford running out of kerosene for my lamp," said Jane.

"No wonder you are now among the first to put up your hand in class," answered Margaret.

Even the rebellious nature of some girls was changing overnight. The principal's sanctions against girls receiving letters from boyfriends dwindled to almost zero during their senior class.

"Who would have thought that Youla would let go of boys?" asked Odile.

"When some of us were saying that there's time for everything, did some of you agree?" asked Maahtou.

"She has become so silent that it's like she is sick," said Gertrude.

Another development resulting from the ultimate exams beckoning in the horizon was the generalized cry against hunger among senior students. It was a threat to their success. Upon returning from home for the second term, Strivers brought along larger quantities of snacks, especially garri.

"Will it not get spoiled before you finish it?" asked Anne to Margaret.

"It will not even last for long enough. The demand is high," answered the latter.

As for the Four Rocks, Maahtou brought a lot of *mbiare* (sun dried sweet potato), and thirty avocados, though the latter was consumed within a week. Eposi brought triple the amount of coconut sweet. Ngwe and Nubodem brought along pleasant surprises. The former had a bag of twelve tiny boxes of chocolate paste. Her uncle who was working in Douala had given her as a reward for passing her exams. Meanwhile, the latter brought four cups of kernels. Her mother had received a special supply from her village.

However, it was not only the students on campus that were registering the effects of reaching a higher level in college. Maahtou's family could not believe the changes in her. She, who used to come on holidays, and relieved everyone, was the one that others were attending to, including her younger siblings. Maahtou was spending almost all of her time reading.

"Take this food to her," her mother said to her younger brother.

"She is sleeping," said Afouomama

"When I woke up this morning at 4:30, I saw the light shining in her room," said Baba, her father.

"Will she survive at this rate?" asked Mama.

"And this is just the beginning," said Baba. "You remember how her elder brothers used to read all through the night?"

"It's becoming as if we've lost our children to the educational system," said Mama.

"Don't you know they have to confront this ultimate battle like soldiers?" asked Baba. "Without that they can't pass their exams."

Baba could explain a lot of what was going on with Maahtou, but Mama was the one who was feeling it the most. Maahtou could no longer spend the whole day with her on the farm. To the affectionate mother, it was not so much about the work to be done as her company.

"Why are they teaching you all these subjects and excluding farming?" asked Mama when they were having dinner.

"Mama, you don't understand. The office jobs pay more than farming," said Maahtou.

"The world has really changed," said Baba. "Your uncle, who was the Agric inspector in this region, used to take his students from one farm to another."

"Exactly," said Mama with emphasis and a nod. "We learned a lot from your elder sisters.

"And even then, they were still in primary school," noted Baba.

Of course, Mama wished her daughter well. Notwithstanding, she was struggling with a deep sense of loss that she could not express in words. She will often think of her children and sigh. Maahtou's elder sisters and brothers were all gone far away, either to further their education or in the cities where they were working.

Each time Maahtou's vacation came to an end, Mama would have prepared a variety of snacks well in advance. She wanted her daughter to succeed, but the melancholy caused by separation between them always caught her unawares. Yet, she could not voice it.

While back in school, Maahtou and her mates began sighing close to the exams. So far, that particular third term was the toughest. By the time exams began, most students were out of snacks. The battle was not just one for comprehension of theories and theorems but also one against withstanding hunger.

Luckily for Maahtou's class, one of theirs came to their rescue unexpectedly and in an unusual manner. She had a knack to tell when a mango was mature. Ju, as she was fondly called, had a raffia bag, with which she would climb from tree to tree and feel the fruits before anyone knew they were getting ready.

On Thursday afternoon, during prep, Ju entered the class with her treasured bag hanging on her left shoulder. She took out the first of five fruits and bit into the green skin lightly. The fruit was just beginning to change from whitish to yellowish.

To the watching eyes of Sarah and Priscilla, sitting next to her, she raised her left hand and head and shook her body in thanksgiving.

"Ju, let me have a taste, please," said Priscilla.

"Take," answered Ju.

"Can I have a taste too?" asked Lem.

"Yes," answered Ju.

Vivian stood up from her desk and came closer.

"You see what you have done?" said Ju to Lem, who had bitten a large chunk. "Next time, I'm not giving you again."

Now Ju was obliged to hold the mango herself while the girls were each biting into it.

"But what are you going to do with all those ones bulging in your bag?" asked Maahtou.

"They are not as mature?" answered Ju.

From that day onward, Ju became a connoisseur. For the rest of the term, she was the saviour of her class. Each day, when hunger became a threat, her mates looked up to her rare ingenuity.

"How did she come about this unusual ability?" asked Eposi.

"It's a kola nut gift, right Maahtou?" asked Ngwe.

"Definitely," said Nubodem.

"I can relate to it," said Maahtou. "We picked mangoes during primary school days, but climbing up the tree to feel for mature ones is a mastered skill."

Chapter 29

Fear of Sexual Harassment

For Maahtou and her classmates, the final year in Virgin Mother's College was marked by significant obstacles to surmount as well as critical decisions to make. What high school were they going to attend? The question haunted them as much as the growing anxiety for the upcoming GCE. Each of them needed to graduate successfully after five years of studies.

The largest and most popular English high school in the country was the Community High School located in the city of Bambili, known as BAST. It was offering courses in art, science, and technology. For years, it had distinguished itself in academic excellence, and was maintaining the lead. Each year, it attracted up to 70 percent of the graduates from VMC. The high level of admission was also due to the proximity between the two institutions. Indeed, senior students of VMC were always invited to attend annual parties at BAST

Among the attendees, the noisiest and most excited girls longing for eventual admission into BAST, would spend hours and days chatting loudly in dormitories about the latest dance. Their prime focus was the ongoing and prominent love affairs. Stories of intimate relations between boys and girls took the centre stage.

Meanwhile, excellent academic performances received only a passing mention. Thus, they painted the Who's Who of campus life at BAST with steamy anecdotes of who was dating who. To them, it had become the rite of passage.

Each time Maahtou overheard those salacious accounts, they sent chills down her spine.

"How can vice be considered a virtue?" asked Maahtou to the other Four Rocks.

"That's why I have decided not to set foot there," responded Nubodem. "I don't have time for distractions."

Nubodem had already applied to the Protestant Community College in Bali. Her cousin, who was a student in Lower Sixth, highly recommended it.

"I don't know much about KAST, but since my family lives in the area, my parents chose it for me," explained Eposi. Indeed, their family home was barely 30 kilometres away from the Community High School in Kumba (KAST).

"I'm venturing out to BAST only because my cousin from Seat of Wisdom college will be sharing a room with me," revealed Ngwe. Ngwe's case was different. She had another option beyond BAST — to eventually travel to the United States to further her studies. Her uncle was living and working there. So, as far as she was concerned, attending BAST was mostly for the experience. In the event where the challenges of social life became untenable, she would simply withdraw and focus on the process to fulfil the requirements to travel abroad.

Maahtou's innate curiosity would have dared her to apply to BAST, but her gut feeling deterred her. She was not ready to put up with constant sexual harassment from hundreds of boys. However, she was at a loss as to how to convince her family, based solely on her misgivings. They would dismiss her fears or classify them as the normal fear of the unknown. After all, they knew dozens of students who had successfully passed through that renowned institution, including girls. What about Moonbih, her elder brother, who recently graduated from there?

Even so, Maahtou thought it was unfair to compare boys and girls. While boys are mainly poised to succeed in their studies, girls face a double challenge. In addition to working hard to earn good grades, aren't girls the ones that would drop out of school if they became pregnant out of wedlock?

Maahtou was even more dismayed by the fact that girls who endeavoured to maintain high moral standards were often derided. Indeed, those who were not willing to start a relationship with a boy were considered as social misfits. That explains why girls who desired to preserve their virginity could not dare divulge their resolve. Maahtou was infuriated. How abnormal that something that should have been hailed was instead guarded as a shameful secret! Having one's priorities right as well as focusing on the goal was abnormal. For example, virginity was considered a taboo in popular cycles.

Maahtou spent sleepless hours in her bed worrying over the predicament before her. Wasn't a co-ed high school a great opportunity to learn how to start and maintain a friendship with the opposite sex? Unfortunately, the reality was out of line with proper moral conduct. Besides, most boys were more bent on having sex with girls than taking genuine interest in the young women. Instead of seizing the opportunity to practice self-control and build character, they prided themselves with their ability to make women either chase them or pine for them.

The glaring example was the case of a handful of boys who became popular, thanks to their family name recognition or for outstanding academic performance. High school carved them out as newsmakers. They took advantage of their status to make advances on several girls. Otherwise, several girls pursued them simultaneously. Some of them ended up with multiple partners. Those guys caused a lot of heartaches and fights between girls.

Maahtou knew that she did not have the stamina to fight against a campus of hundreds of new students. She dreaded the fact that boys were fond of exerting continuous pressure on the so-called 'stubborn' girls until they ceded.

Besides, she loathed the fact that relationships that belonged to the private domain automatically became a community matter. Third parties could make judgements at will and even interfere without limits.

She saw herself in a tiny minority that was not yet ready for relationships. How was she going to express herself in a restrictive social climate? Though Maahtou kept recalling her mother, reminding her the umpteenth time that a girl always has the final say, attending BAST was like being thrown into treacherous ocean waves without the ability to swim. While grappling with all those upheavals, she could neither escape from reality nor arrest the passing of time. Registration into high school was ongoing.

Finally, count-down to the deadline for applications began. Maahtou kept spinning around the house and talking to herself. She was suffering silently. How could she communicate with her parents in an adequate manner? She had never attended a higher co-educational institution. Of all the walls of defence she was trying to raise in her mind, little did she know that the reality was even worse than the stories she had heard. While organizing the room, she stumbled on crucial evidence that convinced her without a shred of doubt that BAST was a no-go zone.

Maahtou was in the room alone. She was looking through her brother's trunk of used books during a hot afternoon. She sighted a photo album belonging to Moonbih. It was looking brand new. She picked it up and began thumbing through it. It was packed full of a recent collection of pictures taken during his graduation ceremony at BAST campus. There were group photos, individual photos, with the couples featuring in the highest number of them. Those students were posing like newlyweds on a honeymoon, if not, in an engagement party.

Maahtou's knees began to weaken instantly. Goosebumps were coming over her arms. Wasn't that the glaring evidence? She knew herself; she was ill-equipped for intimate relations.

Despite her latest findings, she could not advance her fears as an argument before her sponsor, Bongshee, or her parents. They would argue that it was not a sufficient reason to give up BAST. So, she alone had to deal with the psychological pain gnawing at her. At last, she yielded to her family. "If you don't go there, where else will you go?" each of them told her. She could not blame them. BAST was the nearest high school.

While nervously waiting for a response to her application, the results of the GCE were published and broadcast on national radio, Radio Cameroon. It was a Thursday afternoon. What a joy for Maahtou and all the Four Rocks! They passed the GCE Ordinary Level exams. News got to their class that Youla was planning to spend all night at a club to celebrate her success. Unfortunately, three students failed.

After a few weeks, high schools began publishing the list of admitted students. The BAST list came out too. Ngwe and Maahtou were admitted. Maahtou's name featured on the priority list of students granted access to the hostels. Ngwe had not applied for a room.

Maahtou's family was happy. She celebrated with them, but deep down in her heart, she knew that BAST was not for her. Her sole problem was, how was she going to escape? In the meantime, she had heard more stories about boys and girls entering each other's room at will, even in shared rooms. Worse still, some would drop in without warning, including bedtime. Maahtou felt haunted. So, she kept giving excuses and putting off the date to travel to BAST to register.

Thankfully, yet regrettably, by the time that she finally got to BAST to register, the authorities had ceded her place to a student on the waiting list. She had failed to pay her deposit before the deadline. It was sad news for her family. They were unable to afford an off-campus room.

After some investigation, her family realized that they could not afford an off-campus room. Bongshee needed to focus more on her own family than paying for a room for Maahtou. Maahtou should have been sad and sorry, but no. Instead, she was bubbling with joy, though without a clue as to where else to pursue higher education.

The next best alternative was KAST. Unfortunately, Kumba was far away from home; some 300 kilometres away. It was the second of the two choices she had made on her application form.

In terms of social life, KAST was as notorious as BAST. There was also more talk about its multiple campus parties, relegating academics to second rate. As for girls, there were anecdotes of frequent dress competitions as well as rivalries over boyfriends.

Maahtou's family judged that though located further away, she may be lucky to get a campus room.

School reopening was barely in a fortnight, and BAST was still admitting students. Maahtou had to travel to Kumba. Early on Monday morning, on the request of her parents, Moonbih accepted to accompany her to KAST. They woke up at 5.00 a.m. and caught the first bus. After traveling for about six hours, they arrived in the city at1pm.

When they got to the campus, they met a long queue ahead of them. They waited for almost an hour. Their turn finally arrived. Brother and sister entered the principal's office and took their seats.

Moonbih made the introduction. Then, he handed over Maahtou's file to the seemingly overwhelmed middle-aged, dark skin gentleman. Like a robot, he ran his eyes over her transcripts and the GCE results. Then he paused and scrutinized them, subject after subject.

He placed down the file, eased himself back into his seat, looked at the boy and girl before him. He began frowning, seeming visibly upset. Neither Moonbih nor Maahtou knew why. They looked at each other for clues, but there were none. Without any further notice, the principal began his query.

"Why did you consider this school only as a second choice?"

"She instinctively chose the other in the first place because it is nearer home," Moonbih explained.

"And why are you being escorted by your boyfriend?" asked the principal while sternly staring at Moonbih.

"Sir, he is my brother," refuted Maahtou.

The principal shook his head and went on accusing Maahtou of "parading my office with your boyfriend."

Both Moonbih and Maahtou were shocked.

"Sir, I'm her elder brother, not her boyfriend," insisted Moonbih.

The principal shook his head again and insisted that such behaviour was not at all acceptable. At that point, Moonbih almost laughed out, but he quickly held his mouth with his right palm. He could not risk Maahtou's future with a chuckle that the authority in front of them could interpret as insolence.

Nevertheless, after a long silence, the principal announced that he was going to admit Maahtou. However, he informed them there was no more room left in the hostels. Thus, he asked them to make up their minds on the spot. Brother and sister hesitated. They just looked at each other without saying a word.

"Well, if you can't decide, I will give you up till Friday to confirm the admission. Otherwise, that's it," stated the principal.

Moonbih and Maahtou thanked him and walked out of his office. As soon as they got back into the yard, they spoke up.

"Maahtou, I'm sorry that there's no space for you in the hostels," said Moonbih.

"Don't you worry, brother, let's just go home," responded Maahtou.

"So, what's going to happen to you, then?" he asked.

"I don't know," Maahtou said, feigning sadness.

Moonbih kept sighing while Maahtou was rejoicing in her heart. Sunset was already looming on the horizon. They walked past groups of potential students scattered all over the campus. Maahtou merely took a glance and determined in her heart that none of them would see her there again. For the second time, she was grateful to have been rejected. She had no party dresses to flaunt, nor was she going to become a coquette by abiding to indecent norms.

They hurried to the Motor Park. All along, Moonbih could not stop wondering where on earth his sister was going to attend high school. Maahtou was grateful for his companionship and sympathy, but how could she tell him that he was mourning over something that was a source of relief to her?

They were lucky to catch the last bus for the day, heading in their direction. They arrived back in the village at night.

Meanwhile, their parents had suspended dinner to wait for their arrival. As usual, their mother and siblings spent time screening the sound of every passing car as well as the voices of people returning to their respective homes. It was 8.00 p.m. when they finally knocked at the door. Exclamations of joy filled the air even before the door was unlocked.

Moonbih took the lead in recounting what had happened. Everyone was sorry, even Neumour and Afouomama. They sighed repeatedly.

"*Ndaah mba*" (sorry), sympathized Mama.

"My goodness, this is what you went through?" concurred Baba.

"So, where shall we get help for her?" asked Mama.

"I have no idea, Mama," said Moonbih.

Despite all the sympathy shown to her, Maahtou became a dumb observer. She was barely chiming in with the rest to reassure them that she was not going through any mental torture.

Meanwhile, she could not wait to dash out of the kitchen into the room alone. She desperately wanted to shout out for joy. She could not hold it in anymore. So, before she ate, she excused herself and ran into the room and threw her hands in the air. How good it felt that she had evaded the inescapable grip of the monster of obscene campus life! As far as she was concerned, she would be safer skipping high school than putting herself in harm's way.

The following morning, she stared at her despondent mother for long without uttering a word. Would Mama cheer up if someone gave her a clear picture of the indecent social scene on high school campuses? she wondered.

Whatever the case, there was a high probability of Maahtou missing further education. She resigned herself to her fate without any clue as to how else to pursue the journey to discover and hone her kola nut gifts. Despite successfully graduating after five long years of college, she was unable to bring meaningful change to the lives of her parents, much less positively impact her immediate community. What was the worth of a GCE Ordinary Level certificate? How could she translate excellence in Chemistry, Literature, and French into a better way of living in the village? Her mind was blank. And if she does not go to high school, all the sacrifices made during those challenging years in college would go to waste.

Life at home came to a standstill. Lively communication was replaced by continual sighing. Mama managed to cook, but no one had any appetite.

Printed in the United States
by Baker & Taylor Publisher Services